DESTROYED AND *Restored*

THE BARON'S COURAGEOUS WIFE

(# 12 LOVE'S SECOND CHANCE SERIES)

BY

BREE WOLF

Destroyed & Restored

The Baron's Courageous Wife

By

Bree Wolf

This is a work of fiction. Names, characters, businesses, places, brands, media, events and incidents are either the products of the author's imagination or used in a fictitious manner.

Any resemblance to actual persons, living or dead, or actual events is purely coincidental.

Cover Art by Victoria Cooper

www.breewolf.com

ISBN: 978-3-96482-047-1

To our children
A blessing each and every one of them

ACKNOWLEDGEMENTS

My thank-you to all of you who've helped with feedback, typo detection, character and plot development, editing, formatting, cover creation, and the biggie...spreading the word...so that countless readers can now enjoy these stories of love's second chance.

To name only a few: Michelle Chenoweth, Monique Taken, Zan-Mari Kiousi, Tray-Ci Roberts, Kim Bougher, Vicki Goodwin, Denise Boutin, Elizabeth Greenwood, Corinne Lehmann, Lynn Herron, Karen Semones, Maria DB, Kim O'Shea, Tricia Toney, Deborah Montiero, Keti Vezzu, Patty Michinko, Lynn Smith, Vera Mallard, Isabella Nanni, Carol Bisig, Susan Czaja, Teri Donaldson, Anna Jimenez and Tammy Windsor.

DESTROYED AND *Restored*

PROLOGUE

London, spring 1807 (or a variation thereof)

*ou deserve this!" Matthew's father sneered as he glared down at his nephew Tristan, aiming the pistol in his hands at the young man's heart. "You were never worthy!"*

Matthew's own heart tightened painfully in his chest as he watched in shock. As he saw Tristan's gaze shift to his wife, tears streaming down her face. As he saw her scramble to her feet, desperate to save her husband's life. As he saw his own father for the man he truly was.

A madman.

Consumed by greed.

About to become a murderer and rip their family apart for good.

Before Matthew had formed a conscious thought, he felt himself move. He felt himself lunge forward, arms outstretched toward his father. He felt his heart thudding in his chest and his breath catch in his throat as all eyes turned to him in shock.

Then he saw his father move.

Swing around.

Toward him.

The pistol in his hands finding a new target.

And then a deafening sound shattered the peaceful stillness of the early morning air. Instantly, Matthew was thrown backwards into the wet grass of the clearing, red hot pain searing through his left shoulder.

With a groan, Matthew Turner, Baron Whitworth, shot up in bed, his heart beating through his chest as though it was trying to flee his body and seek cover elsewhere. Sweat trickled down his temples, and his breath came in ragged gasps. His eyes were wide open, and yet, they did not see the dim surroundings of his chamber. All they saw were the white clouds that had hung in the pale blue sky that morning. All he heard were his father's angry snarls. All he felt was the fresh pain drilling a hole into his heart.

His fingers travelled to his left shoulder and slipped under his shirt, finding the small scar where the bullet had broken his skin and dug itself into his body. And yet, it had been his heart that had hurt the most. So excruciating had been the pain, that for a moment Matthew had been certain the bullet had found its mark perfectly.

Closing his eyes, Matthew brushed the hair from his face, then flung back the blanket and stepped from the bed. The cool floorboards felt heavenly under his heated feet, and he welcomed the chill of the early morning air as it sent shivers over his body.

Yet another night had ended before it should have, he surmised, pulling back the curtains and staring outside at the darkened sky. His nightmares always found him sometime after midnight, dragging him back to the morning when he had finally realised the truth.

That his father had been a madman. A man willing to murder his own blood in order to steal title and fortune for himself.

And for his son.

For Matthew.

And Matthew had not seen it. In fact, he had always believed his father when the man had spoken harshly of Tristan's faults. He had always agreed that Tristan had brought shame to their family and had not deserved to hold the title passed on to him by his father. Always had Matthew berated his cousin for his inappropriate behaviour, unable to see that all Tristan's demons had been conjured by none other than his own father.

Remembering the crazed look on his father's face, Matthew closed his eyes, inhaling a deep breath. Fortunately—if that was indeed the right word! —Matthew had not died that day.

And neither had Tristan.

In the nick of time, when Matthew's father had once more advanced on his nephew after accidentally shooting his own son, Tristan's sister had arrived on the scene. Henrietta had always been an unusual woman, and as Matthew now knew, she had always protected her little brother from their uncle's destructive plans. It had been Henrietta who had stopped their uncle for good, her dagger's aim true as it always was.

If it had not been for her, Tristan would have died that day, and who knew who else would have followed him to the grave. Matthew sighed. Indeed, it was good that she had come. That she had stopped his father. That she had saved them all.

Matthew knew this to be true, and he also knew that the part of him that felt regret was the most selfish part of him there was. Still, he could not help but regret his father's death for it had robbed him of any hope for closure.

For answers.

Leaning his forehead against the cool pane of the window, Matthew closed his eyes, knowing that his mind would immediately conjure the morning in Hyde Park that had changed his life. Guilt and shame flooded him for having allowed his father to deceive—to manipulate—him so easily.

All his life, Matthew had sought his father's approval, his praise, his attention, and it had blinded him to the truth. Always had he been jealous of Tristan because all his father would concern himself with was his young nephew.

But never his son.

Never him.

Never Matthew.

Gritting his teeth, Matthew felt the strong urge to put his fist through the glass. He had been selfish and vain and foolish, and it had almost destroyed them all.

Still, Tristan had forgiven him. More than that. Tristan had not even wanted to hear of an apology when Matthew had sought him out after the shooting. He had looked him in the eyes and said that they had all been equally blind and that he was not to blame.

Matthew had been thunderstruck by his cousin's kind heart, and the guilt and shame that had taken up permanent residence in his soul had grown tenfold that day. He had vowed then that he would do whatever he could to prove himself to his family.

To prove his love.

His loyalty.

His devotion.

To prove to himself that he was not the man his father had been. To prove to himself that he was a good man. To redeem himself in his own eyes as much as in theirs. To become his own person and not live his life in his father's image.

Again, his fingers curled into a fist, and Matthew had to step away from the window to resist temptation.

As irony would have it, not long after his father's death, Matthew had inherited the title of baron through his mother's line when a distant cousin had died childless in a riding accident. The day he had received the news had been one of the darkest days of his life.

To Matthew, it was as though his father was reaching out his hands from the grave, forcing his idea of right and wrong on him. Forcing Matthew to live the life his father had been willing to kill for.

Would he ever feel at peace again? Would he ever be able to look at himself in the mirror and not feel shame and guilt? Would he ever be his own man? Or was he doomed to follow in his father's footsteps?

He would do anything to gain back even just the smallest piece of respect he used to have for himself.

Anything.

Before it was too late.

1

A WHISPER HEARD

Adelaide Cartwright, daughter to the Earl of Radcliff, smiled when she saw the joy on Tillie's face as the two-year-old girl chased after snowflakes. Bundled up, only the little girl's face was visible, her cheeks reddened from the cold and the exertion of stomping through the snow-covered garden. Her eyes glowed with delight, and even when she stumbled and fell, she quickly pushed herself back up onto her feet, laughter spilling from her mouth with the unhindered joy of the young.

Almost desperately, Adelaide wished she could abandon her concerns for the girl's future as well as her own and join in her happiness. But try as she might, her mind would not relinquish its concerns. They were present day and night, making her heart ache painfully and her head throb with vigour.

Although her unmarried, elder brother had claimed Tillie as his, the little girl was still illegitimate. A bastard. A child without worth as far as society was concerned.

Never would she know respect as others did. Never would she be met with kindness. Never would she know her mother.

Blinking back the tears that threatened, Adelaide inhaled a deep breath of the crisp winter air. If only she could spare Tillie the fate that awaited her. At only two years of age, the girl was not yet aware of the circumstances of her birth. However, before long, she would be, and Adelaide knew that that day would break her heart as well.

Waving to the cheerful little girl, Adelaide vowed that she would do whatever she could to ensure Tillie's happiness…even if she had no idea how to go about it.

Looking up, Adelaide noticed her mother and grandmother coming down the path toward her. Their heads were tilted toward one another, and even from a distance away, Adelaide could tell that their faces held concern.

Instantly, her stomach twisted into knots.

Had her father found her another suitor? Someone who suited his ideas of a son-in-law? Someone with fortune and title? Someone he had become acquainted with on his own escapades all over town? Someone he had met in yet another gambling hell? Someone…he owed money to?

Bright spots began to dance before Adelaide's eyes, and for a moment, she thought she would be ill. Inhaling a deep breath, she willed herself not to despair. As much as she wished to curl up on her bed and forget the world around her, it would not solve her problems. It would not serve her.

Forcing her chin up, Adelaide glanced at Tillie, ensuring that the girl was still otherwise occupied and had not ventured over. Then she met her mother's eyes and understood the pity and regret she saw there exactly for what they were.

Her doom.

After she had lost Lord Arlton's regard—thanks to the interference of a friend of hers! —Adelaide had hoped to find a suitable match before her father could interfere again. However, she had not been fortunate to meet a decent and honourable young man, let alone win such a man's heart. None of the young gentlemen she had danced with and spoken to had appealed to her heart either. Indeed, always had she taken note of something in their character that had warned her to stay away. Either they had been conceited, greedy, ill-tempered or vain. She could not in good conscience have married any of them for they all reminded her of the many darker aspects of her father's character. Was there in all of London not a single eligible, young man of good character and with a kind heart?

If there was, it seemed that she could not find him…at least not in time.

By the time her mother and grandmother reached her side, Adelaide was swaying on her feet. As much as she counselled herself to stay strong, doing so was a different matter. Day by day, her strength seemed to weaken. Her heart no longer hoped, and her soul ached so acutely that she began to feel despair weighing heavily on her. "What is it?" she finally prompted after her mother and grandmother continued to exchange one wary glance after another. "I can tell from the look on your faces that whatever you have to say is not good. Please, do not keep me in suspense."

Her mother sighed, her gaze drifting to the ground.

Stepping forward, her grandmother placed a gentle hand on Adelaide's clenched ones, her kind eyes seeking hers. "Although he's promised otherwise, it seems your father is still gambling."

Adelaide inhaled a slow breath, not surprised by this statement in the least. What was it that her grandmother was trying to tell her?

"However," she continued, "since he has by now lost most of his fortune as well as the smaller estates not entailed, he has been heard to…" Her grandmother drew in a steadying breath, which sent a cold shiver down Adelaide's back, especially since her grandmother was not one to hedge. Indeed, she was one of only a handful of women of Adelaide's acquaintance who always stood tall, who never bowed her head. "He's been heard to…offer your hand in marriage."

Although Adelaide had expected life-shattering news, she still could not prevent the shock to knock the air from her lungs. Her body ached as though someone had truly landed a fist in her belly, and she almost toppled over at the force of such devastation. "Are you certain?" she asked in-between heaving gasps, her hand pressed to her heart, willing it to calm down. "How would you even come to know such a thing?"

Her grandmother sighed, "I've learnt long ago, my dear, to have ears and eyes everywhere. Knowledge can be equally powerful as money."

"Can it?" Adelaide scoffed, repulsed by the despair that rang in her voice. "If what you say is true, then there is nothing that can be done. Father will surely lose my hand soon enough, and then I'll be forced to marry a man of weak character. A man who gambles. A man who indulges in spirits every day of the week. A man who is most likely hot-tempered and ill-mannered, dominating those around him without regard for anyone's well-being other than his own." Her gaze shifted to her mother's tear-streaked face. "I will have a marriage like yours, Mother, and we all know the happiness it has brought you."

Her mother's eyes widened at the veiled insult, and Adelaide cringed at the misery that came to her face. Shaking her head, she grasped her mother's hand. "I'm sorry, Mother. I did not mean what I said. I only–"

"You're frightened," her mother interrupted, her own hands curling around Adelaide's. "I understand very well, my dear. There is no need to apologise. Believe me, if I could, I would give my life to spare you such a fate. If only it would do any good."

"I will not have you speak like that!" her grandmother snapped, her eyes narrowing in anger as she looked from Adelaide to her daughter-in-law. "Neither one of you! Do you hear me? Only weaklings lie down and wait for death. I will not have it. Do you hear?"

Oddly enough, the strength in her grandmother's voice lifted Adelaide's spirits, and she nodded eagerly, desperate for the proffered sliver of hope on the horizon. Swallowing, Adelaide brushed away her tears. "But what can we do? How can we prevent this?"

A sly smile came to her grandmother's lips. "I shall speak to Lady Elton. If anyone can help, it is she. She has the intelligence as well as the daring spirit needed to think of a solution." Squeezing Adelaide's hand, her grandmother nodded to her. "Do not despair. We shall find a way out of the dark." And then she was gone, hurrying back the path they had come, her steps sure-footed and confident.

Adelaide once more inhaled a deep breath, her heart thudding rapidly as she thought of Lady Elton. Would she truly be able to think of a solution? In any case, Adelaide agreed with her grandmother. If anyone could help, it would be Lady Elton. After all, it had been she who had liberated Adelaide from Lord Arlton's intentions a few months ago. With a few well-placed words, the young woman had discouraged the lecherous, old man from pursuing Adelaide further. Adelaide had been thunderstruck by her cunning mind.

Drawn from her thoughts by her mother's anguished sigh, Adelaide turned to look at the woman who had reared her. "You do not believe it possible, do you?" she asked, seeing the downcast eyes that refused to meet hers. "You do not think that Lady Elton will be able to help."

Sighing once more, her mother finally looked at her, the pity in her eyes saying more than a thousand words. "I'm sorry, my dear, but I do not believe that anyone can sway your father from the path he has chosen. I cannot imagine that there is anything Lady Elton can say that would change his mind." Pulling her daughter's hands into her own, Adelaide's mother smiled at her. It was a weak and defeated little smile, and it broke Adelaide's heart. "The best we can do is pray that the one who will win your hand is a good and kind man."

Returning her mother's smile with a half-hearted one of her own, Adelaide nodded, knowing only too well that the fire her mother might have had in her once had been extinguished long ago. Was this her fate as well? Adelaide wondered, knowing equally well that she, too, had all but accepted her lot in life. The only difference between her and her mother was that here and there a spark of hope could still be found in Adelaide's heart. How many more disappointments were needed before hope would never spark again?

Turning away, Adelaide saw Tillie laying in the snow and moving her little arms and legs, making a snow angel. The sight brought fresh tears to her eyes, and she worried about what would happen to the girl if she were to marry. If she were to marry a man of her father's choosing.

Tillie's happiness would be equally affected by such a development as her own, for Adelaide could not imagine that any man—let alone a man like her father! —would want his brother-in-law's bastard child living in his house! The thought of losing Tillie who had been her ray of sunshine in her dreary life these past two years nearly choked the air from Adelaide's lungs.

Would this pain never end?

Pray, her mother had said. Well, so far it had not done them any good, and so Adelaide decided to put all her faith in Lady Elton. After all, the woman had once moved a mountain. Perhaps she could do so again.

2

A CALL FOR AID

fter hastily finishing off his breakfast, Matthew rushed out of the house. His muscles were still sore from yesterday's boxing practise, and so instead of calling for his carriage, he decided that a walk would do him good.

Stretching his limbs, he marched at a brisk pace, feeling his muscles respond in a more favourable manner. He curled and uncurled his fingers, trying his best to shake off the stiffness that often clung to them after crossing fists—as he liked to call it—with an old acquaintance.

Matthew had been boxing almost all his life as he had discovered early on that it helped him handle the frustration that came with competing for his father's attention and approval. Since he had been met by failure at every attempt, the frustration he had initially felt had often threatened to turn into something far more dangerous.

Only when Matthew had accompanied an old friend from his days at Eton to a boxing practise had he discovered the means to control at times raging emotions inside him. Today, even more than before, Matthew relied on the practise to guide him through the treacherous sea of disappointment and anger. Physically exhausting his body calmed his heart and soul, and at least for a time, he felt better.

Felt less like lashing out at the world.

Especially now that he knew the truth about what kind of man his father had been, Matthew knew he needed to keep his own anger at bay. Keep it controlled and locked away…lest he hurt someone.

Who knew what he was capable of?

The mere thought sent cold shivers down his back.

As he climbed the steps to his cousin's townhouse, Matthew wondered what could be so urgent that Tristan had sent a note so early in the morning. He could only hope that he and his wife were fine, and no tragedy had befallen them. Still, there had been something in the brusque tone of the missive that had hastened Matthew's steps.

He could not shake the feeling that something was very wrong.

As he stepped over the threshold to Tristan's study, Matthew found his cousin and his golden-haired wife standing by the tall arched window, their faces intent as they seemed to be discussing something of great importance.

The moment they saw him, they strode forward, greeting him warmly. Still, their open acceptance of him never failed to leave a bitter aftertaste. He did not deserve their kindness. Not after what he had done. Not after what he had allowed his father to do.

"It is good to see you, Cousin," Tristan said, a large smile on his face as he clasped a hand on Matthew's shoulder. Still, tension rested on his face that spoke to the dread Matthew felt curled up in his stomach.

"Good morning, Tristan," he said, returning the greeting. "Lady Elton."

His cousin's wife rolled her deep blue eyes in a rather unladylike, and yet, becoming way. "Matthew, how often must I ask you to call me Beth? It's slowly becoming a bit of a nuisance."

A faint smile tickled the corner of Matthew's mouth, and he almost joined in Tristan's amused laughter. Despite her straightforward manner—or perhaps because of it—Matthew had to admit that he had come to like his cousin's wife. Admired her for her strong and steadfast character.

If only he knew what her secret was. How had she become the strong person she was today?

"You better listen," Tristan advised with a sidelong glance at his wife. "She can become quite unpleasant when she does not get what she wants."

With arms akimbo, Lady Elton glared at her husband. Still, the corners of her mouth betrayed her amusement before she stepped forward and slapped her husband's arm good-naturedly. "Careful what you say, my dear," she threatened, a teasing grin on her face. "Do not forget that I know all your secrets."

Tristan grinned back. "And I yours."

A smile claimed her face, and she laughed. "Indeed, that is true," she admitted before turning questioning eyes to Matthew.

"All right," Matthew said, lifting his hands in surrender. "I admit defeat." Once more, he inclined his head to her in greeting. "Good morning, Beth."

"There," she exclaimed, satisfaction ringing in her voice. "Was that so hard?"

Smiling, Matthew shook his head. Despite his feelings of guilt, he could not deny that he enjoyed visiting with Tristan and Beth. They were genuinely kind and caring people, and their townhouse felt like a home, filled with laughter and teasing and shared memories. If only he could find a woman like Beth. A woman who would believe in him, who would stand by his side and help him defeat his own demons.

The way Beth had done for Tristan.

Without her, Matthew doubted that Tristan would have found the peace and happiness that sparkled in his eyes whenever he looked at his beloved wife.

"May I ask why you called on me?" Matthew enquired, still feeling a bit on edge about what urgency might have occurred. "Your letter sounded a bit…odd. I hope nothing is wrong?"

Instantly, their faces darkened, and Matthew felt his heart clench in his chest. What on earth had happened now? Had they all not suffered enough at the hands of his father?

"Is there anything I can do?" Matthew asked further, observing the way Tristan and Beth exchanged glances as naturally as though they were speaking out loud.

"Indeed, there is," Tristan finally said, turning to meet his eyes. "We need your help."

Matthew nodded. "Anything," he replied, feeling his chest swell with pride that his cousin would call on him in a time of need. He would do anything within his power to prove that he was trustworthy. That he was loyal. That he was not the man his father had been.

Once more, Tristan exchanged a glance with his wife before Beth stepped forward, her blue eyes finding Matthew's. "I have a dear friend," she began, her voice tense and free of the humour he had heard there before. "Unfortunately, her father is a gambler and has been working continuously on ruining the family's reputation. Their fortune is all but lost, and so we've heard it whispered that he has descended to a new low." Beth swallowed, her hands tense as she wrung them nervously.

Never had Matthew seen her so vulnerable. Clearly, this friend of hers meant a great deal to her.

"What did he do?" Matthew prompted, glancing at Tristan, who stepped forward and placed a gentle hand on his wife's back.

Squaring her shoulders, she raised her head, meeting his gaze, her own blazing with new determination. "Apparently, as he is lacking in funds, he has made it known that he intends to wager his daughter's hand in marriage."

Appalled, Matthew all but shrank back, reminded of his own father's disregard for his family. "That is outrageous!" he hissed, his hands curling into fists at his sides. "Who is the man?"

Beth's eyes darkened. "Lord Radcliff."

At her answer, the air was knocked from Matthew's lungs as an image of a raven-haired beauty rose before his inner eye. Her delicate frame and downcast, almost fearful gaze had never failed to conjure his protective side whenever he had laid eyes on her. "Lady Adelaide," he whispered, recalling the ghost of a smile he had here and there seen curl up her lips as though she did not dare allow it to break through.

"You know her?" Tristan asked, and Matthew did not fail to detect the note of suspicion in his cousin's tone.

Matthew cleared his throat. "We've never been officially introduced," he hastened to say. "However, I've…"

"Noticed her?" Looking at him with frank perusal, Tristan grinned from ear to ear.

"Don't tease him," Beth chided, elbowing her husband in the ribs. "Can you be serious for a moment?"

Tristan narrowed his eyes at her. "I'm not teasing. I'm merely making an observation."

"One we can do without at present," Beth concluded, a touch of finality in her voice before she turned back to meet Matthew's reluctant gaze. "Yes, it is Lady Adelaide I was referring to. Are you willing to help us?"

Nothing could stop him from doing so. "What do you need me to do?"

"Since Lord Radcliff already knows me," Tristan explained, the tone in his voice thankfully taking on a more serious note, "I would ask *you* to follow him. In secret. Keep your distance but keep your eyes on the man and find out if he will indeed offer his daughter's hand."

Matthew nodded. "What if he does?" The mere thought twisted his insides painfully.

With lips pressed into a hard line, Tristan held his gaze. "Quite frankly, we don't know yet. But should he lose his daughter's hand, then find out who that man is and report back immediately. Can you do that?"

"Of course," Matthew assured him, pleased when Tristan nodded in acknowledgement, the look in his eyes free of doubt. "Should we not attempt to prevent him from losing his daughter's hand?" Matthew asked, hoping his question would not offend his cousin.

Tristan sighed. "If you have an idea, let us hear it," he replied, a hint of frustration in his eyes. "However, we doubt that Lord Radcliff can be easily persuaded. By now, his daughter's hand and the dowry given to her by her grandfather—funds he cannot touch—are his only bargaining chip. He will not give them up lightly. Only if he sees the promise of a reward."

Matthew nodded, repulsed by the greed some men placed above their own blood. "What if she were to marry?" The question had left his lips before his mind had even fully registered it.

The hint of a teasing smile played on Tristan's lips. "Without a large incentive, he will most likely not accept any suitor we may present. Let us think on it." He glanced at his wife as she stepped closer and another meaningful look passed between them. "However, we must know what happens in the meantime."

"I shall keep you informed," Matthew promised solemnly, hoping against hope that it would not come to it. In his experience, men who lost all connection to reality, men who were consumed by something or other rarely took a step back to rethink what they were doing. Such a circumspect act was no longer within their capabilities. He could only hope that the one who would win Lady Adelaide's hand was a decent man...however slim the chances were.

Still, Matthew could not deny that the thought of her tied to any man—decent or not—was upsetting to him. Swallowing, he took his leave, wondering about the raven-haired lady who haunted his dreams whenever his father did not.

3

A DARK MOMENT

A sennight later, Matthew found himself standing in the back of a crowded room in one of London's most notorious gaming hells.

Over the past week, he had followed Lord Radcliff all over town, watching as the man lost more and more of his remaining fortune. Here and there, he had had a lucky hand. However, his streak—if one could call it that! —had never lasted long, and by now, he was running out of funds.

Smoke hung in the darkened room, stinging Matthew's eyes, and he tried his best to inhale only shallow breaths. Still, he watched with hawk eyes as the earl continued on his downward spiral.

Sweat clung to the man's temples, and he kept wiping his arm across his forehead nervously. All the money he had won earlier that night was gone, and Matthew knew that he was close to playing the last card he had: his daughter's hand in marriage.

With crazed eyes, the earl stared down at his cards, reminding Matthew of his own father and the morning he had finally shown his true face. The shock still clung to Matthew's bones, and he wondered if he would ever be able to make his peace with what had happened. Still, this, here and now, was not about him.

This was about Lady Adelaide, an innocent young woman who was about to be bartered off to the highest bidder.

Matthew felt sick.

His hands began to sweat when the other men began taunting the earl, laughing at him for his misfortune that night, his lack of funds, his hesitation at playing the next card. In turn, the earl's face turned a darker shade of red, and Matthew could see the crazed look in his eyes intensifying. Reason—or what might have been left of it—flew out the window, and in that moment, all the earl was capable of caring about was to win.

At all cost.

No matter what.

Damn the consequences.

Before the earl's voice even rose above the cacophony of voices surrounding him, Matthew knew what would happen. Unable not to, Lord Radcliff would up the game and offer the only thing left to him that still possessed value in order to save face. "My daughter's hand in marriage," he boomed as though announcing certain victory, "as well as the vast dowry her grandfather bestowed upon her."

Silence fell over the room as men stared at him, their disbelief apparent in the way their eyes nearly crawled out of their sockets. Although they had all heard the earl boast of his intentions of wagering his daughter's hand, none seemed to have taken his words at face value.

Then laughter soared high as men slapped each other on the back, their eyes eager as they turned them back to their cards. Even those not in the game stepped closer, their attention captivated as the final round played out. Lewd comments were passed back and forth about the lady, which had Matthew's hands curl into fists once more. It took all his willpower not to strike men down left and right while Lord Radcliff seemed oblivious to the words aimed at his daughter, his gaze fixed on the cards in his hands.

Loss or gain had never been more closely tied to a single moment.

Holding his breath, Matthew watched everything unfold. His gaze shifted from the earl to the other players, one of which would win Lady Adelaide's hand—he was certain of it. He was equally certain that none of these men deserved to call her his wife, and he hoped with fervent intensity that Tristan had come up with a good plan to circumvent the earl's blatant disregard for his daughter's happiness.

With a triumphant grin on his reddened face, Lord Radcliff placed his cards on the table.

Groans rose from the other players as they tossed their cards aside, anger and disappointment marking their features, their reaction giving Matthew a moment of hope as he stepped forward, relief tickling the corners of his heart.

Until his gaze fell on one remaining player by the name of Harkin, who was still holding on to his cards, a pleased smile slowly spreading over his face as his glassy eyes stared at the earl's cards.

Matthew's heart crashed to the ground and shattered into a million pieces.

Closing his eyes, he inhaled a deep breath before willing himself to face the truth. Reluctantly, Matthew opened his eyes once more, his skin tingling at the stillness in the room, and watched as Harkin placed his cards on the table.

Slowly.

Ever so slowly.

One by one.

Everyone held his breath.

Including him.

Including Lord Radcliff.

Before raucous laughter erupted from the spectators, they saw Harkin's winning hand.

Barely a second later, all blood drained from the earl's face, and he turned ash-white so that momentarily Matthew thought he might pass out. Then he shot to his feet, threw his drink across the room, shattering against the opposite wall, and stormed out without another word.

Swallowing, Matthew turned his attention to the man who would now have every right to claim Lady Adelaide for his wife.

A commoner, Mr. Harkin had made his fortune in trade and had, by the looks of it, adjusted to privileged life quite well. With others to tend to his business, he spent most of his time drinking and gambling, and Matthew had encountered him more than once as he had followed the earl all about town. His balding head shining with perspiration, he slapped his large belly as triumphant laughter spilled from his mouth. Quite obviously, he was more than pleased with the evening's outcome.

Feeling bile rise in this throat, Matthew stumbled outside in desperate need of fresh air.

The moment he stepped across the threshold and the night engulfed him, Matthew knew that there was nothing to be done. His heart sank as he stumbled onward, his thoughts a jumbled chaos in his head as he desperately tried to think of a solution. Perhaps the man could be bought off.

Sighing, Matthew closed his eyes, resting his back against the brick wall behind him. If there was one thing Mr. Harkin possessed in spades, it was money.

Certainly, he would not relinquish his claim on Lady Adelaide for something that had little value to him. Also, as a commoner, he certainly knew that it would raise his standing within society if he were to marry a lady of the upper class.

Cursing under his breath, Matthew hastened down the street toward the better part of town and his cousin's home. He could have hailed a hackney-coach, but his muscles seemed to burst with pent-up energy and were in dire need of release.

What on earth were they to do now?

Again, Lady Adelaide's gentle features and fearful downcast eyes rose in his mind, and Matthew cringed at the thought that he had failed her. A part of him counselled that he had done exactly as asked, and yet, he knew it was not enough. He ought to have protected her. He ought to have found a way to stop her father from ruining her life. Wasn't that what good men did? Did they not protect the innocent?

What did this say about him?

4

A HELPLESS PAWN

ringing her hands, Adelaide took the seat on the settee next to her grandmother, her gaze travelling around Lady Elton's elegantly furnished drawing room. Out of the corners of her eyes, she could see the tension resting on both her grandmother's as well as Lady Elton's face, and yet, Adelaide did not dare admit defeat yet.

For one more moment, she wanted to pretend that all was not lost.

That she would not be forced to marry a stranger.

A man like her father.

A man who had won her hand in a card game.

Still, unable to shut out her surroundings completely, Adelaide felt her stomach twist and turn when she became aware of her grandmother's nervous fidgeting. Alarm bells went off in Adelaide's head. Never in her life had she seen her grandmother like this.

Always composed, the dowager countess stood for strength and character, her sharp mind and dauntless courage a beacon of light in the darkness that had always been Adelaide's life.

But no more.

Smiling at her, Lady Elton took a seat on the armchair opposite them, her kind blue eyes glancing from Adelaide to her grandmother. "I'm glad you were able to come on such short notice," she said, her features tense. "I'm afraid what I have to say cannot wait."

Holding her breath, Adelaide looked at her grandmother.

Squaring her shoulders, the dowager countess nodded. "I see," she gritted out, her eyes narrowing with suppressed anger. "What is it you've found out, my dear? Please, do not keep us in suspense. What has my son done?"

Adelaide knew that it was a proforma question as they all knew beyond the shadow of a doubt what he had done.

Lady Elton inhaled a steadying breath, her eyes unwavering as she spoke. "I'm afraid the worst has come to pass," she said, her blue eyes travelling to Adelaide. "I'm sorry. There is no use in holding back, so I will tell you in as few words as possible what has happened."

"We'd appreciate that," the dowager countess said as she reached out a hand for Adelaide's, pulling it into her lap and holding it tightly.

"We had Lord Radcliff followed for the past sennight," Lady Elton began, a hint of anger in her voice as she spoke. "As expected, he mostly frequented gaming hells, in one of which he lost your hand, Lady Adelaide, to a commoner by the name of Harkin last night."

Adelaide felt as though her heart stopped beating, and yet, it was the fearful squeeze of her grandmother's hand upon her own that crushed every last bit of hope she had still clung to. Tears came to her eyes as she glanced at her grandmother, her face haggard and without strength as she closed her eyes attempting to shut out the pain Lady Elton's words had caused. What were they to do?

"Thank you for your efforts," her grandmother said to Lady Elton before she leaned forward, her eyes fixed on the young lady. "Is there anything that can be done to prevent this? I assume this Mr. Harkin is not a man worthy of my granddaughter."

With a sidelong glance at Adelaide, Lady Elton shook her head. "I'm afraid not." Then she drew in a deep breath, and Adelaide found herself frowning at the sudden spark of mischief she saw in the lady's eyes.

Her grandmother had to have seen it, too, because she almost jumped off the settee as she exclaimed, "You have a plan! I can see it in your eyes. Tell us, my dear. I assure you we will do what it takes to prevent this marriage from happening."

A hint of a devious smile came to Lady Elton's face. "I had hoped you would say that."

Paralysed, Adelaide stared from one woman to the other and back again as they discussed her future as though she were not in the room. Still, Adelaide was grateful for she had never possessed even an ounce of the strength she so admired in her grandmother.

Holding the dowager countess's eager gaze, Lady Elton leaned forward conspiratorially. "What we must do is fairly simple," she said, a devilish smile on her face, one that reminded Adelaide of her grandmother, and she wondered what her grandmother had looked like when she had been young. Oddly enough, Adelaide felt that Lady Elton made a fitting representation of that image.

"We must win her hand back," Lady Elton announced, drawing a delighted chuckle from the dowager countess. "I've already spoken to my husband, and he will ensure that everything is in place. The friend whom I've already mentioned before will once again assist us in tempting Mr. Harkin to offer up Lady Adelaide's hand once more."

"Marvellous!" the dowager countess beamed, turning glowing eyes to Adelaide. "Don't worry, my dear. All shall be well. I'm certain of it."

A tender smile came to Adelaide's face as she nodded. Still, she could not shake the sense of doom that had come over her at the sight of her grandmother's fear. Even though Adelaide was not a young child any longer, her grandmother had always seemed larger than life.

Invincible.

Infallible.

Impeccable.

A moment ago, she had just become human like the rest of them, and that thought frightened Adelaide more than anything she had ever known. What if things went wrong? What if this was something her grandmother and Lady Elton could not solve?

"However, time is of the essence," Lady Elton continued, "as we should not wait for Mr. Harkin to demand Lord Radcliff hand over your granddaughter and give his blessing for their union."

"Of course not," Adelaide's grandmother agreed, her hand squeezing Adelaide's with renewed strength as she inhaled an invigorating breath. "When shall it take place?"

"As early as tonight," Lady Elton replied. "We can only hope Mr. Harkin will not seek out Lord Radcliff today." She glanced from the dowager countess to Adelaide. "It might be a good idea to instruct your butler to excuse you to all visitors today."

Nodding alongside her grandmother, Adelaide did her best to fight the sense of doom that still lingered. All her life, she had felt like a pawn, unable to decide which path to walk, what direction to go. Always had it been her father's decision, and she knew very well—even before this unfortunate development—that he did not base these decisions on his regard for her.

Sighing, Adelaide wondered if she would ever find herself in a position to choose.

For herself.

Would it make a difference if she finally gathered the courage to voice her objections to his decisions? To his plans for her?

In all likelihood, her father would simply ignore her as he had ignored her all her life so long as she was not of use to him.

Was there not a man anywhere in England who would see her as more than a bargaining chip?

5

A LUCKY HAND

eated around a large table in yet another darkened room in one of the many gaming hells men like Lady Adelaide's father frequented, Matthew found himself glancing to his right at none other than the loathsome Mr. Harkin.

Over the past three days, Matthew had done his utmost to gain the man's trust, relieved to have been awarded that time as Mr. Harkin seemed in no hurry to claim Lady Adelaide as his bride. He seemed to be perfectly content boasting about his prize at every possible opportunity, bathing in the admiration of the other gamblers and drunkards, especially those who had gone a long while without Fortune smiling on them.

Still, despite being preoccupied with flaunting his prize, Mr. Harkin had proved himself more of a suspicious man than Matthew had anticipated. Even though his pale eyes were glassy more often than not, there was a sharpness to his mind that Matthew feared might be their downfall. What if he began to suspect Matthew's intentions? Certainly, Lady Adelaide would be lost.

Matthew could not allow that to happen.

And so, he reminded himself to be patient…again and again, forcing his hands to remain still, his face to portray nothing of the turmoil he felt as he drank alongside that loathsome man and joined in the laughter at Mr. Harkin's retelling of how he had won the fair lady's hand.

This endeavour was made all the more difficult as the look of superiority in Mr. Harkin's blood-shot eyes only served to remind him of Lord Radcliff as well as his own father. The loss of one's faculties as well as the complete obsession with a meaningless object or pastime in these men proved that such afflictions did not adhere to class, standing or rank. No, they attacked those who were weak enough to allow it entry the same.

Matthew could only hope that he would not end up like one of these men, and so he fought all the more strongly against the urge to succumb to his baser instincts and solve the matter as his father might have.

Through bodily harm…and even murder.

Still, tonight Matthew would stoop as low as using deceit and manipulation to achieve his goals, and although he knew he had a very good reason to do so, he wondered if that reason truly justified the means. Did not all crazed men *think* they had a good reason to do what they did? Did they not all believe that the reason justified the means? Had his own father not thought so as well?

Pushing these thoughts from his mind, Matthew tried to focus on the task at hand. As discussed with Tristan, he had guided Mr. Harkin to that very room that night after ensuring that the man had indulged in spirits for the first half of the evening. The man's unsteady walk and slurred speech were testament to Matthew's success.

All was in place.

All was as planned.

Glancing around the table, Matthew took note of the other gamblers, men he had seen here and there and knew to be in his cousin's employ. Trustworthy men who tonight posed as bored noblemen seeking to gamble away their fortunes. Only Mr. Harkin remained oblivious to the fact that he was surrounded by men who sought to rob him of his prize.

As the evening progressed, Matthew began to feel lightheaded as the pulse in his veins continued to beat at a rapid pace. If they could not resolve the matter soon, he might pass out from the sheer stress of it.

Conjuring an image of Lady Adelaide's shy smile, Matthew forced himself to focus. Unobtrusively, he glanced at Mr. Harkin, who half hung on the table for support as he blinked at his cards, trying to discern his hand.

Was now the right moment to bait the man to up the stakes? Or was it too soon? Mr. Harkin might get suspicious? Or he might pass out and end the night prematurely?

As the evening wore on, Matthew's nerves slowly wore thin as he continued to observe the man to his right. Mr. Harkin's skin was pale and shining with sweat, and his eyelids began to droop.

Swallowing, Matthew decided that it was time. He did not dare wait any longer, nodding to one of Tristan's men when the cards were dealt for the next round.

Inhaling a deep breath, Matthew picked up his cards, breathing a little easier when he saw his superb hand. Then he turned to Mr. Harkin, a triumphant grin on his face. "Harkin, old man," he slurred as best as he could, "I can tell from a single look that your hand is awful." He snickered. "I've never seen anyone lose that much in one night."

Harkin chuckled, his elbow sliding off the table as he did so. Before his chin could connect with the hard surface though, he caught himself, once more bracing himself on his lower arms.

Matthew tried to swallow the lump in his throat, wondering if he had underestimated the man. Still, there was no turning back.

Turning his unsteady gaze to Matthew, Mr. Harkin chortled. "I wouldn't be so sure, boy," he stated after glancing at his cards.

"You're bluffing!" Matthew accused him.

Mr. Harkin's eyes narrowed. "Care to up the stakes?" he challenged, a spark of clarity in his otherwise glazed eyes. "Or can you only talk big?"

Matthew laughed. "I don't need money," he boasted, padding the leather pouch resting beside him on the table. "I have enough." He grinned. "And now thanks to you, I have even more."

"What do you suggest then, boy?"

Matthew felt the little hairs on the back of his neck rise as he prepared to lay out the final step of their plan. Now or never.

Matthew chuckled before gulping down half his drink. "For the past few nights, I've heard you boast of that fine lady you've presumably won." He shrugged, glancing around. "And yet, there is no proof that says you truly have a claim on her."

Mr. Harkin's eyes narrowed. "Her father knows," he slurred, a touch of resentment in his voice, and Matthew knew he had hit his mark. "Many were there that night. They can attest that he lost her to me." A sly grin spread over the man's face as he sat back, looking smug. "I will father noble heirs."

Matthew swallowed the bile that threatened to rise in his throat, willing himself not to show how he truly felt. "Well, if that is truly the case," he challenged, leaning forward his gaze fixed on Mr. Harkin's, "then offer her hand now…if indeed you do have a claim on her." Sitting back, Matthew grinned. "If your hand is indeed as good as you say, then there is no risk to you."

Mr. Harkin's brows drew down, and Matthew could sense that the man was reluctant. "Or are you too much of a coward?" Matthew taunted.

Raucous laughter erupted around the table as Tristan's men sneered at the aging merchant.

Matthew held his breath, watching Mr. Harkin carefully. It was obvious that he was reluctant to offer Lady Adelaide's hand. Still, the attack on his pride stung, and men like Harkin or Radcliff or Matthew's own father feared nothing more than to be reduced in the eyes of others.

"Done!" Mr. Harkin hollered, pounding his fist on the table for emphasis.

Matthew nodded, and they all placed their cards on the table.

For almost a fortnight, Matthew had searched for a way to protect Lady Adelaide, first following her father and then getting closer to Mr. Harkin. He had moved slowly and with care, always afraid that one wrong step would shatter their hopes of reclaiming her hand. Patience had been key, and at times, the need to be patient had been excruciating.

And now, the one moment he had been working for was here…and over before he knew it.

In an instant, Mr. Harkin's triumphant grin turned into an angry sneer as he looked from his own cards to Matthew's. A growl rose from his throat, and he shot to his feet, his eyes shooting lightning bolts at Matthew.

Still, as inebriated as he was, he could not keep upright, swaying on his feet. Two of Tristan's men rose immediately, clasping him on the shoulder and offering him another drink. "It was a good game," one said, seeking to soothe the man's anger. "Let us drink to a night well played."

Although reluctant, Mr. Harkin joined in and allowed himself to be guided out of the room. "I cannot believe I lost," he all but pouted as he clung to the other man for support. "I lost her hand!"

As the door closed behind them, Matthew sagged forward, resting his face in his hands. His eyes closed as he inhaled one slow breath after another, feeling all tension leave his body.

"Well played, my lord," one of Tristan's men commented, an appreciative smile on his face. "I suppose there is no harm in having half the gaming hell hear him complain about losing her hand."

Matthew shook his head. "There is not. Will you see to it?"

The man nodded and then turned and left with the rest of his companions.

Indeed, if Mr. Harkin did not remember in the morning that he had lost Lady Adelaide's hand, then there would be enough people to remind him of it.

As the night's success slowly sank in, a small smile tugged on Matthew's lips, and his thoughts inevitably turned to Lady Adelaide.

He had won her hand.

She was his.

At least for tonight, he could pretend that it was true. Tonight, she was safe. But what would happen the next time her father offered up her hand?

Matthew knew that only once she was married for real would she ever be truly safe.

6

ALL SHALL BE WELL

The past three days Adelaide had barely slept a wink. Her mind had been too preoccupied with all the what-ifs that loomed in her future, and her heart ached with the fear of the unknown that lay ahead. Not even Tillie's innocent smiles could distract her for long, for they only served as a reminder of what she had to lose.

Rising early, Adelaide wandered the house like a ghost, her eyes unseeing as she mulled over everything that might come to pass, unable to concentrate on anything for too long. As she walked by her father's study, she noticed that the door was ajar. Glimpsing inside, Adelaide found him seated behind his desk, head resting in his hands.

Stepping forward, Adelaide lifted her hand to knock. Perhaps her father knew something. As she had yet to receive a note from Lady Elton, Adelaide had no way of knowing what had transpired in the last three days, and not knowing was slowly driving her mad.

Perhaps her father knew something.

Perhaps.

Swallowing, she knocked, flinching slightly as her father's head snapped up, his red-rimmed eyes finding hers through the gap between door and frame.

"Come in," he ordered, and yet, his voice held no strength.

With shaking hands, Adelaide pushed open the door and stepped across the threshold. Slowly, she approached her father's desk, suddenly realising that she had rarely been in his study. It was his most private place. A place that no one was allowed to enter without express permission.

Adelaide had never dared challenge that.

"Are you all right, Father?" she asked feebly as it seemed the most inconspicuous thing to say.

Sighing, he looked up, then gestured for her to sit. "It is fortunate that you are here," he began, and yet, the resignation in his voice made it clear that what he was about to say did not please him in the least, "as I've been meaning to speak to you."

"Yes, Father," was all Adelaide could say as her skin crawled with a sense of foreboding. Was there a hint of resignation in her father's eyes? Never had she seen him like this. Always had he seemed strong, in control.

Clearing his throat, he finally met her eyes…though reluctantly as though he felt ashamed of what he had to tell her. "I'm…*pleased* to inform you," he began, a grotesque imitation of a smile coming to his face, "that I've…received another offer of marriage for you."

Although the news was not news to her and Adelaide was very much aware of the circumstances of said offer, her heart still stopped for a short moment as though it truly had not known.

"Although he is not titled," her father continued, "he is very wealthy and has gained great respect in society over the past decade. I'm certain it will be a most advantageous match for all of us as it is always a good idea to align oneself with influential people. I have no doubt that you will want for nothing."

Adelaide swallowed, willing herself not to faint on the spot.

Again, her father sighed. "You'll be doing your family a great service." For a moment, he held her gaze, looking at her as he had never done before in all her years. "If you'll excuse me, I have matters to attend to."

Nodding, Adelaide retreated until her back collided with the door. Then she mumbled a quick goodbye and all but fled her father's study. By the time she reached the front hall, tears were streaming down her face, and her heart hammered so hard in her chest that she felt certain her ribs would crack at any moment.

"Lady Adelaide, this missive was delivered for you."

At their butler's words, Adelaide stopped in her tracks, shame sneaking into her heart that he would happen upon her in such a state. Quickly, she wiped the tears from her face, blinking her lids and encouraging a small smile to curl up the corners of her mouth.

Then, and only then, did she turn to face him. "Thank you, Walton." Reaching for the letter, she nodded her head, then turned and hastened up the stairs and toward her chamber.

When the door closed behind her, hiding her away from prying eyes, Adelaide exhaled the breath she had been holding. All but stumbling toward the armchair by the window, she sank into it as her shaking legs would no longer support her. Then Adelaide glanced down at the letter, wondering how much more she could take before crumbling into a thousand pieces.

It was then that her eyes recognised Lady Elton's handwriting, and her pulse hitched even higher.

Instantly, her fingers reached to break the seal, but then stopped. What if Lady Elton wrote to tell her that all had gone horribly wrong? That she would truly have to marry this Mr. Harkin?

Closing her eyes, Adelaide pressed her fingers to her temples as a throbbing pain began to beat against the insides of her skull. Could she face this truth here and now? Alone?

What if it is good news? a small voice whispered.

"What if it is good news?" Adelaide repeated almost dazed, once more glancing down at the envelope as though she could tell by the look of it what it contained.

Then without conscious thought, her fingers moved, breaking the seal and pulling forth a folded parchment. The envelope glided to the floor as her hands hurried to reveal the words written on the crisp, white paper.

All shall be well. Call on me this afternoon.

Never had Adelaide received a shorter letter, and yet, none had ever brought her the relief that flooded her being in that moment. All tension left her aching muscles, and bereft of all strength, Adelaide slid off the chair and onto the floor. Her head came to rest on the soft Persian rug, and she closed her eyes feeling the warm morning sun on her face.

All will be well.

With all her being, Adelaide clung to these words, a balm to her battered soul. All her life—but especially lately—she had felt like a piece of driftwood tossed about by the stormy sea, unable to hold on to anything to steady her. Would this never cease?

Bless Lady Elton, her mind whispered, and a small smile came to Adelaide's face. Even when they had not yet known each other, the young woman had come to her rescue, redirecting Lord Arlton's regard elsewhere. And now, once again, she had worked tirelessly to ensure Adelaide's future did not lie in the hands of another old man. Why Lady Elton tended to her so devotedly, Adelaide could not say, but then and there, she did not care.

All she knew was that she was blessed to call her a friend.

7

UNDER ONE CONDITION

nce again, Matthew stepped over the threshold into Tristan's study. Only this time, he found his cousin alone.

Stepping forward, Tristan embraced him warmly, a bright smile on the man's face. "You've gotten some sleep," he observed as a teasing grin formed on his lips. "Good. Last night you looked quite the fright."

Matthew chuckled, quickly remembering the ease he always felt in his cousin's presence. Tristan as well as his wife were sincere and honest people who always spoke their minds and were at times painfully direct. Still, that trait only served to prove that there was no hidden agenda or whispers behind his back. Without a doubt, Matthew knew that if his cousin were to disapprove of him, he would say so outright.

"I'm glad everything worked out," Tristan said, honest relief on his face as he offered Matthew a drink. "I was worried we might not succeed."

Declining the drink, Matthew swallowed. "Were you worried I could not do it?" he asked before he could stop himself, knowing that his self-doubt was nothing he wished others to be aware of.

Exhaling loudly, Tristan looked at him. "I never doubted your commitment nor your honour," he said, his gaze steady as it held Matthew's. "All I meant to say was that given that you're a painfully honest man, I felt that deceiving another even if for a good reason might be asking a lot of you. That is all."

Nodding, Matthew felt the tension flow from his muscles. Again, he had interpreted a comment based on his own insecurities, his own low opinion of himself. Although Tristan's words soothed the ache in his soul, Matthew could not deny that he himself was the one who was unable to free himself of these doubts. He could not help but wonder if he indeed was a good man. An honest man. Everything that had happened in his life had made him doubt himself, his own worth.

First, his father's disregard despite Matthew's countless efforts to be the son his father desired. And then, the life-shattering realisation that he had indeed been a man of weak character, allowing his father to manipulate him so effortlessly.

It gnawed at Matthew day in and day out, and he wondered if he would ever be able to put these thoughts to rest.

Perhaps it was true and there was no need to prove himself to those he held most dear. However, it was also undeniably true that the need to prove to himself that he was—or could be—a man of worth was a constant struggle.

Still, only those who tried could eventually succeed.

Tristan's gaze remained on his for a good while, and Matthew could see that his cousin was not oblivious to his struggle. Clasping a hand on Matthew's shoulder, he said, "All went well. You did good. You saw her safe."

The ghost of a smile brushed over Matthew's lips, and his heart warmed at the thought of Lady Adelaide. "I must admit that I feared it would not work until the last moment when Mr. Harkin placed his cards on the table, and I saw that I beat him." He shook his head, sighing with relief. "I cannot remember ever having felt that anxious."

Still watching him, Tristan's gaze narrowed as the hint of a mischievous smile came to his lips. "You have never even spoken to her, have you?"

Matthew swallowed. "Who?"

Tristan's grin widened. "Lady Adelaide, of course."

"I have not," Matthew replied, his mouth suddenly beginning to feel dry as he saw the speculation in his cousin's eyes. "I...saw her here and there at a ball, but we were not in the same circle so...." His voice trailed off, and he wondered what he had wanted to say.

Sighing, a hint of regret came to Tristan's face. "I apologise for not including you more, Matthew. I admit at the time I was fairly preoccupied with my own demons to think of you. I should have introduced you."

Matthew shook his head. "I do not blame you, Tristan. After all, it was my own father who had conjured your demons." Swallowing, he licked his lips, his mouth drier than before. "I want to apologise for my role in–"

"Don't!"

The vehemence in Tristan's voice made Matthew flinch, and for a moment, he stared at his cousin rather dumbfounded.

Inhaling a deep breath, Tristan shook his head. "I'm sorry for my outburst. However, I do hate to see you torture yourself so." Stepping forward, Tristan once more placed a comforting hand on Matthew's shoulder. "You, my friend, are a good man, and no one can fault you for believing in your own father. You were not wrong to trust him, to trust his word. None of us knew what he had done. None of us knew what his intentions had been. You need to forgive yourself. Now. Before you waste a lifetime regretting something that was not within your power."

Touched beyond words, Matthew nodded. Never had he felt so close to anyone the way he now felt in Tristan's company. His cousin was a truly good and loyal man, and Matthew was fortunate to call him family. They ought to have been as close as brothers from the start, and they would have been if his father had not interfered.

Still, that was of the past, and the future now rested in their hands, not his father's.

Nodding his head in agreement, Matthew smiled when he saw relief come to his cousin's face.

"Good," Tristan said, stepping back and crossing his arms in front of his chest. His gaze once more narrowed as he watched Matthew with a hint of contemplation. "Now, tell me, what do you think of Lady Adelaide?"

Taken aback, Matthew felt his eyes go wide and then saw a knowing smile come to his cousin's face.

Averting his gaze, Matthew cleared his throat. "She seems kind," he croaked, knowing that his comment fell far short of the goodness that always rested in her eyes. All too well did he recall the gentleness that clung to her features as well as that fleeting smile that would cross her face now and then as though she did not dare smile a real smile, unwilling to trust even the smallest kind of happiness. "And sad," he added, meeting his cousin's gaze once more. "Now, I know why."

Tristan's face sobered as he nodded in agreement.

Feeling his muscles tense, Matthew shook his head in disbelief. "How can her own father do this to her? This is a far cry from an arranged marriage based on mutual benefits. This is outrageous!" Dimly aware that his voice rose, Matthew tried his best to control the sudden outburst that had sneaked up on him when he had least suspected it. "He lost her hand in a card game, for goodness sake! That man has no honour, giving her to scum like Harkin. Neither man deserves her."

"I agree," Tristan said. "Then what kind of man do you think would deserve her?"

Although deep in his soul, Matthew understood the reason behind his cousin's words, he could not stop himself from saying, "A true gentleman who would treat her with the utmost respect and truly understands how fortunate he would be to have her in his life."

In answer, Tristan's grin grew wider. "Again, I agree." His brows rose. "A man like you?"

Even though he had seen it coming, Matthew felt the air knocked from his lungs at his cousin's suggestion. His eyes opened wide, and for a moment, he was unable to form a conscious thought.

"You won her hand after all," Tristan pointed out rather matter-of-factly. Still, the grin on his face continued to linger.

The lady's fearful eyes rose in his mind, and Matthew shook his head, taking a step back. "That was not our agreement," he stated, knowing in his heart that it would be wrong to force her hand as her father had no doubt done all her life.

Tristan's eyes narrowed. "Do you not want her?"

Cringing at the words, Matthew almost growled in agony at the memories they conjured. "Men ought not to act on want alone," he forced out through clenched teeth. "Those who do will all too quickly lose themselves to a darker place from whence there is no return."

Concern drew down Tristan's brows as he once again stepped toward his cousin, his gaze seeking to understand. "I hear what you're saying, Matthew, and I assure you that you are the only one who thinks of you thus. There is not a single doubt in my mind that you are an honourable man and that Lady Adelaide would be fortunate to call you her husband." Then his brows rose in question yet again. "Do you want her?"

Feeling his shoulders slump, Matthew exhaled a deep breath as exhaustion stole over him.

"I suspected as much," Tristan chuckled when Matthew lifted his head once more. "The moment I spoke of her, something changed in you."

"She…I…" Matthew stammered without knowing what he wanted to say.

Still, Tristan nodded as though he understood. Perhaps he did. Perhaps he remembered his own muddled brain when he had first met Beth.

"Listen, despite our best efforts," Tristan stated, his voice sobering, "we will not be able to keep her safe indefinitely. One day, her father will succeed in tying her to another, and then there will be nothing we can do." His eyes implored Matthew to listen. "The only option is to see her married to a good man before her father can destroy her happiness for good."

Torn between temptation and his fear of failing yet again, Matthew nodded. "I know. That thought has been with me ever since I returned last night. At first, I was euphoric, but then I realised that it was only a temporary solution."

"Then what are you afraid of?" Tristan asked, straightforward as always.

Gritting his teeth, Matthew held his cousin's gaze, knowing that now was not the time for false bravery and pretend reasons. "That I…may not be good enough for a woman like her."

"You've felt like this all your life, have you not?" Tristan asked, a strange sense of understanding in his blue eyes. "As have I. No matter what I did, I could never live up to your father's expectations, and I always thought the fault lay with me. I never once contemplated that he might be the one to blame." He sighed, and for a moment, utter relief washed over his face. "And then I met Beth, and she showed me that I did not need to change in order to be the man I wanted to be. All I had to do was open my eyes." Gripping Matthew's shoulders with both hands, Tristan held his gaze. "Do you want her?"

His teeth pressed together almost painfully. "Yes."

"Good," Tristan stated. "Then marry her, and keep her safe, and then allow her to do the same for you."

Bewildered, Matthew stared at his cousin. Not in a million years would he have seen this coming. Certainly, he had been aware of his regard for Lady Adelaide despite his best efforts to ignore it. However, never would he have expected this turn of events.

As a new thought registered, Matthew's eyes opened wide. "Does she know?"

"Beth invited her over," Tristan said, his eyes as watchful as before. "She should be here any minute."

The mere thought of seeing Lady Adelaide again warmed Matthew's heart in such a way that he could not deny that she was exactly what he wanted. Still, he could not act upon his own desires alone. He could not become the man his father had been. "I will marry her," he finally said, meeting his cousin's gaze, "but only if she agrees. I will not force her hand. I will not marry her against her will."

Grinning widely, Tristan sat down leisurely on the corner of his desk. "I would have expected no less from you."

8

A GOOD MAN

Clutching her grandmother's arm so tightly she feared it might snap in half, Adelaide ascended the stairs to Lady Elton's townhouse. The blood rushed in her ears, drowning out all other sounds, including the butler's greeting. As though she was attached to her grandmother, Adelaide moved whenever the older woman moved, stepping into the large foyer, her eyes almost unseeing.

Only when Lady Elton rushed toward them, a kind smile on her face as though she knew exactly what fears clawed at Adelaide's heart, did she inhale a deep breath, doing her best to shake off the strange sense of detachment that had befallen her.

"Welcome," Lady Elton greeted them warmly. "I admit I've been waiting by the window." A wide smile came to her face, making her shine like the sun on a dreary day. "Please follow me to the drawing room." She looked at Adelaide. "I promise I shall answer all your questions."

As they turned toward the adjacent room, Adelaide caught a glimpse of Lady Elton's fair-haired husband currently deep in conversation with another gentleman as they stood close to where one of the back corridors led to the front hall.

Even from a distance, Adelaide could see the tension that seemed to hold the unknown man almost rigid, his head jerking up and down as he listened to Lord Elton. Every once in a while, his right hand would rise and run through his dark brown hair as though for the mere reason of having something to do. Then his gaze suddenly swerved in her direction, and the slow rise and fall of his wide chest stopped as their eyes locked.

If only for a moment.

A gentle smile curled up his lips as he respectfully inclined his head to her. Still, there was a shyness in the way he quickly averted his eyes.

He touched something deep within her.

If only she knew what…and why.

Stepping over the threshold into the drawing room, Adelaide felt a small stab of regret when the doors were closed, effectively ending her rather daring observation of the unknown gentleman. Still, within moments, her mind worked to remind her why they had come, and Adelaide felt her hands grow damp. Her knees trembled, and she was relieved to sink down onto the settee next to her grandmother, their hands still wrapped around one another as though holding on to an anchor. "I received your letter," she suddenly blurted out, unable to contain her need to know any longer.

Lady Elton smiled at her kindly. "I suspected as much."

"I'm sorry. I…"

"There's no need," Lady Elton said, waving Adelaide's concerns away. "If it were me, I would feel equally ill at ease. Then allow me to inform you that Mr. Harkin no longer has a claim on you."

Almost sagging against her grandmother, Adelaide closed her eyes, her head spinning with relief as she forced one deep breath after another into her lungs. Dimly, she became aware that her grandmother was brushing a hand up and down her back, mumbling words of comfort. "I'm all right," she whispered, looking up and into her grandmother's concerned eyes. "I'm all right. I simply…"

"I know, dear," her grandmother whispered, brushing a gentle hand over her cheek. "You've had to deal with a lot as of late. It is understandable that you would be overwhelmed."

Nodding, Adelaide turned her eyes back to Lady Elton. "What happened?" was all she could ask, her mind still too muddled for anything more meaningful.

"As I said before," Lady Elton began, "we tempted Mr. Harkin into another game. Eventually, he…let's say, bowed to social pressure and upped the stakes, offering your hand. The friend I mentioned before then won the game and with it your hand." A soft smile on her face, Lady Elton held Adelaide's gaze. "All will be well."

"Thank you," Adelaide whispered, wondering why this woman was so determined to protect her.

"What if he hadn't won?" her grandmother asked, and Lady Elton's gaze moved to her. "What if something had gone wrong? What if another had won? Or even Mr. Harkin again?" Despite the positive outcome of the previous night, worry hung on her grandmother's face.

A devious smile lit up Lady Elton's face. "Let's just say we ensured that that wouldn't happen."

A deep chuckle escaped her grandmother's lips, and her eyes lit up with renewed vigour. "You cheated," she stated, open admiration in her voice.

Despite the large smile on her face, Lady Elton batted her eyelashes innocently. "I would never say that," she replied before her voice dropped to a whisper, "nor would I deny it."

Both women laughed, and Adelaide wondered at the obvious connection between Lady Elton and her grandmother. For a reason she could not understand, there was not only mutual trust between them, but also a deeper understanding that eluded Adelaide. And yet, both women had known each other less than a year.

"Breathe, dear," her grandmother instructed, taking Adelaide's hand. "You look pale."

Doing as she was bid, Adelaide once more turned her gaze to Lady Elton. "Thank you again for what you did. Again. Whenever I've needed a friend, you have always been there. I hope one day I will be able to repay you for your kindness."

Smiling, Lady Elton held her gaze, and yet, it seemed to darken with something Adelaide could not understand. "There is no need, Lady Adelaide. It was my pleasure. After all, family…and friends protect each other. You don't owe me anything. All I want is for you to be happy."

Overwhelmed by such kind words, Adelaide did not know what to say. All she knew was that she was blessed to have these two devoted women in her life who did not hesitate to do all within their power to protect her.

When Adelaide's attention returned from her inward reflection, she took note of the looks being cast back and forth between Lady Elton and her grandmother. Something silent was passing between them, and judging from the concern darkening their eyes, it was nothing good. What were they keeping from her?

"Is something wrong?" Adelaide finally asked, unable to bear the renewed doubts any longer. "Is there something you're not telling me?"

Lady Elton sighed. "There is nothing wrong," she replied. "At least not yet."

Adelaide frowned. "What do you mean?"

Once again, her grandmother took her hand, her eyes gentle as they looked into hers. "What she means is that no one can say when your father might act rashly again and give your hand to a man without thinking." Squeezing her hand, her grandmother sighed, "I'm afraid you will not be truly safe, my dear, until you marry."

"I know," Adelaide whispered, wishing she could ignore that fact, "but I—" Her voice broke off as she took note of the strange way her grandmother glanced at Lady Elton. Looking back and forth between the two women, Adelaide felt her blood run cold as her eyes widened with sudden realisation. "You want me to marry," she breathed, feeling her head spinning as though it were not attached. "Now?"

Reaching for both her hands, her grandmother held them tightly, her soft and yet determined gaze imploring Adelaide to understand. "It is the only way to keep you safe from men like Mr. Harkin and Lord Arlton."

Terror gripped Adelaide's heart, squeezing it within an inch of her life. "Who?" she asked, her voice trembling as her eyes drifted to Lady Elton.

"The man who won your hand last night."

Panic surged through Adelaide's being at the thought of being married off to a stranger. Shooting to her feet, she tried to put some distance between herself and the other two women. Her breath came in heavy pants as she tried to fight down the overwhelming panic reaching out its talons for her. Her gaze travelled to the window, then the door before it returned to the settee and her grandmother.

Rising to her feet, Lady Elton came toward her, gently drawing Adelaide's hands into her own. Her kind blue eyes sought to meet hers as she squeezed her hands reassuringly. "Please listen."

Swallowing, Adelaide nodded, knowing very well that she had very little choice in the matter.

"The man I spoke of," Lady Elton began, "is a cousin of my husband's. He is a good man. I assure you that he is kind and loyal, decent and honourable. He would never hurt you. You'd be safe with him."

"Equally important," her grandmother added from the settee, a teasing chuckle on her lips, "he is not an old man, but has a handsome young face with piercing green eyes."

Adelaide frowned. "You've met him before?"

"In passing," her grandmother replied as she stepped toward them. "As have you."

"I have?"

Her grandmother nodded. "As far as I know you've never spoken to him, but I've seen him look at you now and then."

At her grandmother's words, Adelaide felt her insides twist and turn. As much as she had always tried, she had never managed to completely ignore the leering way some men tended to look at her. It never failed to bring on a sickening feeling.

"Not like that," her grandmother said, her knowing eyes holding Adelaide's. "He looked at you…in awe and admiration. Sometimes even shyly as though he deemed himself unworthy of you."

Lady Elton nodded. "Matthew is a wonderful man, and I promise you you have nothing to fear from him."

"Matthew," Adelaide mumbled, liking the gentle sound of his name on her lips. Dimly, she remembered the stranger she had seen with Lord Elton upon entering the house, and she wondered if he could be the one her grandmother and Lady Elton were urging her to marry. There had been a shyness in his gaze that had made him feel safe, and he had been handsome indeed. But above all, he had seemed truly kind.

Adelaide's heart calmed a little when she looked up and met Lady Elton's gaze once more.

"I beg you to consider this," the young woman all but pleaded as though her own happiness depended on this as well. "Consider the consequences of your decision. I know that it is not fair, but it is what it is, and next time, we might not be able to protect you."

Swallowing, Adelaide nodded, knowing Lady Elton's words to be true. Had she not feared such a situation ever since her coming out? That her father would choose a man her heart rejected?

As though reading her mind, Lady Elton asked, "Does your heart belong to another?"

"It does not," Adelaide whispered with a sigh, remembering the dream she had once harboured in her heart of finding true love. A dream she had given up upon long ago. Even before her coming out.

Life could be a harsh teacher.

"Then perhaps," Lady Elton said, a little smile playing on her lips, "in time, Baron Whitworth, Matthew, will claim it as his…in exchange for his own."

Adelaide inhaled a shuddering breath, not knowing whether it was fear or hope that made her heart tremble. Still, she could not keep herself from whispering his name once more, its sound soft and gentle, making her wonder if the man who carried it possessed an equally tender soul.

Meeting Lady Elton's gaze, Adelaide nodded. "Then I will marry him," she whispered, feeling all dread fall away.

Almost.

What if he learnt of her secret? Would he still be kind to her then? Or would he turn on her?

Adelaide prayed that she would never find out.

9

A LADY'S CONSENT

taring at his cousin's note, Matthew felt as though he had strayed into a dream.

He blinked his eyes.

Still, the words remained.

"She agreed," he whispered, unable to believe that it could be true. Lifting his head, he stared out the window at the slowly blossoming gardens. "She agreed."

Stumbling a few steps across the room toward the armchair in the corner, Matthew sank into it, his gaze still distant as he recalled Lady Adelaide's soft features. When he had seen her that morning at Tristan's townhouse, the air had been knocked from his lungs. Like a fool, he had stared at her, taken with the power of his emotions as they had surged to the surface.

Certainly, he had seen her before, but only from a distance, and it had been a long while since he had last laid eyes on her. She had lost nothing of her loveliness. Unfortunately, her gaze had been as fearful as he recalled, not that he could blame her.

Now, Matthew understood even better than he had then why she always seemed to shrink away from the world. In a strange way, it was something that connected them. The way she looked at others with mistrust was not unlike the way he looked at himself, full of doubt and concern, expecting only the worst.

Matthew scoffed, realising that oddly enough they seemed to complement one another.

Glancing back down at the short note, he inhaled a deep breath.

I shall procure a special license so that you can be married within three days' time.

Certainly, it was wise to remove Lady Adelaide from her father's influence as soon as possible. Matthew, however, could not help but feel overwhelmed at the thought of marrying the woman he had admired from afar with such haste. They had never even spoken to each other. He had yet to hear the sound of her voice.

He swallowed, reminding himself that she, too, had to be taken aback by these sudden developments. Did she fear him? He wondered. Did she think of him as the lesser of two evils?

The thought twisted his insides painfully, and although he knew he ought to take a step back and release her from her commitment to him, he could not. Selfishly, he realised that his cousin had been right. He wanted her. He wanted her more than he had ever realised when he had harboured no hope in his heart to win hers…let alone her hand.

Rising from the chair, Matthew put away the note, steeling himself for what lay ahead. In order to see Lady Adelaide protected—at least from her father's influence—he needed to take the first step and call on Lord Radcliff, inform the man that he would marry his daughter in three days.

Although the thought of facing Lady Adelaide made him nervous, Matthew felt nothing but anger when he thought of her father, fuelled even more by the resentment and disappointment he harboured toward his own. Emotions he had not yet been able to lay to rest.

Stalking to the earl's townhouse, Matthew asked to speak to the man right away as the matter he needed to discuss was of utmost importance and concerned the man's daughter. When the butler returned, he bade him to follow. Falling into step behind the elderly man, Matthew glanced around the house. It lay as still and dead as his own, poisoned by the men who had done nothing but bring suffering to their families.

Unexpectedly, light footsteps echoed to his ears before a soft giggle travelled through the still air.

Turning his head, Matthew found himself looking at a little girl with dark curls framing her laughing face. As she beheld him, she stopped in her tracks, a finger coming to her lips as she cocked her head in innocent perusal of him.

"Hello," Matthew greeted her, surprised to see her and wondering who she was. "I bid you a good day."

"My lord," the butler said, the look in the old man's eyes urging him to follow. "Lord Radcliff is expecting you in his study."

With a mischievous twinkle in her eyes, the little girl held out her skirts in a child-like attempt at a courtesy. "G'day, my lord."

Unable not to, Matthew smiled before his ears detected more footsteps echoing closer. A moment later, Lady Adelaide swept around the corner, her gaze fixed on the little girl. "Tillie, I've asked you not to run off by yourself," she chided the little girl. Her eyes, however, remained gentle, and Matthew could see a smile tickling the corners of her mouth as she looked down at the mischievously grinning girl.

The sound of Lady Adelaide's voice made his blood sing, and he stared in open-mouthed wonder.

Placing a gentle hand on the girl's head, she leaned down to look into her eyes. "We do not want to disturb his lordship, remember? Will you promise to be quiet?"

The little girl—Tillie—sighed in a fairly annoyed way for such a young child before her eyes shifted back to Matthew, their depth twinkling with curiosity.

Noticing the girl's distraction, Lady Adelaide gazed over her shoulder. Upon seeing him standing there, she all but jumped back in fear, hand to her chest as her breath came in rapid bursts, her eyes widening as she recognised him. "My Lord Whitworth!"

Matthew almost cringed as his title flew from her lips, feeling that it misrepresented him in a strange way. Deep down, he realised he wanted her to know him as Matthew, plain and simple and honest.

"My lord," the butler pressed once more, impatience in his voice.

At the interruption, Lady Adelaide took a step back, her hand coming to rest on Tillie's shoulder as she urged the young girl back the corridor they had come. Her hands trembled as she held his gaze, and Matthew wondered what she saw when she looked at him. Did she see someone here to protect her? Or did she see in him a man like her father, forcing her hand? After all, the choice had not truly been hers, had it? Would she have agreed to marry him if she had had any other option?

With a last glance Lady Adelaide disappeared around the corner, and Matthew heaved a deep breath, trying his best to gather his wits. There would be time later to dwell on how to put her at ease. But for now, he first needed to ensure that she would be his to protect.

After a short knock, the butler opened the door to the earl's study, bidding him to enter. As Matthew crossed the threshold, he felt assaulted by the stench of spirits that lingered on the air. Judging from the earl's dishevelled and stained clothing, he seemed to be the most likely source. His eyes were blood-shot as he lifted his head to gaze upon his visitor through squinted eyes. "Who are you?" he drawled, wiping a forearm over his sweat-streaked face.

Anger rose in Matthew's veins at the sight of the man who so thoughtlessly had gambled away his daughter's happiness. "I'm Lord

Whitworth," Matthew stated, his voice harsh as he regarded the earl with unveiled contempt.

Frowning, Lord Radcliff pushed to his feet, then braced himself on the desk as he began to sway. "Whitworth you say." Squinting his eyes even more, he looked at Matthew. "That cannot be. You're not Whitworth's son. I know the look of him. What is your purpose in coming here?"

Matthew wondered if his cousin had been more closely acquainted with the earl before his death. However, as it did not signify, he chose to disregard it for now. "I'm not the man's son," Matthew explained, loathing every second he had to spend in the earl's presence. "I'm his second cousin. After an unfortunate accident that claimed his son's life, the title passed to me."

Mumbling something unintelligible, Lord Radcliff shook his head. Blinking his eyes, he seemed to be able to focus his attention on Matthew with more precision. "A shame when a man dies before fathering an heir. I always say it is never too early to ensure the continuation of one's line." He cleared his throat, once more reaching for a thick glass with a honey brown liquid within. "If what you say is indeed the truth, what then can I do for you?"

Forcing his hands to remain where they were, Matthew met the earl's gaze head-on. "I've come here today to inform you that I shall marry your daughter within three days' time."

Choking on his drink, Lord Radcliff coughed, his face turning dark red. "How dare y—?"

"How dare I?" Matthew thundered, unable to hold back his outrage any longer. Two strides carried him up to the man's desk, his jaw tense as he leaned forward, a snarl on his face. "How dare I? Was it not you, *my lord*, who lost her hand in a game of cards?"

Momentarily taken aback, Lord Radcliff swallowed before he flung the glass in his hand across the room. It shattered against the opposite wall, spraying shards all over the floor. "You imbecile! My daughter does not concern you. How dare you speak of marrying her?" The earl's lips pressed together tightly as he regarded Matthew with disgust. "I would never give her in marriage to a man like you. She will marry a gentleman of the highest rank. A man—"

"Like Mr. Harkin?" Matthew demanded, fixing the earl with a hateful glare. "You may call him a gentleman of the highest rank. I call him a gambler and a drunkard. A description you ought to be familiar with as it not only fits him perfectly but also you as well."

Sputtering in shock, Lord Radcliff stomped around his desk, anger fuelling his steps as he advanced on Matthew. "What do you want? How do you know of this?"

Drawing himself up to his full height, Matthew looked down upon the earl even though there was little difference in height between them. "I was there the night you lost her hand to him. I saw the man you are."

A hint of doubt came to Lord Radcliff's eyes as he took note of the anger that shook Matthew, barely contained in the clenched fists by his side. Finding himself facing a worthy adversary, the earl seemed to rethink his next steps. The man's shoulders relaxed before he took a step backwards. "Then why do you believe you have any right to claim her if you know I lost her to Harkin?"

Renewed anger rushed through Matthew when he thought of all the times the earl had intimidated his daughter into compliance. Of all the times he had thundered toward her, yelling in her face, threatening her with the power he held over her. The thought of what she had had to bear made him cringe. No wonder she rarely smiled.

Gritting his teeth, Matthew leaned forward. "Because he lost her to me." Unable not to, Matthew took another menacing step toward the older man, rejoicing in the way he retreated. Finally, the man was receiving a glimpse of what his daughter had endured at his hands. "She is mine," he growled. "I have every right to claim her."

Lord Radcliff swallowed, his mouth opening and closing, probably at a loss for the first time in his life. The look in his eyes suggested that he did not care for it in the least.

Inhaling a steadying breath, Matthew lowered his voice to a menacing whisper. "She is no longer yours to do with as you please.

Now, she is mine to protect." His gaze narrowed as he drove his point home. "I will see to it that you will not ruin her future for good. I will see to her happiness from now on, *my lord*." Gritting his teeth, he hissed, "Will you give us your blessing?"

Closing his eyes in defeat, the earl nodded.

10

A MAN WITH TWO FACES

After returning Tillie to the nursery, Adelaide felt drawn back to her father's study. Her heart hammered in her chest as she quietly approached the closed door, her eyes glancing about her to see if she would be discovered. Her sense of decorum chided her for what she was doing, trespassing on another's privacy. However, her curiosity would not be denied.

After seeing Lord Whitworth up close for the first time, Adelaide felt the desperate need to learn more about the man she was to marry. Lady Elton's words still echoed in her mind, and Adelaide had clung to the lady's description like a woman drowning.

He is a good man. I assure you that he is kind and loyal, decent and honourable. He would never hurt you. You'd be safe with him.

All day, Adelaide had repeated these words to herself, hoping that indeed Lady Elton truly knew the man she was entrusting her to. That he was indeed kind and honourable, a man quite unlike her father.

Unlike Mr. Harkin. And yet, when she had looked at him across the corridor only a few minutes past, her trained eyes had glimpsed evidence that spoke to the contrary.

The knuckles of his hands—as far as she could tell from such a short glimpse—had seemed reddened, the skin roughened and even broken here and there as though he had only recently found himself in a physical confrontation. Only too well did Adelaide know these signs as her brother—and even on occasion her father—often showed similar signs. Her brother, John, frequently ended up in drunken brawls provoked by minor differences that escalated due to lack of reason as those involved were generally inebriated.

Could Lady Elton be wrong? Was Adelaide's betrothed a man like her own brother? Did he drink and perhaps even gamble? Did he have a short temper? An aggressive streak like her father?

Had she made a monumental mistake by agreeing to marry him?

Recalling the note she had received from Lady Elton not an hour ago, Adelaide groaned. It had informed her in a few words that everything was going as planned. A special license would be procured with haste so that the ceremony could take place in three days hence.

To see Adelaide safe.

Safe?

Would she be safe with a man like Lord Whitworth? Or had she just given her agreement to a life not unlike her mother's? Constantly fearing her husband's anger? Not even safe from physical harm?

Adelaide sighed. How often had she seen bruises on her mother's arms? She did not know. Too often. Once even on her face. Would that be her fate also?

How would it feel to be safe? Adelaide wondered, unable to recall the feeling. All her life, she had lived in a constant state of anxiety. Safety was nothing she had ever been accustomed to. What would it feel like not to worry even in her own home? To walk about with ease? What did it mean when people said they felt carefree?

Adelaide flinched as the sound of something shattering echoed through the door, followed closely by her father's angry voice. "You imbecile! My daughter does not concern you. How dare you speak of marrying her?"

Holding her breath, Adelaide remained stock-still as though even the smallest movement might draw their attention. Her teeth were clenched, and her jaw began to ache from the tension.

After his outburst, her father's voice returned to a menacing low and she could not make out what was being said. She strained her ears, and yet, it was no use. Not knowing what was being discussed sent cold shivers up and down Adelaide's back, and tears began to prick the backs of her eyes.

Still, they did not spill until Lord Whitworth's voice, matching her father's in a most shocking way, slammed against her ears. "She is mine," he growled, his voice dripping with menace. "I have every right to claim her."

Shrinking back instinctively, Adelaide felt tears streaming down her face at the sight of her shattered hopes. All strength left her, and she felt like sinking to the ground and burying her head in her hands.

He had come to claim her? Claim her? Like one claimed a possession?

Shaking her head, Adelaide tried to fight off the haze that descended upon her, cushioning the blow and easing the pain. It had served her well countless times. Still, now she could not let it. If she were found outside the door, eavesdropping, what would they do? What would her father do? What would her betrothed do to her once she was his?

How often had she heard her mother cry out at her father's harsh treatment? Adelaide could not remember. It had been too often.

With trembling hands, Adelaide backed away from the door as she desperately tried to calm the panic that had seized her heart, threatening to overpower her. Gritting her teeth, she forced her gaze from the door, spun on her heel and forced her legs onward, away from the threat that loomed over her.

When she had almost reached the corner, the faint sound of a door opening reached her ears, stilling her movements. Trying to swallow the lump in her throat, Adelaide closed her eyes when footsteps echoed closer.

"Lady Adelaide."

The sound of Lord Whitworth's calm voice chased away her paralysis, and she quickly lifted her hands, hastily brushing away the tears that still clung to her face. Only once she felt reasonably certain that her emotions were once more concealed behind a mask of polite obedience did she turn to face him.

His hands were curled into fists, and the pulse in his neck beat angrily as he looked at her, his gaze drifting over her face as though he had never seen her before. Tension held his shoulders rigid, and anger stained his face a darker shade of red as he slowly stepped closer.

Forcing herself not to back away, Adelaide dropped her gaze from his, trying her best to appear unobtrusive.

Measured steps carried him closer, and there was a hint of caution about him, reminding her of a hunter not wishing to spook his prey. He was more than a head taller than she was, and the sheer size of his body made her feel weak and helpless.

There was no feeling she hated more.

No feeling she knew better.

"I wanted to apologise," he said, his voice surprisingly gentle, and Adelaide's head all but snapped up at hearing it, "for the strangeness of this meeting. I'm aware we have never even been properly introduced, and yet, we find ourselves betrothed to one another." A soft smile came to his lips, and his green eyes shone brightly as they looked into hers.

Unable not to, Adelaide stared at him, not knowing what to make of the man who suddenly stood before her. A moment ago, he had appeared as threatening as her own father on his worst days, and now, he seemed genuinely kind. Was it a mask to fool her? Was he simply more adept at hiding his aggression? But why would he bother? After all, she had already agreed to marry him.

Allowing her gaze to travel over his features, Adelaide felt reminded of earlier that morning when she had seen him from a distance, speaking to Lord Elton. She recalled the subtle shyness that had rested in his eyes as well as the respect he had shown her. His clear green eyes, soft and kind, had proved him to be the man Lady Elton thought him to be. And yet, later that same day, Adelaide had seen and heard evidence to the contrary.

How could she be certain of his character?

When she remained quiet, he nodded, understanding coming to his gaze. "I can see that these developments have unsettled you, my lady. Are you…," he swallowed as though suddenly nervous, "are you aware why I'm here?"

Unable to recover her voice, Adelaide nodded, feeling the effect of his gentle smile all the way to her toes. What a strange effect he had on her! A moment ago, she had been terrified. And now…she could not say how she felt.

"Good," he replied, taking another step forward.

Instantly, an alarm went off in Adelaide's head and she shrank back, unable to prevent it. Groping for words to avoid his anger, she opened her mouth…but the words remained stuck in her throat.

However, instead of anger, he showed her kindness once more. "I apologise if I've alarmed you, my lady. I merely sought to assure you that all is settled."

Carefully, Adelaide lifted her gaze to meet his. When their eyes met, the corners of his mouth once more curled into a gentle smile, reassuring as well as encouraging. Adelaide could not believe her eyes.

He nodded to her. "Soon, you will be able to leave this house, and I promise that I will do all that I can to ensure your safety from here on out. You have my word." For a long moment, he held her gaze, seemingly wishing to say more. However, he did not. Instead, he granted her one last smile before taking his leave.

Watching him stride toward the foyer, Adelaide did not know what to think or feel. Her hands shook with a myriad of emotions that assaulted her, pulling her in different directions. When he stopped at the corner and looked at her over his shoulder, her breath caught in her throat, and her heart felt as though it would jump from her chest.

Still, his eyes shone brightly, full of promise and hope.

With all her heart, Adelaide wished that it could be true, that he could be the man Lady Elton thought him to be. And yet, she did not dare believe so. Life had taught her time and time again that men could not be trusted. They knew only their own desires, deceiving and manipulating to achieve their goals, and if need be, using their physical superiority to ensure that none stood against them.

Sighing, Adelaide wondered what Lord Whitworth's goal was. Why had he agreed to marry her? Was it the dowry her mother's father had bestowed upon her? Certainly, it could not be for any other reason as her own family's reputation was slowly going up in flames as her father continued on this downward spiral.

Her heart and mind ached with an intensity Adelaide had rarely known, and so she decided to retreat to her chambers, knowing herself to be in desperate need of some peace and quiet to sort through the chaos. However, when she turned to go, a gentle voice humming a child's lullaby drifted to her ears.

Unbidden, a deep smile came to Adelaide's face, and she immediately changed direction, stepping up to the drawing room to her right. The door stood ajar, and she slowly pushed it open, her gaze falling on Tillie's dark curls as she knelt by the coffee table, her dolls arranged around it and their best china used in her make-believe tea party.

"Did I not ask you to stay in the nursery?" Adelaide asked as she approached, unable to hide her smile. "How did you escape Miss Harmon yet again?"

Grinning rather mischievously for a two-year-old, Tillie shrugged as though there was nothing to it. "I was bored," she said, not answering Adelaide's question. Perhaps she did not wish to give away her method, so she would be able to use it yet again another time, Adelaide thought, wondering if there was more to Tillie than met the eye. After all, she often seemed a bit too wise for her age.

As though to prove her right, the little girl cocked her head and looked at Adelaide with that sort of wisdom that only young children had. "You're sad," she observed openly, her deep blue eyes lingering on Adelaide's face.

Forcing a smile onto her features, Adelaide sat down on the settee beside the little girl. "I'm fine," she assured her.

Still, her attempt had to have been unconvincing because Tillie rose to her feet, climbed onto her lap and wound her little arms around Adelaide's neck, hugging her close. "All will be well," she whispered the same way Adelaide always did when Tillie woke up at night afraid of the dark.

Blinking back tears, Adelaide sighed, hugging the girl closer, knowing only too well that in three days' time she would have to say goodbye to her. Her heart filled with sorrow, and she almost crumbled under the weight of it. After all, Tillie was her ray of sunshine. How would she survive without her?

She could only hope so.

11

A NEW BEGINNING

Escorting his new bride into the parlour of his townhouse, Matthew revelled in the feel of her delicate hand in his. Although her skin seemed chilled, her hand fit perfectly within his own as though they were meant to walk through life together.

Hand in hand.

Due to the circumstances of their wedding, not many guests had been invited. In fact, only family had been present at the ceremony and now took their seats around the large table for the wedding breakfast. A certain amount of tension rested on almost all their faces. However, only Matthew's new father-in-law did nothing to hide his displeasure. With a drink in his hand, he sat in his chair, grumbling something unintelligible—but no doubt hateful—under his breath.

In turn, Matthew was glad to see his mother conversing animatedly with the countess as well as his wife's grandmother. All three women seemed to be at ease with one another, occasionally glancing in their direction before sticking their heads together again. "What do you think they're talking about?" Matthew asked, turning his gaze to his new bride.

Paler than he had ever seen her, the new Lady Whitworth sat beside him, her hands trembling as they rested in her lap. Upon his question, she turned her gaze to meet his. However, after a mere second, her eyes dropped to her hands, and she mumbled something under her breath like a frightened child.

Matthew swallowed, realising he had been a fool to think that merely removing her from her father's influence would set her free. Years of fear and obedience had left her a mere shell of herself. It would not be easy for him to gain her trust.

And yet, Matthew knew he would try. He would do whatever she would ask of him in order to prove himself to her. As well as to himself.

After all, after his initial hesitation to admit to himself how he felt about his betrothed, Matthew had come to realise that too much time in life was wasted by lying to oneself. His heart already knew the truth even if his mind refused to acknowledge it. Why continue this charade?

Lies had brought him nothing but doubt and pain and regret, and Matthew refused to continue to lead the life his father had forced on him. His own family, his own wife, would know peace and happiness. He would make certain of that.

Glancing around the room, Matthew realised that the house still looked the same as when his father had been alive. In a strange way, it was as though he were still there. His influence finding his son even from the grave.

That would not do.

Determined to turn over a new leaf, Matthew vowed to speak to his wife the next day and discuss with her what changes to make and how to turn the house into a home for their family.

Once more, his eyes travelled to her as she sat beside him, her back rigid and her hands clenched in her lap. The sight pained him greatly, and yet, it was to be expected. After all, the past few days had changed her life fundamentally. Torn from the only home she had ever known, his new wife suddenly found herself among strangers. Certainly, that alone was enough to make one fearful.

As the subdued celebration of their wedding continued on, Matthew found himself watching his wife as she spoke to her family as well as his cousin's wife Beth. While her mother and grandmother seemed to be trying to coax a smile from her, Beth spoke with more vehemence. Matthew wished he could hear what was being said. How did they even know each other? When Tristan had first called upon him for help, Beth had referred to Lady Adelaide as her friend. Still, the bond that seemed to exist between them appeared far deeper than a new friendship would allow. After all, Beth had only recently come to town herself about a year ago.

Hers and Tristan's had been a whirlwind romance. Or it would have been if it had not been for his father's interference.

As dark thoughts rose once more, Matthew put them firmly away. They had no place on his wedding day. No, today he would concentrate on his new bride. Nothing else.

As he continued to watch her, Matthew observed a few things that had eluded him before. She always seemed to keep a safe distance from her father, never looking in his direction for more than a second. Her shoulders seemed to relax whenever she drew near to her mother and grandmother, the look in her eyes growing less fearful. And when her eyes would meet his own by accident, he saw nothing short of sheer terror there.

"Lost in thought?"

Almost flinching at the sound of Beth's voice, Matthew forced a smile onto his face. In truth, the sight of his wife's fearful retreat made him feel sick to the stomach.

A charming smile on her face, Beth looked from him to his new wife, her gaze watchful. "She's afraid," she observed, direct as always.

Swallowing, Matthew nodded. Then he forced his gaze away from his wife and looked at Beth. "Tristan said she had agreed to marry me."

Beth nodded.

"Why?"

A hint of humour as well as disbelief came to her face. "Why?"

Matthew nodded. "We had never even been introduced. Why would she agree to marry me?" His heart raced as doubts clawed at his heart. All these past three days, he had told himself that he was doing this to keep her safe, and yet, he had known all along that at least partly he was marrying her because he wanted her.

Had he been selfish? Should he have tried to find another solution? One that would not have forced her hand?

"Because I told her that she would be safe with you," Beth replied, her blue eyes lingering on his face as though trying to see into his mind.

"You did?" Matthew asked, touched to know that she would think of him thus. "Did she believe you?"

Beth chuckled, "She married you, did she not?"

"Then why is she afraid?"

Sighing, Beth looked at him as though he had asked her why the sky was blue. "She's scarred," his cousin's wife whispered, her gaze holding his as though to ensure that he was truly listening. "You need to be good to her," she said, a gentle smile on her lips, "and patient." The look in her eyes grew in intensity, filled with a deeper meaning. "She will not give her trust lightly. She can't."

Understanding what Beth was saying, Matthew nodded. "I promise. I shall keep her safe."

"I know you will," Beth replied before a teasing gleam came to her blue eyes. "But do make her happy as well, won't you? Safety is nothing without happiness."

Returning her smile, Matthew nodded. "I promise," he said once again, determined to seek out his wife as soon as possible and set her mind at ease.

When it came to arranged marriages, the wedding night was generally a bit of a precarious situation. Two strangers sharing something immensely intimate could easily lead to an even greater distance between them than there had been initially. The look in his wife's eyes told him that she all but feared the night ahead, and the thought of her submitting to him against her will was one of the vilest ones Matthew had ever known. He would never want to see her hurt, especially not by him. No, in order to gain her trust, he would have to prove that she had nothing to fear from him.

Still, despite his intention to seek her out immediately, Matthew found himself detained, first by his own cousin and then by his wife's brother. While Tristan claimed the opportunity to once more tease Matthew about his partiality toward his new wife, Adelaide's brother John simply looked at him for a long moment before ordering Matthew to treat his sister kindly. Then he wandered off, yet another drink in his hand. Not unlike his father.

By the time, Matthew had reclaimed his senses from such a strange encounter, he found his wife already climbing the stairs to the upper floor. Her mother and grandmother were by her side, speaking to her in hushed tones. Still, his wife's face looked tense, and yet, expressionless as she held herself rigid. Moments later, she was lost from his sight, and he cursed himself for missing his chance to put her at ease.

Of course, Matthew had no intention of changing his mind with regard to their wedding night. However, he wished he did not need to keep his wife in suspense. Judging from the look in her eyes, she would no doubt worry about what lay ahead when in truth there was nothing to worry about.

If only she knew.

12

BEHIND A MARRIAGE

Stepping over the threshold into her new bedchamber, Adelaide felt the air rush from her lungs. Panic encroached on her from all sides as her gaze travelled from the vanity to the slow burning fire in the hearth to the large bed. Her own trunk had been unpacked during the celebration and all was ready, the room awaiting its lady.

"Everything shall be all right," her mother whispered, coming to stand beside her left shoulder. Gently, she placed a hand on Adelaide's cheek, her pale eyes finding her daughter's. "Do not worry. He seems like a kind man. I'm certain it will not be so unpleasant."

Closing her eyes, Adelaide inhaled a deep breath, her legs trembling with the need to get away. How had she ended up in this situation? How had this happened? Only a mere few days had passed, and now all of a sudden she was married. Married to a man she did not know. A man she had hardly spoken to. A man who knew nothing about her.

And she could only hope he never would. If he discovered her secret, what would he—?

"My dear, you look like a lamb being led to the slaughter," her grandmother observed with a chuckle, cutting off her daughter-in-law's objections with a quick wave of her hand. Stepping closer, she smiled at Adelaide, wrapping her warm hands around Adelaide's chilled ones. "I agree with your mother in one aspect, your new husband truly is a kind man, and I urge you not to see him as a threat."

Adelaide swallowed as her fears rose before her, taking shape.

"He will not hurt you," her grandmother said kindly, and yet, there was an urgency in her voice that Adelaide had rarely heard before. "If you're afraid, which I can see that you are, then tell him so. Ask him to be patient. Ask him to wait."

"Do you truly believe that would be a good idea?" Adelaide's mother stepped forward, deep concern resting in her eyes as she looked at her mother-in-law. "Will that not upset him? Make him angry with her?"

Regret came to her grandmother's eyes as she looked at her daughter-in-law. "I know you do believe so, but not all men are like that." Her gaze shifted back to Adelaide. "I assure you your husband is not the kind of man to be angered by honesty. On the contrary, I do believe it will bring the two of you closer."

Trying to swallow the large lump in her throat, Adelaide nodded, wanting more than anything to believe her grandmother's words, to believe that her counsel would guide her someplace safe. And yet, deep down, her own experience told her otherwise. There was no place that was truly safe.

"He might be understanding," her mother objected once again, "but even kind men might get upset if their wives refuse them and on their wedding night no less." Shaking her head, she looked almost sternly at her daughter. "No, you'd be wise to hide your fears and submit to his wishes." Tension came to her eyes before she briefly dropped her gaze. "I assure you it will be less painful that way."

Torn, Adelaide looked from her mother to her grandmother. Two women. Two stories. Two marriages. Both as different as night and day.

Knowing only too well the nature of her parents' marriage, Adelaide was not surprised by her mother's counsel. Neither was she surprised by her grandmother's as her marriage had been a true love match. Adelaide's grandfather, a man she barely remembered, had been a sweet and kind man, utterly in love with his wife, and she had mourned him deeply when he had passed before his time. It had broken her in a different way than Adelaide's father had broken her mother with his cold demeanour and complete disregard for her feelings.

Adelaide sighed. Which counsel ought she to heed? Which road ought she to travel?

Reminding herself that there was no love between herself and her new husband, Adelaide suspected that where her own marriage was concerned she would do well to heed her mother's advice. Her husband might not be as hot-tempered as her father, but she had heard with her own ears the force of his anger.

A shiver ran down her back as she remembered the sound of his voice echoing through the door of her father's study. That day he had come to claim her—those had been his words—and tonight she had no doubt that he would demand she submit to him. Indeed, he would expect it. Would not any husband? Even those in love? No, she would not dare incite his anger tonight and have it directed at her. She could not refuse him.

Her body tensed as she looked up at her grandmother, her gaze darting to her mother as well, as she gave voice to her greatest fear. "Do you think he will know?"

While her mother dropped her gaze, Adelaide found her grandmother's holding hers, unwavering. Even now, Adelaide marvelled at the strength she often saw in her grandmother, wishing she had inherited at least some of it. Certainly, it would serve her tonight.

"Do not worry, my dear," her grandmother counselled once again, the certainty in her voice pulling on Adelaide's heart, making it yearn for a world of which her grandmother spoke. "Trust your instincts. It is something you need to learn as your old life only taught you how to be afraid." Grasping Adelaide's hands, her grandmother looked at her with emphasis. "Believe me when I say that I would never have urged you to accept him if I'd thought for a moment that he was not worthy of you."

Could her grandmother be right? Adelaide wondered. Was her husband such a rare specimen of a husband? A man who could not be angered by his wife's refusal? Did such a man truly exist?

"But you hardly know him," Adelaide objected, afraid to trust in hope. Too often had she been disappointed. "You said so yourself."

"You're right," her grandmother admitted, the look in her eyes no less intense than before. "But Beth knows him. Knows him well."

"Beth?" Adelaide mumbled, once more taken aback by the depth of her grandmother's relationship with Lady Elton. It seemed they knew almost everything about each other, their trust in one another utterly complete. How had this happened? How had this bond formed?

"She only wants to protect you," her grandmother continued, "and if she says that you'll be safe with him, then I believe her. And I urge you to believe me." Her hands tightened on Adelaide's. "You have nothing to fear from him." Again, she shook her head for emphasis. "Nothing at all. He is not the villain in this story, my dear. He's your knight in shining armour."

13

A MISUNDERSTANDING

After bidding everyone goodbye, Matthew headed upstairs to seek out his wife. A soft smile played on his lips as he remembered her grandmother's stern look when she had told him to be good to her granddaughter upon taking her leave. Still, despite the severity in her tone, there had been crinkles of humour around her eyes as though she knew and whole-heartedly believed that he would be.

Matthew had to admit he liked the dowager countess. Oddly enough, she reminded him of Beth, always speaking her mind, direct and unflinching. It was a rare trait.

One he greatly admired.

As Matthew walked up to the door, it suddenly opened, and a maid stepped out of his wife's bedchamber. Upon seeing him, she quickly curtsied and leaving the door ajar walked briskly down the corridor.

Inhaling a deep breath, Matthew gently pushed open the door, the warm glow of the room beckoning him forward. The fire in the hearth cast a beautiful light over his surroundings, and the lamp on his wife's vanity gently illuminated the soft blush on her cheeks.

Dressed only in her night rail, she stood in the middle of the room, her eyes slightly widened as she stared at him.

Unprepared for the sight, Matthew felt overwhelmed by the softness she radiated. Her dark curls were undone and trailed down over her shoulders. Her blue eyes, wide and deep, seemed pale even in the darkened room as they held his own.

As his eyes trailed further down, tempted by the way the soft fabric of her night rail hugged her delicate frame, Matthew took note of the slight tremble in her hands. Lifting his gaze, he found hers darting from his, looking past him at something off to the side.

Turning to look, Matthew saw her robe lying over the back of a chair. "Allow me to assist you," he said, a gentle smile on his face as he walked over to the chair and picked up the soft garment. Then he approached her, holding it open so she could slip her arms into the sleeves.

Standing barely an arm's length in front of her, Matthew watched as she lifted her gaze to his—if only for a split second—before she turned and allowed him to help her into the robe. "If you're cold," he whispered, inhaling the rose scent of her hair, "come and stand closer to the fire. The days and especially the nights do still get a bit cold this time of year."

Stepping around her, Matthew tended to the fire, ensuring it would burn throughout the night and keep her warm. The thought of her chilled in her new bed, in her new home, made him feel neglectful. After all, she was his to protect now…in every way.

Even if only from a cold.

The thought warmed his heart, and when he turned back to look at her, his mind darted to a future of a shared home. Of happiness. Of companionship. Even of love.

"Is there anything else you require?" he asked as he stepped closer, his gaze caught by the way the light made her hair shimmer like diamonds. "You only need to ask. All I have is yours." He sighed. "Ours."

At his words, her gaze lifted and met his, her own unsteady, and yet, her eyes were slightly narrowed as though she tried to see past his offer to a deeper understanding. For a moment, it seemed to Matthew as though the distance between them was decreasing, as though the foundation for a bridge to bring them together had been set.

His heart danced with joy, and he could not help the smile that drew up the corners of his mouth.

Inhaling a shuddering breath, his wife dropped her gaze, and a midnight black curl danced forward, framing her face in a most becoming way.

His gaze trailed it from her temple all the way to its tip, his fingers itching with the need to feel it against his skin. Instinctively, Matthew reached out a hand to tuck it back behind her ear.

As his hand moved forward, her eyes widened in alarm, and with a sharp intake of breath, his wife shrank back.

Matthew froze, his jaw dropping as he stared at the panic now all too evident in her pale eyes.

Seeing his expression, she suddenly stilled. "I'm sorry," she whispered, her voice almost choked as her hands curled into fists at her sides. All too evident was also the tension that rooted her body to the spot, not permitting her to retreat further. "I'm sorry. I didn't mean to…" She swallowed hard, watching him fearfully like a deer expecting the wolf to strike.

The sight pierced Matthew's heart, and he realised that he had been wrong. Closing his eyes, he inhaled a deep breath, cursing himself inwardly for not seeing it sooner. Too lost had he been in his fantasy of a loving family and a welcoming home. He had forgotten Beth's words as well as his promise to her.

Lifting his gaze, Matthew looked at his wife, wondering how he could have been so blind. "You're not cold, are you?" he all but mumbled, seeing her muscles twitch with each word he spoke. "You're not cold. It's me, isn't it? You're…you're afraid." Holding her gaze, he nodded. "Afraid of me."

At his observation, the panic in her eyes grew in intensity, gripping her as though wishing to squeeze the life from her. He could see that she wanted nothing more but to retreat, to put a safe distance between them, but she held herself in place. Sheer willpower kept her where she was, her mouth opening as she clearly searched for words to appease him.

What had he done to deserve such terror be directed at him? Matthew wondered, knowing even as the question rose in his mind that he was not being fair. After all, it was not he who had taught her to be afraid. And yet, he could not expect her to unlearn in a single moment what had been drilled into her for years. A few kind words were not enough to conquer the fear that shone in her eyes. It was as though it had a mind of its own, a separate will, one she had no control over.

The look of utter fear in her eyes almost brought Matthew to his knees. Had she struck him hard across the face, it would have hurt less. Unbidden, an image of his mother rose before his inner eye, of the many times he had seen her back away from his father when anger had seized him. Fear and terror had been in her eyes then, and even as a child, Matthew had wondered about the nature of his parents' relationship. Was there supposed to be fear in a marriage?

Still, no one had ever acted as though the kind of marriage his parents had was not perfectly normal. And yet, it had always bothered him. After all, fear meant that there was no love, did it not? How could anyone love someone they feared?

Looking at his wife, Matthew could have groaned in agony. If she feared him, she would never be able to love him, would she? One did not allow for the other.

As much as he had known that she would be fearful, that she would need time, that she was scarred as Beth had said, Matthew had not been prepared to see her react to him in such a way. And as much as he tried not to, in that moment, he saw himself as his father, intimidating his wife, watching her shrink from him in fear.

Taking a step back, he all but hung his head in defeat. Perhaps walking in his father's footsteps was a curse he could not escape. Perhaps it was too late, and he had done too much that could not be undone. Turning toward the door, Matthew halted his steps when a tiny spark of hope claimed his attention. No, he could not walk out the door without declaring his position, without assuring her that indeed she had nothing to fear from him. Even if she could not believe him, he had to say the words. It was all he could do.

As he turned to look at her once again, her body tensed anew, and for a moment, Matthew felt tempted to ask her to slap him hard across the face in order to offset the pain that radiated in his heart. Still, he held himself back, willing the expression on his face to underline his words. "I can see that you're afraid."

Again, she tensed as though he was striding toward her with a raised hand.

"And I cannot fault you for it. I know my words might ring hollow to you as you have reason to believe that men cannot be trusted, but I cannot leave this room without assuring you that I am not like your father, nor am I like mine. You have nothing to fear from me, and I promise from this day on, I shall assure your well-being, your happiness with everything I have, everything I am. If need be, I shall give my life to guard yours, and I will gladly take upon me any pain that might come your way to prevent it from hurting you…for I could not bear to see you suffer."

Seeing her wide-eyed stare, Matthew nodded his head to her. "You have my word, and I will do what I can to prove that it can be trusted." Inhaling a deep breath, he swallowed. "Good night, my lady. Sleep well…and safely. I promise that I shall not cross the threshold into your chamber without your express invitation." Before she could say a word or shrink back yet again, Matthew turned on his heel and left, hoping that at least a small part of her wanted to believe him.

14

A NEW LIFE

The moment the door closed behind her husband, Adelaide sank to the floor in front of the hearth, her breath coming fast and her limbs trembling, unable to hold her upright any longer. Bright spots danced before her eyes as her chest rose and fell with each rapid intake of breath. Still, her head began to spin, and before long, Adelaide allowed herself to slide down completely, her head coming to rest on the soft rug.

Tears poured from her eyes, running down the side of her face and into the rug below her head. Slowly, ever so slowly, the panic began to recede, removing its talons from her heart and allowing her to breathe more calmly.

Only then did Adelaide's mind take her back to the words her husband had spoken to her that night. With the threat removed from her room, her mind could focus once again, and her heart did not quake with fear and terror any longer. Clarity came, and with it, a feeling of shame.

Had she truly done him wrong? Had his words been genuine? Honest? From the heart?

When he had seen her terror, when he had realised that she feared him, anger had sparked in his eyes. She had been certain of it. Nothing else could Adelaide detect with such certainty than anger. It was a survival instinct, one developed over years and years of living in fear. For the sooner she was able to discern another's anger, the easier it was to quell or at least deflect. This ability, though not free of error, had served her well.

And yet, it seemed to have blinded her to all else but anger. Was she no longer capable of seeing other emotions? Did kindness and honesty slip by her? Certainly, she had no trouble detecting them in women like her grandmother or Lady Elton. However, men…men were different. Always had they set themselves apart in certain ways. Always had Adelaide seen the difference in their position. Men had power. Women did not. Men could do what they wished. Women had to live with the consequences. Men could not be trusted. Women could.

But was her thinking correct? Again, her grandmother's urgings to be honest with her husband rang in her mind. What if she had been honest? What if she had told him straight-out that she feared him and why? What if she had asked him to be patient? How would he have reacted?

Her mother's opinion was clear on the matter. And yet, her husband had retreated. He had left her chamber…even though she had not asked him. Somehow he had seen her desire to be left alone and complied. Indeed, the realisation that she feared him had come as a shock to him. Only too well did Adelaide remember the way his face had paled, the way his muscles had tensed, the way his eyes had darkened.

The realisation had been like a blow to his chest, knocking the air from his lungs.

But why? Why did it bother him? It had certainly never bothered her father. Was it not what husbands did, terrify their wives into submission? Adelaide had seen it many times. Or at least the subtle signs of a wife fearing her husband. His anger. She knew beyond the shadow of a doubt that it was not only her own parents. It made her wonder who else suffered silently at home and only knew how to hide the signs when stepping out in public. What was the truth? And what was a lie?

Closing her eyes, Adelaide inhaled a slow, deep breath. She could no longer tell. The line between truth and lie had blurred, leaving her in ever-present doubt.

On her hands and knees, Adelaide finally crawled over to the bed, her limbs heavy as lead. Climbing under the covers, she curled up, hugging a feather-soft pillow to her chest as tears of loss and helplessness slowly ran down her cheeks. Exhaustion washed over her, her heart and mind aching with the overwhelming developments of the past sennight. And yet, sleep would not come.

Long into the night, Adelaide lay awake, feeling her eyes begin to sting with lack of sleep. Her body ached, and her heart longed for the warmth of the little girl who had often climbed into bed with her when monsters had chased her from her own room.

When the sun finally rose, Adelaide was still tossing and turning, hoping to find a reprieve from this constant turmoil, but sleep continued to refuse her. Finally, she decided to rise early, unwilling to prolong this agony. Perhaps the activity of her morning preparations would do her good. Something familiar. Something to give her a sense of normalcy.

As Adelaide sat at her vanity, looking at her pale face and red-rimmed eyes in the mirror as her maid worked on her hair, she reminded herself that she would soon be facing her husband as well as his mother across the breakfast table. Again, tears stung her eyes at the thought of her own mother, her grandmother and above all little Tillie. Would she ever learn how to live without them?

During breakfast, Adelaide kept her gaze down, answering her mother-in-law's questions after her comfort politely but in a rather monotonous way. Her mind felt heavy with fatigue, and she had trouble focusing on maintaining a politely interested, while still indifferent demeanour. Out of the corner of her eyes, she could see her husband's gaze travel to her again and again, his mouth opening and closing a few times before he finally spoke. "I wanted to speak to you about changes I'm planning to make to the house."

At his words, his mother's gaze flew up, a touch of surprise on her face.

Turning his head, her husband gave his mother a small smile before turning his attention back to Adelaide. "This…this still feels like my father's house," he said with a sigh, and yet, the muscles in his jaw tensed with suppressed anger.

Adelaide felt her skin crawl.

"I do believe it would do us good to make it our own," he said, his voice once gentler as he looked at her. "I want this to be a true home for all of us."

Feeling her husband's gaze on her, Adelaide forced her eyes up, worried that he might find her unresponsiveness offensive.

When their eyes met, a soft smile curled up the corners of his mouth. "I do want you to be happy here," he whispered as though they were alone at the table. "I want *us* to be happy." For a second, his gaze darted to his mother, and Adelaide saw a gentleness in the way he looked at her that had not been there before.

Perhaps she simply had not seen it because she had not been looking, afraid of what she might find.

"I'd like that," Adelaide whispered, attempting a smile of her own, knowing that it fell far short and hoping that he would not notice.

"Feel free to make any changes you want," he continued before shifting his gaze from her to his mother and back again. "Perhaps we should all talk about what we would like to do."

Sighing, his mother smiled. "That is a marvellous idea, my son. I should truly like to brighten up the place a little." Looking at Adelaide, she added, "And I'm certain you would like new furniture in your bedchamber. I admit that I never cared for it. It always seemed daunting and dark." She shrugged. "But my husband preferred it, and there was no changing his mind."

Adelaide once again felt reminded of her own mother's marriage as she saw the look of resignation in her mother-in-law's eyes. "Perhaps," was all Adelaide could mumble in reply as she tried to recall the furniture her husband's mother so disapproved of, only to realise that with all the turmoil in her heart she had barely taken notice.

Carefully, Adelaide glanced at her husband from under her eyelashes, wondering about the two different faces he often portrayed. Although anger seemed to be strong in him, he did have a breathtakingly gentle side. Or was it only a mask to get her to drop her guard? But why would he bother? After all, her position was by far the weaker one. He did not need her approval. All he needed was her obedience, and she could only hope that she would soon convince him of her commitment to it.

From what her mother-in-law had said—as well as her husband the previous night—Adelaide wondered about her late father-in-law.

From what she had gathered, he seemed to have been a man like her own father. The evidence of that still rested in his widow's eyes and lingered about the house. And although her husband did wish to make changes to the oppressive atmosphere that still clung to the walls, Adelaide wondered how far he resembled his own father. After all, she knew only too well how a son could follow in his father's footsteps even without his intention. Her own brother, John, came to act like their father more and more every day.

Over the next few days, Adelaide spent most of her time evading her husband. Oh, she knew it was foolish and childish and possibly dangerous. However, alone in an unfamiliar house with only strangers around her, Adelaide felt almost cornered as though danger lurked in every nook and cranny. Still, the more she continued to evade her husband, the more she felt like a hunted animal as she silently walked around the house, trying her best to prevent drawing any attention to herself.

And yet, he did not confront her. Neither did he seek her out in her chamber. He kept his word, which only served to bring a new ache to Adelaide's heart. Was she doing him wrong? Was he a truly kind-hearted man who deserved better? But if that were the case, why did his body often tremble with suppressed anger? Where did he get the bruises on his knuckles if not from a physical altercation?

Adelaide's head spun with all the questions that assaulted her, and her heart knew not what to feel. All she knew for certain was that she missed her family. Not daring to call on them lest she cross paths with her father, Adelaide often looked out the window at the street, hoping to see her father's carriage draw up at the kerb. Still, days passed without a word, and Adelaide told herself that they were merely giving her time to settle into her new life. Certainly, they would come to call on her soon.

Adelaide told herself all that and more, and yet, it did not ease the loneliness in her heart. So, when the butler found her in the library one afternoon and announced that she had a visitor, Adelaide all but flew from the room, not even bothering to ask who it was despite the questions that raced through her head. Was Tillie with them? Oh, how she longed to feel the little girl's soft embrace!

"Oh, how I've missed you!" Adelaide exclaimed as she sailed through the door into the drawing room. However, the smile on her face died a quick death when her gaze fell neither on her mother or grandmother but on her father instead.

Never would she have expected him to call on her! What a fool she was!

Despite the fact that his clothes were in order, her father looked as he always did. His eyes were blood-shot, and every pore in his body seemed to ooze the stench of spirits. And yet, he held himself tall, shoulders back and chin raised as he glared down at her as though she were the source of all his troubles. Had he been out gambling the previous night? Had he lost money he did not have? Was that where the desperate look in his eyes came from?

Adelaide swallowed, momentarily contemplating fleeing the room. But flee where? There was no one here who would come to her aid. After all, this was her father. Why would anyone think it odd that he would come to call on her?

"Hello, Father," Adelaide finally said, trying to keep her voice steady as she offered him a seat. "Would you like some tea?"

Remaining on his feet, her father continued to glare at her, his eyes narrowing as though trying to determine what she hoped to accomplish. Apparently, he could not see that all Adelaide did hope to accomplish was to protect herself from his anger. "Is your new husband to your liking?" he asked in a snarl.

Adelaide almost jumped out of her skin. Swallowing, she looked at her father, trying to gauge what he wanted to hear.

Her father continued to stride around the room, the muscles in his jaw twitching. "I never would have thought that you'd ever betray me." His voice was low as he spoke, but all the more menacing for it.

Adelaide froze, the little hairs on the back of her neck rising in alarm. "I assure you, Father, I had no intention of ever–"

"Don't lie to me!" he thundered, angry feet carrying him closer. "You plotted against me! You forced my hand. I'm the one who ought to have chosen your husband. It was my right as your father."

Swallowing, Adelaide kept her eyes downcast, a part of her wishing she had the courage to contradict him. After all, he had made his choice, had he not? He had chosen to offer her hand in a game of cards and lost. Everything else that had followed had merely been a natural consequence. And yet, Adelaide had to admit that she had indeed plotted. Would her father truly have been happier if she had married Mr. Harkin? What would that have gained him?

"I had an agreement with Harkin," her father continued in his tirade. "The man was to provide us with funds to save our estate, and all he wanted in return was your hand and my assistance in introducing him to upper society. Was that so much to ask?" He was all but yelling at her now, and Adelaide prayed that her mother-in-law was nowhere within earshot. How humiliating would it be to have her happen upon such a scene? It was certainly bad enough that at least one or two servants was overhearing this.

"Now, that this deal is off," her father continued undeterred, "we need to find another solution."

Looking up, Adelaide felt her skin crawl with dread.

Her father's eyes focused on hers as he stepped closer, bringing his face level with hers. "You will ask your husband for money."

Adelaide sucked in a sharp breath.

"Tell him it's for you. For new dresses and such," her father advised, rolling his eyes as he continued. "He will not be able to deny you anything. And if he seems reluctant, use your…female assets to get what we need. Do you understand?"

"I cannot do this," Adelaide stammered without thinking before clasping a hand over her mouth in shock.

Her father's face, too, showed the same surprise. "What did you say?" he growled, a threat clear in his voice.

Although a part of Adelaide began to suspect that her father was right, that her husband would not hesitate to give her anything she asked for, she could not in good conscience rob him in order to provide for her father's gambling needs. "He would refuse me," she stammered. "He only married me because—" Her voice got stuck in her throat.

…because Lady Elton and her husband asked him to, and perhaps he owed them a debt.

Although Lady Elton had never said such a thing, Adelaide could not fathom why a young man would give up his future in order to help a friend. After all, with his new title and in possession of a fortune of his own, her new husband had no need for her.

Not even her dowry would tempt him.

Nor her family's former acclaim.

Or their dwindling connections.

Only a man like Mr. Harkin would still see value in those. But not Adelaide's husband, and she realised that it was not knowing why he had agreed to marry her that kept her from taking a step toward him. If she did not know his motivation, how could she hope to trust anything he told her? How could she trust his kindness above his anger?

Stepping even closer, her father snarled into her face. "Then you'd better find another way to provide the funds you robbed me of, or I will ensure that your husband knows everything there is to know about you."

His words felt like a slap to the face, and Adelaide stared up at him in shock. He could not mean—? Surely, he did not know that—

Adelaide's mind reeled as for the first time in her life she held her father's gaze, reading in his blood-shot eyes the very truth she had always feared. It was no bluff. No guess. No gamble. For once, he knew exactly what he spoke of. He meant to ruin her as she had ruined his plan. But how? How could he know? Had someone betrayed her? Only a handful of people knew her secret, and she had thought she could trust them with her life.

After all, they loved her. They were her family. How could they have done this? Who?

Closing her eyes, Adelaide felt all strength leave her body, knowing beyond the shadow of a doubt how her father could have extracted the information from one of them. In all likelihood, it had been her mother. Never had she been strong enough to endure his raging anger. Always had she given in for fear of the consequences. Had he threatened her? But how had he known that there was something to know in the first place?

"I will be back," her father hissed before he strode toward the door. "Do not disappoint me again."

Then the door banged shut behind him, and Adelaide sank down onto the settee, her mind reeling with what to do. Ought she truly betray her new husband? Tell him she wished to refurnish her bedchamber and then give at least some of the money to her father? If she did so, would he not always come back and ask for more? Would she then not find herself forever locked in his threat?

And what if she did not? Did her father truly know? And if he did tell her husband, what would he do? Would anger finally overrule kindness?

Adelaide prayed that she would never find out. There had to be another solution. If only she could think of one.

15

A MOTHER'S HONESTY

Sitting in his study, Matthew found himself unable to concentrate.

Day after day passed, and he could not shake the look in his wife's eyes. It rose in his mind whenever he closed his own, whenever his mind was unoccupied, whenever he drew breath. A look of sheer terror. And although his mind reasoned with him, tried to remind him of her past, his heart would not listen.

Matthew knew that he was wallowing in self-pity, allowing it to conjure the greatest fear he had ever known. That she feared him not because she had learnt to fear men in general, but because she recognised something in him. Because her trained eyes could see that deep down he was slowly turning into his father.

Was it not his anger that frightened her beyond anything else?

Matthew knew that he must never allow it to escape his tight control, fearing what he might do if that should ever happen. Only when he stood up with an opponent for a boxing match did he allow himself to inflict physical pain, and even then he held his anger under tight control. Never would he wish to truly wound someone. But the exercise—even when it was accompanied by an occasional jolt of pain—eased the strain in his muscles. Afterwards, he felt more like himself, almost free of the shadow that hung over him.

Again, Matthew recalled the moment he had entered her chamber. How could he not have seen it from the first? He had helped her into her robe, stoked the fire and attempted to draw her into a friendly conversation, and all the while his wife had been terrified of him. Had she feared that he would strike her? Force himself on her?

How could he not have seen this? Most certainly, he was the greatest fool to ever walk the earth! And blind at that!

A knock on his door jarred Matthew from his thoughts, which immediately conjured an image of his wife's gentle features. He all but shot to his feet and they carried him toward the door with quick efficiency. His hand reached out, all but yanking the door open.

His heart fell.

"You expected someone else," his mother observed, a gentle smile on her face as she stepped forward, brushing a hand down his arm. Her eyes held his until he nodded. Then she inhaled a deep breath and stepped into the room.

"Is something wrong?" Matthew asked, concern encroaching on his heart as he took note of the slight tension creasing her forehead. "Are you all right? Is Lady Adelaide all right?"

The hint of a grin came to his mother's face. "Lady Adelaide?" she asked as he realised his mistake. "Is she not your Lady Whitworth now?"

Gritting his teeth, Matthew hung his head as he walked across the room, focusing his gaze out the window and away from his mother's watchful eyes. Although he wished he could, he did not yet dare think of her as his. Not in that way. His to protect, certainly. His to care for, possibly. But his to claim? To love?

Soft footsteps echoed closer. "I never meant to meddle in your marriage," his mother said, her voice tentative as though she was not certain whether or not to speak.

Matthew hated the hesitation in her voice. It always reminded him of his father, of the way she had spoken to him, always weighing her words, hoping not to offend him, to anger him.

"However, I cannot in good conscience remain silent," she continued, "when I see two people so miserable. You've been avoiding each other for days, and I cannot help but fear for your future." She sighed, "I remember when you came home and told me you would marry her. I remember the way your eyes lit up. I remember how you tried your best to keep at bay the joy that wanted to break forth." Stepping around him, his mother looked up into his face. "I know very well that yours was not a love match. And yet, I can see as plain as day that you care for her."

Matthew gritted his teeth, hearing the question in her tone. "I do," he finally admitted, his jaw aching painfully.

"Then why do you hold back?" his mother asked. "Please talk to me. I am your mother. Allow me to help you."

Inhaling a deep breath, Matthew said, "She fears me." Despite the turmoil of the past few days, Matthew was surprised at the pain he felt when these three simple words left his lips. Instantly, he wished he could take them back.

"No, she does not," his mother objected, her head going from side to side as her eyes held his.

"She does," Matthew forced out. "You don't know what happened. You didn't see the terror in her eyes when I entered her chamber. I…"

Reaching up, his mother grasped his chin, turning his gaze back to her. "She does not fear *you*," she said, and Matthew wished he felt the same conviction in his heart that he heard ring in her voice. "She fears that you might be the same kind of man like your father, like hers. She does not know you."

Frowning, Matthew took a step back, his eyes gliding over his mother's face. "What do you know of her father?"

His mother shrugged. "Only what everybody does. He's a drunkard and a gambler."

"There's more," Matthew pressed, seeing the way his mother's gaze dropped from his.

Sighing, she closed her eyes for a long moment before her gaze returned to his. "People don't speak of it, the same as they didn't speak of your father and me. And yet, they know…and they whisper." Again, she sighed, and Matthew wished he had been there when she had needed him. Never had he seen his father strike her or harm her in a physical way, but he had seen her fear and wondered where it had come from. Yet, he had never dared to take a closer look. "More than that though, I know how to spot men like your father." An apologetic look came to her eyes as she reached for his hands. "I'm sorry to speak of him thus. I never meant to speak ill of him, least of all to you. He was your father."

Matthew scoffed, "Why would you not? After all, it is the truth. There is no falsehood in what you say, and why should you not speak the truth now that he is dead. We should have spoken truthfully long ago. He deserved no less. We deserved no less." Turning his gaze back toward the window, Matthew crossed his arms in front of his chest, knowing only too well that he had failed his mother. He ought to have realised the truth sooner. He ought to have seen it. Instead, he had allowed his father to terrorise his mother for years. Not only his cousins Tristan and Henrietta had suffered, but also his own mother.

Only because Matthew had not dared look at what had been right in front of him. Just as he had not seen his wife's fear…because he had not wanted to see it. He had allowed himself to live in an illusion. An illusion that was now slowly crumbling around him, burying him under the rubble of a wasted life.

"Look at me," his mother urged as her hands came to rest on his arms, pulling him toward her. "I know that you fear becoming like your father."

Matthew swallowed, shocked to hear her say so. Then he nodded, reminding himself that if nothing else he could give her the truth. He owed her that much…at the very least.

"I've always known," his mother said, guilt suddenly clouding her voice, "and yet, I've never done anything to convince you otherwise. I saw the way you always looked at him, the longing to be accepted as a worthy son and I hated him for not giving it to you." Briefly, she clamped her mouth shut as though shocked by her own words.

Then his mother inhaled a deep breath, and her gaze seemed to clear. "I've thought about this, my life, our lives a lot lately. In a different way than before. More honestly, I suppose, and while I've always believed or rather told myself that if I had been a better wife to your father, he would have treated me better. I now know that the fault did not lie with me, but with him. It was a realisation a long time coming, and it changed how I saw the world in general. I know now what is right and wrong. Now, I can say that what he did to us was wrong and that we are not to blame. It was him. No matter what, he would never have changed. He saw no need to. He did not care for us, not the way a man is supposed to care for his family." The look in her eyes focused, and once again, she smiled up at him, her left hand reaching out to cup his cheek. "But you care. As much as you've tried to live up to your father's expectations, you have never been able not to care. I always saw your turmoil, and it pained me greatly that I could not help you. But I can now." Nodding her head, she held his gaze, her own growing in intensity. "I can tell you the truth. I can make you believe it as well."

Matthew swallowed. The truth? He thought. Always had it been a fickle subject. Never had he been able to tell what was true and what not. Did truth not lie in the eye of the beholder? If that was so, then there was no universal truth, was there? Only each person's subjective view of the world? Could one even speak of truth in such a case?

"You, my son, you care," his mother repeated as though trying to drill these words into his mind until he truly would believe them. "That is what matters. That is what sets you apart from your father.

You care. He did not." Her hand squeezed his. "Go and talk to her. She is a sweet girl, but she seems to have lived a life where she was never taught to stand tall." A sad smile flitted across his mother's face. "She reminds me of myself when I was younger, when I was a young bride. Only I did not grow up with a father like hers. I only learnt how to be afraid from my husband."

Matthew gritted his teeth. Never had his mother spoken so openly to him. Never had she revealed so much about how she felt, about how she had suffered. And although he felt the pain of her words like a stab to his heart, her words also warmed him for they meant that he held her trust. Indeed, if he were like his father, would his mother dare speak to him thus? Would she not also fear him? The fact that she did not, did it mean that her words were true? Could be true?

Heaving a long sigh, his mother met his gaze once more, a soft smile coming to her lips, bright and hopeful. "Your father taught me how to be afraid," she said, her voice strangely uplifting for such a dark statement. "Now, you need to teach your wife how not to be afraid, how to stand tall, how to raise her chin and meet the world without fear. For only when you're equals, when she sees herself as your equal in every way, will she be able to stand up to you, to refuse you, to speak honestly. And only then will you be able to win her heart."

Amazed, Matthew stared down at his mother, wondering how it was possible that he had never seen the wisdom that now rested in her eyes. All her life, she had hidden it away out of fear to anger his father. What would the man have done if he had known the true strength of the woman he had married? Matthew was glad he never had to find out.

"Thank you," he finally whispered, his heart feeling a thousand pounds lighter.

Nodding in understanding, his mother smiled at him, and her eyes glowed as she saw the hope that returned to his heart. "I never thought I'd ever say such a thing, and yet, I need to say how glad I am that he is finally gone from our lives so that we can be ourselves again. So, you can be the man I always knew you were."

Hugging his mother tightly, Matthew sighed, wondering what his wife would look like with her head held high, her shoulders squared and a look of determination in her eyes. She would be even more radiant than she already was. He was certain of it.

Now, he had to find a way to speak to her without instilling fear. It would not be an easy feat, but he had to try for if he did not, he would become a bitter, hateful old man like his father.

And he would never let that happen.

His mother deserved better than that.

His wife deserved better than that.

And deep down, Matthew thought that he himself deserved better than that as well.

16

A FATHER'S VISIT

undled up against the cold of early spring, Adelaide strolled through the garden of her new home, a mournful sigh flying from her lips. In the house, she was constantly fighting to avoid her husband, not knowing what to say to him, while out here, she could not help but picture little Tillie chasing across the lawn and playing hide-and-go-seek behind the evergreen bushes. These days, no matter where Adelaide went, her heart ached. Fear and loss were her constant companions, and she was beginning to wonder if that would ever change.

Nights found her restless, tossing and turning, until her body succumbed to exhaustion and she cried herself to sleep. In the mornings, her heart and soul ached with a deep longing to be with her family and she wished she could simply go to see them. Still, the fear of encountering her father held her back. Was he the reason they did not come to see her? Was he keeping them away in order to isolate her? So, she would give in to his demands?

That thought only served to remind Adelaide that she still did not know what to do about her father. What would she tell him when he came to call on her next time?

Hearing the gravel crunch under her feet, Adelaide strolled onward, her eyes unseeing to the soft greens that poked their heads out of the dirt here and there. Although her husband made her uncomfortable, she had to admit that he did not instil the same fear in her as did her father. And yet—or perhaps because of it—she could not bring herself to ask him for money. Money she would then hand over to her father, who in turn would gamble it away, no doubt coming back to demand more sooner rather than later.

Adelaide sighed, stopping in her tracks. Lifting her face to the brilliant blue sky, she closed her eyes. "What am I to do?" she mumbled, hopelessness falling over her shoulders like a heavy cloak.

Hearing her name called, Adelaide flinched. Then she turned back toward the house and found her mother-in-law walking toward her. Relief chased away the dread that had gripped her heart when she had feared it might have been her husband.

"Are you all right, dear?" her mother-in-law asked, her soft eyes lingering on Adelaide's face as though she truly cared to know. "You seem a bit forlorn."

Returning the woman's greeting, Adelaide smiled as best she could. "I'm fine," she replied, turning away and allowing her gaze to sweep across the garden. "I simply thought to take a short walk as the weather is so promising today."

"It is indeed," her mother-in-law agreed, and yet, there was something in her voice that made Adelaide think that she was not merely referring to the weather.

A hand settled on Adelaide's arm, and when she turned to look, her mother-in-law met her gaze with an enquiring one of her own. "Are you all right, dear?" she asked once again. "I know it must be hard to be away from your family and to start over with people you hardly know." A soft smile came to the woman's lips, and Adelaide felt tears form in her eyes. "I know that everything was a bit rushed and overwhelming, but I simply wanted to welcome you into this house and into this family. You'll always have a home here, and we will always be here for you. If there is anything you need, please do not hesitate to come to me."

Blinking her lids rapidly, Adelaide felt an honest smile tugging on the corners of her mouth. "Thank you," she whispered, not knowing what else to say. Always had she guarded what lived in her heart, and the thought to share it with someone she hardly knew would never have occurred to her.

"Call me Clara, will you?"

Smiling, Adelaide nodded, feeling a sudden warmth sooth her aching heart. Although she had always been afraid, she had never been lonely, and the last fortnight had shown her how miserable she was when separated from her family. Why would they not call on her?

"My son is a good man," her mother-in-law suddenly said, and Adelaide could not prevent the slight jerk that went through her at the mention of him.

The almost imperceptible narrowing of her mother-in-law's eyes told her that she had noticed, and Adelaide could only hope that the woman would not come to think of her as lacking as her son's wife. Almost desperately, Adelaide wished for someone who was kind to her in this house. Someone who might come to care for her…even if only a little.

Stepping forward, Clara reached out to place a gentle hand on Adelaide's arm. "He is a good man," she repeated as though saying it again would make it true. "I know you have reason to doubt him, but I am urging you to give him a chance. Try to see him as he is, not as you fear he might be. I assure you you will not be disappointed."

Torn between the desperate desire to be thought well of, to be liked by this woman and her own instincts, Adelaide could not so easily abandon the caution that had guided her all her life. Clara's words touched her, and yet, she wondered if her husband's mother knew her son as well as she thought she did or if she simply chose to ignore the more aggressive side of his character. After all, Adelaide reminded herself, it was not all in her head. She had seen and heard evidence that clearly spoke to a less than collected side of his. What was true?

Could anyone truly say that with certainty?

"Excuse me," a young footman said, clearing his throat.

Blinking, Adelaide tensed as she had not even heard his approach. Had she not taught herself to always be aware of her surroundings?

"I apologise," he said to Adelaide's mother-in-law before his gaze turned to her. "My lady, you have a visitor."

Adelaide's blood froze in her veins. What were the odds of her family calling on her today? What if…? "Who is it?" she asked in a voice that would have been befitting for someone on their deathbed.

"Lord Radcliff, my lady."

Adelaide felt the deep desire to faint right then and there on the spot. Still, all that would accomplish was to postpone the conversation with her father for when it came to money, he could not be persuaded to reconsider. Best to get it over with as soon as possible. Perhaps he would accept her allowance. Perhaps it would be enough. It had to be as she did not have more to give. But what if he refused? What if he insisted?

"Are you all right, my dear?" Clara asked, her eyes watchful as they studied Adelaide's face. "Do you want me to accompany you?"

For a moment, Adelaide hesitated, wondering if her mother-in-law could tell how uncomfortable she felt at the thought of meeting her father. "No, that is not necessary. Thank you." Hoping the smile on her face was convincing enough, Adelaide took her leave and followed the footman back into the house to the drawing room.

Each step felt more reluctant than the one before, and Adelaide took a few deep breaths, hoping to slow the rapid beating of her heart. Her hands balled into fists as she stepped across the threshold and the doors were closed behind her.

"Do you have the money?" her father asked without bothering to offer a greeting. His gaze fixed her with impatience, and when she failed to answer right away, two large strides carried him closer. "Speak!" he snapped. "Or have you lost your tongue?"

Adelaide swallowed, carefully stepping around her father as she retreated deeper into the room…farther away from the door. Still, she could not bear to have him stand so close to her. "I can give you this," she said, stepping up to the mantle where she had hid a small purse in an old vase. Turning around, she held it out to him. "It is all I have."

Her father's eyes narrowed as he approached and then snatched the small pouch from her hands. "What is this?" he demanded, loosening the string and peering inside. "You must be jesting!" he exclaimed, his blood-shot eyes glaring at her once more. "This is nothing! This is barely enough for one evening!"

Wringing her hands, Adelaide felt her skin crawl as she found herself the object of her father's wrath. All her life, she had done her utmost in order to prevent this from happening, and now, when she was supposed to be safe, the moment had finally come. Was that not why she had married? Why her family had urged her to marry? To keep her safe from her father's influence? It would seem *safe* was not a place she would ever find.

"All I have is my allowance," she stammered, trying to think of a way to dissuade her father from pursuing this…but her mind failed her as fear rose, claiming her wits and stealing her thoughts.

"Your allowance?" her father thundered. "Did I not tell you to ask your husband for more?"

Swallowing, Adelaide nodded.

"And did you?"

Gritting her teeth, she shook her head.

In a flash, her father stood before her, his large hands wrapping around her upper arms, their grip painful as he shoved his face into hers. "Why not?" he growled, anger darkening his face.

Feeling her teeth chatter with fear, Adelaide bowed her head, unable to hold her father's gaze. "I c-could not," she stammered. "He w-would have wanted to know w-what it's for."

"Then lie!" her father snarled as though it were the most natural thing in the world.

Unable to speak, Adelaide all but hung in her father's arms, her body aching with the strain of keeping herself upright when all she wanted to do was sink onto the floor and bury her head in her hands.

"Answer me!" her father growled, shaking her as though she were nothing but a doll.

Adelaide's teeth clucked together painfully, and she began to see bright spots before her eyes.

It was in that moment when Adelaide was ready to give up and surrender everything she was, everything she had clung to that the door burst open with a loud bang that reverberated through the entire room.

In stormed her husband, his face dark red and his gaze narrowed into slits as his eyes slid over her for the barest of moments before he turned them onto her father.

Adelaide gasped at the sight of him, feeling the strength of his presence in every fibre of her body. Never had she seen him like this before, and fresh terror seized her heart. What would he do?

Like a predator, her husband stalked into the room, his gaze unwavering as he stared at her father. "I'd ask you to kindly remove your hands from my wife, *my lord*."

Despite his words, the threat was unmistakable, and Adelaide gasped anew when she saw the effect of it in the way her father took a step back, his hands finally releasing their hold on her.

What did it mean when someone who had always intimidated others suddenly showed fear himself?

Adelaide wished she did not have to find out.

17

A HUSBAND'S WORD

tanding by the window in his study, Matthew looked out at the far corner of the garden visible from his position. Although he knew he ought to see to the papers on his desk, his thoughts continued to stray from the task at hand. All he could think of was his wife…and his mother's advice to him.

But how? How could he teach her to stand tall?

Matthew hung his head. He did not even know how to approach her without sending fear into her heart. Whenever he drew near, she would shrink away and had done her utmost to avoid him ever since their wedding day. It was hopeless.

Without warning, the door was suddenly flung open and his mother rushed in. She was still wearing her coat and gloves, and her cheeks were flushed and her eyes wide. "Matthew!"

"Mother, what's wrong?" Grasping her hands, Matthew looked down at her, feeling his chest tighten with the worry he read on her face. "What happened?"

"Lord Radcliff is here!"

"What?" Fear gripped Matthew's heart. "Where?"

"In the drawing room, speaking to your wife." Momentarily, Matthew froze. "You should have seen the look in her eyes when he was announced," his mother rushed to explain, her face tense with anxiety. "She looked all but terrified, and yet, she insisted to meet him alone."

Swallowing the lump in his throat, Matthew stepped around his mother and rushed toward the door.

"Something is very wrong," his mother continued when he stepped across the threshold and out into the corridor. "You need to protect her."

As he rushed down the hallway toward the front of the house, Matthew felt his heart beating wildly in his chest. Never in his life had he known fear like this. Not even when his father had turned on him that fateful morning.

Approaching, he could hear the earl's angry snarl even through the closed doors, a threat hanging in the air even though the barrier between them muffled his words. Still, the message was loud and clear, and Matthew felt a growl rise in his throat at the knowledge that it was directed at none other than his wife.

His sweet, innocent, delicate wife.

Matthew thought he was prepared for anything, and yet, when he threw open the doors, the air caught in his throat.

The earl stood menacingly above her, holding her limp body in his claw-like hands as though he wished to devour her. With her head bowed in defeat, Adelaide all but hung from his hands as they gripped her around the arms, no doubt leaving marks that could be seen for days.

Anger surged through Matthew, and he had to fight to remain in control or he would have acted as a man of low character. Instead, he stalked toward the other man, seeing the slight widening of his eyes and knew that his presence alone took the wind out of the earl's sails. As much as the man liked to intimidate his family, he was not immune to fear himself. "I'd ask you to kindly remove your hands from my wife, *my lord*."

Dimly, Matthew heard his wife gasp, but his attention was focused on her father as he swallowed and then finally loosened his grip on her arms. Stepping back, he met Matthew's stare, his own suddenly lacking strength if not determination. His eyes were blood-shot and his face red. He was clearly angry, but even more so, he seemed desperate.

"What are you doing here?" Matthew demanded, stepping forward and in-between his wife and her father.

The earl swallowed, but then raised his chin. "That is none of your concern. I came to speak to my daughter. Alone."

Matthew scoffed, "What I saw did not look like a polite conversation," he snarled, his gaze daring the man to show his true colours.

Still, the earl remained silent, clamping his lips together in annoyance, refusing to see reason.

At this clear show of defiance, Matthew took a threatening step closer to the man he had come to loathe as much as his own father. "You're not welcome here," he hissed. "If you refuse to treat your daughter with the respect she deserves, then I must *ask* you to leave this house immediately."

Though his confidence was clearly shaken, the earl glared back at Matthew. "She is *my* daughter, and I will speak to her any way I see fit."

"You will not!" Matthew threw back, squaring his shoulders as he fought to keep his fists at his sides. "She is now *my* wife, and I will not allow you to threaten her."

Throwing back his head, the earl laughed. "I would never threaten my own daughter. Clearly, you misunderstood."

Frowning, Matthew glanced from the earl to his wife, wondering what the man was hiding. Why had he come here today? What did he want? No matter what he said to the contrary, Matthew was certain that he wanted something. From his daughter. From him. What could it be? Money? It was the most logical answer, and yet, how could the man threaten his daughter when he could no longer decide her fate. What was he missing? Matthew frowned, wondering if there was something he did not know. Something his wife kept from him.

"I doubt that," Matthew finally said, crossing his arms in front of his chest. "What do you want, Radcliff? I'll never believe you came here to see your daughter. What are you hiding?"

At his words, the earl's gaze drifted to his daughter and a slow smile—a clear threat—came to his face. And yet, he remained silent…as did his daughter.

Annoyed with the man's refusal to answer him, Matthew asked, "Do you not think that there will be marks on your daughter's arms after the way you grabbed her? Is it common practice for you to harm your own blood?" Holding the earl's gaze, Matthew took a step toward him. "You better believe that if I see you harming *my wife* ever again, I will call you out. Have I made myself clear?"

The man's face paled visibly as he tried to swallow the lump in his throat. Then he glanced at his daughter and quickly took his leave.

As his footsteps receded, their echo growing smaller, Matthew turned to look at his wife. Her hands were trembling, and her eyes were as round as plates as she stared at him, fear lingering on her face as though it belonged there.

Knowing that there would never be a perfect time, Matthew inhaled a deep breath, trying to calm himself as best as he could, and braced himself for the greatest challenge he had ever been faced with: speaking to his wife.

He could only hope he would find the right words.

Staring at her husband, Adelaide did not know what to make of him. Although anger was still radiating off him, only moments after he had come through the door, she could have hugged him. The sudden desire to do so had caught her off guard, and she was still reeling from the shock of it. Never had anyone come to her defence. Not like this. But why had he? Simply because she was his? Because he considered it an insult to him that another would threaten his wife and by extension him?

Or…?

Utter curiosity rooted her to the spot where she would have otherwise retreated. Her eyes flitted over his face as he clearly fought to calm his anger. She could see him watching her, gauging her reaction. He stood back and did not approach, giving her space, and Adelaide wondered how he knew. How did he know so well what frightened her? And why would he care whether or not she feared him? Her father certainly never had been bothered by it. Instead, he seemed to consider it a great achievement on his part.

"Are you all right?" her husband finally asked, his gaze dropping from hers and touching the spots on her arms where her father had held her with his iron grip.

Glancing down, Adelaide felt learnt behaviour take over. "It is nothing," she said, shaking her head in dismissal, the hint of a smile on her face.

Her husband, however, did not seem reassured at her words. Instead, his eyes narrowed, and she could see doubt come to his face. She could see that he did not believe her, but for once the knowledge did not frighten her, but merely made her wonder why.

Absentmindedly, she rubbed a hand over her left arm, flinching as she touched a spot that sent a jolt of pain through her body. Instantly, she tensed, and her gaze returned to meet her husband's.

"It is not nothing," he said, his gaze insistent as it held hers, as he took a step toward her. "Your father had no right to treat you as he did." Again, he stepped closer, and Adelaide inhaled a slow breath, fighting the urge to retreat…not out of fear, but out of habit. "No one has the right to lay a hand on you. Not your father. Not me. Not anyone."

The green in his eyes darkened, warmed, and Adelaide once again found herself staring at the man she did not understand, the man she could not make sense of. Still, his words touched her as did the sincerity she heard in his voice.

But old instincts died hard.

A feigned smile returned to her face as she shook her head yet again, seeking to dismiss his concern. "My father would never hurt me," she said, her voice flat and without conviction. "This was an accident. He lost his temper and–"

"It was not," her husband interrupted, his eyes grew harder as he approached. "You know it was no accident, no exception." He swallowed, and she could see the hints of a battle waging within. "I…I know the signs of a woman mistreated." Gritting his teeth, he met her gaze openly, allowing her to see the turmoil that claimed his heart. "My…father used to treat my mother the same way, and for a long time, I believed that that was simply the way between husband and wife. I was a child then. Now, I know better."

Adelaide felt her skin crawl as his words washed over her. Had he grown up in a household similar to her own? Had he escaped his father's anger merely because he was a man? Had that saved him?

One look into his eyes told Adelaide that it had not been so for what she saw there spoke of a man haunted. He still carried his childhood with him as she carried her own. The realisation that there was something to connect them, something they shared, something that bound them together was all the more startling to Adelaide as she would have never expected a man to feel as she did.

He took another step toward her, and again, she flinched…unable not to. Still, there was nothing threatening about him now. In truth, she had never seen a man look so vulnerable, and she wondered why he would allow her to see him thus. Did it not speak of great trust? But why would he trust her? How could he? They hardly even knew each other.

When he saw her tense, her husband immediately halted his step. "I am not my father," he said, his voice loud and clear as though he was not trying to convince her but himself. "Nor am I yours." He swallowed. "I do not want you to fear me. What I want is your respect. I want you to respect me as much as I respect you."

For what felt like the thousandth time that day, Adelaide stared at her husband. Never had anyone surprised her as greatly as he had in a single day. Her heart urged her to believe him, told her that his words sounded genuine. And yet, fear urged her to be on her guard, reminding her what her past had taught her.

Men could not be trusted.

"May I ask," he began, his gaze watchful as he looked at her, "is there anything about me that makes you fearful? Is there something I need to be careful about? Something I might not even be aware of? Please, help me understand."

At a loss, Adelaide shook her head, afraid to anger him if she indeed were to answer honestly.

Her husband inhaled a deep breath as though his patience was wearing thin, and yet, he did not lash out at her. He continued to hold himself back, his narrowed gaze telling her that he had seen her renewed apprehension. His mouth opened to speak, but then he hesitated. Gritting his teeth, he closed his eyes, and she could see his hands curling into fists.

Still, it was not anger she saw when he looked at her once more. It was rather a sense of frustration, even fear, and when he finally spoke, Adelaide felt herself respond to the honesty she heard in his words. "I'm afraid I will become a man like my father," he admitted, not dropping his gaze although he clearly wished to. "He was a cold man, uncaring and dismissive of others. He did what he wanted, and he never saw a reason to change. He was strong, and we were weak, so why would he?" He took another step until he stood barely an arm's length in front of her, his gaze almost pleading as he looked at her. "I would ask for your help. Help me see the signs so that I may avoid a fate like my father's. Will you do that?"

Adelaide swallowed, and yet, the lump in her throat would not move. Again, she saw kindness in him as well as vulnerability, and it made her heart ache. What had made him reveal this weakness to her—a stranger! —of all people?

Would she be a fool to dare and trust him in return?

If only she knew.

.

18

THE MEANING OF ANGER

Indecision rested in her blue eyes, and Matthew all but held his breath.

Although his muscles trembled with the truth he had just shared with her, he held himself still, knowing that sudden movements frightened her. And so, he held her gaze, felt it sweep over him, study him. He saw temptation come to her eyes, sending a jolt of hope to his heart, before fear once more chased it away.

Matthew had seen how close she was to the women in her family, but had no man ever proved himself worthy of her trust? Certainly not her father to be sure. But what of her brother?

Despite a period of estrangement, his cousins Tristan and Henrietta had always been close, sharing with each other what they would not share with the rest of the world. Always had Matthew envied them, wondering what it would have been like to have had a brother or sister.

The room had grown still around them, and when she spoke, Matthew almost flinched at the sound of her voice. "Your anger frightens me." The moment these words left her lips, she clasped a hand over her mouth, her eyes going wide with shock as she took a step backwards, seeking cover.

Matthew nodded, fighting the urge to step closer and offer comfort, knowing she would not see it as such. "I can understand how that might make you fearful," he said calmly. "However, my anger stemmed from fear for your safety, your well-being. I was afraid your father would harm you. I only sought to protect you, not harm him or anyone else."

Her eyes dropped from his, and he could see that she contemplated his words. Her brows drew down into a frown as she lifted her gaze to meet his once more. "But…?" She broke off, and her eyes travelled downward and came to linger on his right hand.

Seeing the direction of her gaze, Matthew lifted his hand, seeing the faint bruising on his knuckles. Air rushed from his lungs as he understood. "These are not from a fight," he explained. "These are from a boxing match, nothing more but a friendly competition. I swear it."

Her blue eyes returned to his. "Why do you box?" she asked, her voice unsteady. "Is it not a sign of anger? To hurt someone?" The moment she had finished, her gaze once more dropped to the floor as though it had taken all her courage merely to ask what was on her mind.

Matthew sighed, "I admit that anger was the reason why I started boxing, but I never allow it to fuel my actions. Boxing is…" Inhaling deeply, he searched for a way to explain. "Anger has a way of settling into your bones. It lingers, and if you let it, it will harden your heart. I find it liberating to…push myself, my body to extremes. It clears my head and unburdens my heart for I do not wish to carry anger wherever I go. I'd rather let it go, and boxing is the only way I've discovered which accomplishes this for me."

Although his words seemed to have calmed her, the look in her eyes spoke of incomprehension. "And so," Matthew asked, "what do you do when you get angry? How do you deal with it?"

She blinked, and then she shook her head.

Matthew frowned. "You cannot tell me you never get angry?" His voice was light, and yet, filled with disbelief. Was anger a truly foreign concept to her? Did she truly only ever witness it in others? Did she never feel it herself? How was this possible?

"It serves no purpose," she whispered. "It only brings pain. The world would be a better place without anger."

Holding her gaze, Matthew exhaled loudly, taken aback by her confession. "I admit anger does not have the best reputation," he admitted, "but it is not all bad. Anger tells us when something is important to us. It speaks of passion and even deep affection. Of course, it always needs to be tempered by reason and respect for others, but it does serve a purpose. It shows boundaries, defines them, allows others to see them."

A smile curled up the corner of his mouth as Matthew glanced down at the tip of her shoes. "If I were to step on your toes while dancing, would that not upset you?" he asked, his voice teasing as he watched her carefully.

Frowning, his wife shook her head.

"Truly?" he asked, doubt in his voice as he smiled at her. "Would you not get upset? Or would you simply not show it?"

Staring up at him, she opened and closed her mouth a few times before he saw her gaze harden with decision. "I ignore these emotions. I—"

"But you feel them?"

"Sometimes," she admitted, her voice stronger than it had been before. "But I've been ignoring them for so long that now I hardly ever feel them. Now, they're only a mild echo of what they once were. An echo easily ignored."

Staring at her, Matthew shook his head. "That is awful," he said, unable to believe that she truly did not feel anger. In all likelihood, she had merely learnt to suppress it. What happened to someone if they spent a lifetime suppressing all they felt? "You must re-learn it, reacquaint yourself with these emotions."

Stunned, she looked up at him, her lips moving before she could weigh her words. "Do you truly wish for me to be angry?"

Grinning, Matthew nodded vehemently, pleased that they were finally speaking to one another. Once again, he glanced down at the tip of her shoe before lifting his own and gently stepping onto hers. "Oops," he said, a wide grin on his face, amazed at the lightness of heart he suddenly felt. It had been a long time since he had teased someone, and it felt utterly liberating. More so than any boxing match ever had.

His wife's gaze widened as she looked at him, her face immobile. For a long time, they simply looked at one another trying to see the other for who they truly were before—out of nowhere—the right corner of her mouth gave a slight twitch.

By all means, it was not a smile, and no one would have called it thus. Nor was it the ghost of a smile. And yet, it was…something.

As though deep inside, her true self was still there, alive and kicking, fighting to break free, only held back by her iron will. Although she had always seemed fragile and delicate, Matthew realised that she was not. Indeed, she had a hidden strength, a strength that had allowed her to survive thus far and remain the kind-hearted woman she was. Somehow, she had been able to protect herself from the anger that surrounded her, not allow it to affect her, alter her, corrupt her.

Perhaps one day she would share her secret with him.

But for now, he would find a way to make her angry, to help her feel safe in order to be herself. If she could show him anger, Matthew knew there would be no reason for her to hold anything else back.

Still smiling at her, he held her gaze, his head lowering toward hers only a fraction. "I give you my word, my lady, that in the days to come I will strive to make you angry. Be prepared, for I can be relentless. I shall annoy you with everything at my disposal until you cannot bear to look at me any longer without yelling in my face." Seeing her stunned expression, he laughed. "And that day shall be the day of my greatest triumph."

After all, anger meant passion, and a life without passion was no life worth living.

Matthew sighed, wondering if teaching his wife to reclaim her anger as well as her passion would help him reclaim that piece of himself he had lost a long time ago. Perhaps they could help free each other with the burdens of their pasts. Perhaps this was the first step toward a shared future.

Matthew could not remember when he had last felt this hopeful.

19

A CHANGED MAN

Over the next few days, Adelaide noticed a change in her husband's demeanour.

In the beginning, while he had never acted unkind or intimidating, he had still always seemed tense. His gaze whenever it had sought hers had been hard and even pained. Adelaide could not recall ever having seen a smile curl up his lips. In truth, he had seemed as miserable as she herself had felt, and Adelaide wondered how she could not have seen it.

Perhaps her fear of him, of what he might do, had blocked out everything else.

Now, he was no longer the same man he had been only a few days ago.

Now, whenever he saw her, whenever their eyes met, his own seemed to light up with such delight as though he were truly happy to see her, as though he had longed to see her. Still, a bit of a wicked smile always played on his lips, and every once in a while, he would wink at her as though they shared a most improper secret.

When he first had looked at her thus, Adelaide had almost fainted on the spot. Her heart had jumped a mile high, and her breath had been sucked from her lungs. She had stared at him with a rather dumbfounded expression on her face as her mind had raced to make sense of what her eyes were seeing. Never in her life had she encountered such a man.

It was quite unsettling.

And yet, as the days wore on and he continued to wink and smile at her, to tease her—for now there was no doubt in Adelaide's mind that that was exactly what he was doing—Adelaide was shocked to find herself respond without thought. For despite his wicked smile, he never failed to treat her with the utmost respect. He always kept his distance, never invading her personal space. He spoke calmly and kindly, asking her opinion as they set to refurnishing the drawing room. He encouraged her to speak honestly, to say what was on her mind, and whenever they happened to disagree, Adelaide would hold her breath, expecting an angry outburst, while he would simply smile at her, suggesting flipping a coin.

In consequence, the drawing room now showed a rather interesting array of colours and fabrics, and yet, Adelaide could not bring herself to regret their choices. Whenever she set foot in it, she remembered their compromises fondly and found herself unable to keep from smiling when her mother and grandmother finally came to visit, their curious glances gliding around the room.

Judging from the sparkle in her grandmother's eyes, Adelaide knew that the old woman suspected something. However, as Adelaide herself was still at a loss as to what was happening with her husband, she said not a word, ignoring her grandmother's watchful eyes.

Over time, Adelaide slowly felt her unease dissipate, and before she even knew it, she was no longer actively avoiding her husband. However, what was most shocking to her was when she caught herself returning his smile one afternoon with a weak one of her own.

Seeing it, his eyes widened, and his own smile deepen in such a way, that Adelaide shrank back, shocked at her own response.

"Don't ever hide your smile," her husband had whispered before he had walked away, once more allowing her the room she needed.

Closing her eyes, Adelaide had sagged back against the wall behind her, inhaling a deep breath as her emotions ran rampant in her heart. Had he not promised to make her angry? She wondered. Now, instead, he was making her smile. What was he thinking? Was there a plan involved? What exactly did he hope to achieve with it?

Adelaide's mind raced as she tried her best to make sense of her husband's odd behaviour, wondering if she would ever find out. Finally, she got her answer one afternoon as she sat reading in the library.

Snuggled into one of the tall-backed armchairs, she quickly found her thoughts absorbed by the words on the page before her. She did not hear him approach, and her heart skipped a beat or two when the book was suddenly yanked from her hands.

Air rushed from her lungs, and Adelaide pushed to her feet and found her husband standing behind her chair, flipping leisurely through her book as her own heart hammered wildly in her chest. "My lord?"

Looking up, he grinned at her, then closed the book.

Adelaide swallowed as his eyes lingered on hers. "I did not hear you enter."

A teasing twinkle came to his eyes as he took a step toward her. "Does that upset you? Would you wish for me to announce myself when entering a room?"

Although Adelaide could see that his words were not meant as true criticism or even a threat, she could not help the sudden tension that rose in her body. Whenever her father had spoken to her thus, *he* had been the one dissatisfied with something *she* had done.

As her pulse hammered in her veins, Adelaide forced herself to remember her husband's promise. He wished to anger her for a reason she still could not understand, and so she decided to answer his question honestly. "Not at all."

The delight in his eyes dimmed, and she could tell that he was dissatisfied with her answer. Still, he did no more but return his gaze to the book in his hands, leisurely flipping through it once more. "This is a good book," he commented, apparently unaware that he was holding it upside down. "I've read it at least three times." His eyes rose to meet hers as he closed the cover. "I can't seem to get enough of it. You should finish it." Holding it out to her, he held her gaze.

Deep down, Adelaide knew that something was up. There was a strange gleam in his eyes that she had not seen there before, and she wondered what it was that he hoped she would do. Still, as silence began to linger, she could not think of anything else to do but take the book he offered.

Stepping forward, Adelaide reached out. However, the moment her fingers expected to feel the book's leather binding, her husband once more snapped it away, holding it out of her reach.

Staring at him, Adelaide blinked.

Her husband, however, seemed to have trouble suppressing a grin. "It truly is a good book. Perhaps I ought to read it yet again. What do you think?" His eyes widened then as though he had suddenly realised something. "Oh, I apologise. I forgot that you were right in the middle of it. I can wait. Here, you take it." Extending his arm, he held the book out to her once more.

Adelaide felt her eyes narrow as she looked at him, knowing beyond the shadow of a doubt that if she were to reach for it again, he would tug it out of her reach once more. "Keep it, my lord. If it means this much to you, you should read it."

"Oh, I couldn't," he replied, taking a step closer until the book's edge almost touched her hand. "It is yours. I insist." His green eyes held hers with such an intensity that Adelaide could almost feel their caress. And yet, there was a challenge in them.

Beginning to feel annoyed with his game, Adelaide gritted her teeth. Then quick as lightning her hand flew forward. Her fingertips brushed the book's binding, but she could not grasp it as her husband yanked it away again.

Delight lit up his eyes and he laughed. "You're quick," he complimented her. "I barely saw your intention before you moved."

Inhaling a slow breath, Adelaide tried to still her trembling hands, belatedly realising that it was not fear which had caused the slight tremor in them. "As a boxer, I suppose your reflexes must be good," she commented, taking a step back…refusing the challenge.

Unwilling to let her escape, her husband closed the distance between them. "They must be indeed." Then he once more held out the book to her.

Adelaide sighed, "Why are you doing this?" she asked, glancing down at the book. "You must admit that this is rather childish."

"It certainly is," he agreed, a wide smile on his face as he leaned forward confidentially. "And no one knows better how to give their emotions free rein than children, wouldn't you agree?"

Adelaide swallowed as an image of Tillie rose in her mind and her heart immediately ached with longing. Over the past weeks, she had forced herself not to think of the little girl, knowing it would only be all the harder to say goodbye to her if she did so.

"So, you want me to reach for the book again?" she asked, trying to determine what goal he had in mind.

"Yes."

"And then?"

He shrugged.

Adelaide sighed, "I don't understand why you would−?" Breaking off mid-sentence, she shot forward…and almost collided with his chest when he moved the book sideways.

Her husband laughed, "That was quite clever of you and rather sly. I would never have thought you had it in you to deceive others."

Adelaide froze staring up at him. "I didn't−"

"You certainly did," he objected, that increasingly annoying grin still on his face. "You acted as though you had no intention of retrieving the book, and then when you thought me distracted, you reached for it."

Clamping her mouth shut, Adelaide inhaled a slow breath, feeling a rather unfamiliar emotion stirring in her body. "Fine, if you will not return it, then neither will I try to retrieve it. There."

Leaning forward, her husband looked at her, his eyes travelling over her face. "You're angry," he observed, his eyes twinkling with delight.

"I'm not!" Trying to relax her shoulders, Adelaide held his gaze, wondering how on earth they had ended up in this ridiculous situation.

"Then prove it," he dared her, lifting the book so she could see it. "Take it."

"I don't understand how that would prove anything," Adelaide countered, surprised by her own bravery to contradict him. Had she lost her mind? Years of experience had taught her how *not* to anger a man. What on earth was she doing? This was a game she could not win.

"Well, it's either or," her husband concluded with a quietly patient demeanour that was getting hard to ignore. "Take the book or yell at me."

"Even if I were to yell at you, it would not mean I was angry. I–"

"Then do it," he dared, his gaze hardening on hers as he leaned forward as though unwilling to allow even the subtlest of her facial responses to slip by him. "Yell at me. Berate me for teasing you because we both know exactly what I'm doing here. You can't deny that!"

"I'm not. I simply–"

"Then yell at me."

"No!" she snapped, feeling her blood begin to boil.

"Why not?"

"Because–"

"Believe me, it'll be liberating." His grin dared her. "You'll feel so much better if you simply–"

"Give me the blasted book!" The moment the words left her lips, Adelaide clasped both hands over her mouth, heat rising to her cheeks. Her eyes were wide as were her husband's, and for a long quiet moment, they simply stared at one another.

Then he broke out laughing. He laughed so hard that a tear ran down his cheek.

Ashamed, Adelaide turned away, unable to believe that he had been able to bait her thus. Always had she thought herself in control. She had to be. If she lost it, the consequences would be unthinkable.

"Don't hide," he urged, his voice gentle as he stepped around her, blocking her escape. "I'm proud of you. I did not mean to laugh about you. I was only so relieved to see you angry, to see these emotions bubbling out of you."

Trying to hide her face in her hands, Adelaide barely heard a word he said. All she could think of was her lack of control and what it would mean for her future. Only when a warm hand came to rest on her shoulder did she look up…

…and into her husband's green eyes, soft and gentle and kind.

His hand moved from her shoulder, and she could feel the gentle caress of his fingertips as they slid across her cheek, brushing away a tear she had not even known was there. "I'm proud of you," he said once more, his voice serious and without humour. "You're magnificent when you're angry. I've never seen you more alive."

Staring up at him, Adelaide finally understood why he was trying to anger her. It had been so long that she had felt her heart beating in such a way, her body fuelled into action, strong and confident. And he was right. It did feel good. Liberating.

But was it safe?

"Here, take the book," her husband said, once more holding it out to her.

Adelaide opened her mouth to respond, felt the need to do so rise in her like a reflex, something without thought.

But he stopped her.

"I promise I won't pull it away. You have my word."

Exhaling a slow breath, Adelaide swallowed, trying her best to regain her composure. Then she reached out, half-expecting him to pull it away, and found her fingers close round the book's spine.

"See?" he said, his own hand still curled around the other side.

"Thank you." Pulling on her end of the book, Adelaide found him unwilling to relinquish his. He held on, and her eyes narrowed when a teasing grin came to his lips. Before she knew what was happening, her hand yanked on the book, throwing him off balance and propelling him toward her.

Her husband's other arm came around her middle, holding her to him as he sought to regain his balance, his breath warm as it brushed over the side of her face.

Adelaide stilled as she felt his embrace. No one had held her like this, not since…

Moving back a little, her husband looked down at her, his arm still holding her to him while his other hand held on to the book…as did hers.

"You promised," Adelaide whispered, not knowing where to direct her eyes while his studied her face with such intensity. "You said you wouldn't–"

"I didn't," he interrupted, his voice teasing as he finally released the book. "You did. You pulled. Not me."

Adelaide inhaled a deep breath, overwhelmed by his nearness. "You tricked me," she whispered, feeling her skin crawl in a rather unfamiliar and surprisingly pleasant way. "Why? To make me angry again?"

At her question, the teasing grin vanished and her husband's face sobered. He swallowed, and she could see a hint of nervousness in his green eyes before they dropped from hers and travelled downward to briefly linger on her lips.

Adelaide drew in a sharp breath.

A moment later, his gaze was back on hers, and she could feel both his arms pulling her closer against him. "One day," he whispered, lowering his head to hers, "I will ask you for a kiss…but not today."

Adelaide's heart skipped a beat, and she dimly wondered why.

"Not before I can be certain," he continued, "that you have the courage to refuse me if that is your wish." For another long moment, his gaze held hers before he finally stepped away, his arms releasing her. "One day," he repeated, and then he turned and walked away.

Minutes passed, and Adelaide was still staring at the door through which her husband had left, desperately trying to catch her breath. It seemed anger was not the only emotion that made her feel alive, and try as she might, she could not keep a deliciously smitten smile from showing on her face.

Fortunately, her husband was nowhere in sight or she was certain he would have revelled in his triumph.

Still, Adelaide had to admit that it had been a long time since she had felt anything resembling the emotion her husband had stirred within her that afternoon. Never had she expected to feel it again. Never had she thought herself capable.

It would seem she had been wrong.

Her hands trembled, and she wrapped them more tightly around the book he had finally returned to her, realising that part of what she felt was disappointment.

Despite her initial attempts to avoid him, Adelaide realised that she had come to enjoy her husband's company. She could not deny that the way he smiled at her, the way he treated her as though there was nothing and no one more important than her affected her.

And now he had held her.

Always had he kept his distance, careful not to touch her, and then today he had tricked her into his arms. Indeed, there was a bit of a devious streak in him, and yet, it was tempered by kindness and respect. It did not frighten her.

Shock her.

Surprise her.

But not frighten her.

Recalling his last words to her before he had walked out the door, Adelaide felt a shiver run over her and she wondered when the day would come that he would ask her for a kiss. For even now, she knew that she would not be able to refuse him. Not out of fear, but out of curiosity.

What would his kiss feel like?

20

A STROLL IN HYDE PARK

fter another short visit from her mother and grandmother, Adelaide found herself strolling through Hyde Park with Lady Elton two days later. The sun was shining, the world was filling with different shades of green and cheerful chatter hung in the air, mingling with the first calls of spring. And yet, Adelaide was lost in thought.

"There is something on your mind," Lady Elton observed, a teasing grin on her face as she stopped to meet Adelaide's gaze. "Tell me."

Adelaide swallowed, then licked her lips, unable to put into words what currently occupied her mind.

"Is it about Matthew?"

At the sound of his given name, Adelaide blushed, feeling emotions rush to the surface that only recently had made themselves known to her.

"I see," Lady Elton observed with a twinkle in her eye. "Can I assume that married life is treating you well? That Matthew is treating you well?"

Adelaide nodded. "He is."

"You sound surprised?"

"I…" How was she to explain what she could not quite understand herself? Lately, the mere mention of her husband seemed to have the strangest effect on her.

"You've come to care for him, have you not?" Lady Elton exclaimed, joy on her face like that of a child finding a jar full of biscuits.

Feeling her heart tighten in her chest at Lady Elton's observation, Adelaide quickened her pace, her thoughts racing to find something to say. "Why…?" She swallowed, belatedly realising that Lady Elton had fallen behind. When she had caught up, Adelaide asked, "Would you mind telling me…? May I ask why…?"

"Why what?" Lady Elton prompted, her blue eyes holding kind amusement. Not the kind that thought it a sport to make fun of others' embarrassments, but the kind that teased out of affection.

Again, Adelaide swallowed. "Why did you ask…Matthew for help when Grandmother and I came to you? Why him?" For weeks now, Adelaide had wondered about that. Had it simply been for the reason that he was family to them? That they trusted him? Gritting her teeth, Adelaide willed her traitorous heart to keep silent and not whisper the small hope that had begun blossoming in her heart ever since…

Oh, she could not quite say since when, but it was there, whether she admitted to it or not.

Lady Elton sighed, all amusement leaving her eyes, replaced by a sadder emotion. "After realising his father's betrayal, Matthew lost his way. Even before then, all he did was strive for his father's approval. To make matters worse, he had to face the fact that he had been his father's pawn, and to a man like Matthew, who deep down has a strong sense of right and wrong, that was devastating." A soft smile came to Lady Elton's face. "I didn't know him that well then, but I've come to know him since, and I can see that he was misled like my husband was. And yet he still blames himself."

Listening intently, Adelaide wondered about the gentle, teasing man she had come to know in the past few days. The man who feared to become like his father while at the same time striving to restore her sense of safety, security…and respect.

"No one blames him for what happened," Lady Elton continued. "His father betrayed him as much as us, but Matthew still cannot forgive himself. It does not seem to matter that we do not hold him accountable. He does and continues to do so. He feels the need to prove himself, to prove his loyalty, to prove that he is a man different than his father."

"That is why you asked for his help?" Adelaide asked, feeling her heart sink for a reason that could only be foolish. "To help him?"

For a moment, Lady Elton's watchful gaze lingered on Adelaide's face, and she quickly returned her own to the far horizon. With her eyes fixed on the nearing treeline, Adelaide heard Lady Elton inhale a deep breath, a touch of amusement in her voice. "I admit it was not the sole reason."

Unable not to, Adelaide turned to look at Lady Elton, hoping her curiosity to learn more was not written all over her face.

Lady Elton's smile, however, said that it was. "Ever since I became aware of your father's intention to marry you off to the highest bidder," shaking her head, she rolled her eyes, "I've been thinking about who a good match for you would be. After all, it was clear that you would not be safe from his schemes unless you got married." Stopping, she held Adelaide's gaze. "I've noticed the way he looked at you, the way he always stopped to listen whenever your name was mentioned, the way he did not hesitate when we asked for his help. You did not see the tortured expression on his face when your father lost your hand to Mr. Hawkin. He looked sick to the bone, and yet, there was a murderous gleam in his eyes I had never seen before."

Adelaide inhaled a sharp breath as her fears returned in full force. Had she been wrong about her husband? Was he as hot-tempered as her father and brother? Did he merely know how to hide that side of himself better?

"I can see what you're thinking," Lady Elton observed, her eyes slightly narrowed as she watched Adelaide's face, "and I can tell you that you're wrong. Do not fear him. The anger in him only came from a place of deep affection, a deep desire to protect you, to ensure your safety. He would never be violent, not even when his father pushed him to the limit. Not even then did he harm my husband. Instead, he risked his life to save him. And I have no doubt he would risk it yet again in order to protect you."

Closing her eyes, Adelaide inhaled a deep breath. Her hands trembled even though her heart rejoiced. And yet, her own reaction only served to prove that her husband still frightened her, not because of his anger, but because he was a different man than her father. As much as she hated her life, hated the fear she constantly lived in, it had become normal. Now, living with a man who actually sought to protect her was terrifying in a strange way. It was the unknown that frightened Adelaide. What would her life be like now? What was expected of her? How ought she to behave?

Her head spun with all the uncertainties that suddenly rushed toward her, and she had to clamp her teeth tightly together in order to keep herself upright.

"He is a good man," Lady Elton stressed once more, misinterpreting the reason for Adelaide's undoubtedly pale cheeks. "His own doubts only serve to prove that. You have nothing to fear from him."

Was that true? Adelaide wondered. Certainly, she slowly came to believe—even in her heart—that he would not harm her, would not strike her or force himself against her will. Still, did that mean there was nothing to fear?

Judging from the way her heart reacted these days whenever they crossed paths, Adelaide knew that there was a great deal to fear. Only now this fear was a completely new one. One that was unfamiliar to her, and therefore, all the more terrifying.

Although she could see the affection between happily married couples like Lady Elton and her husband, Adelaide only ever saw it from the perspective of an outside observer. Whereas, the only marriage she had ever witnessed from a closer perspective was that of her own parents. Well, if her new husband was nothing like her father, then what kind of marriage did she now find herself in? Behind closed doors, how did Lady Elton and her husband—?

"Addy!"

Adelaide's head snapped up at the sound of Tillie's voice, her gaze swivelling back to the path in front of her. Not too far ahead, she saw her mother and grandmother strolling toward them, little Tillie running ahead, her arms spread wide as she raced toward Adelaide.

In an instant, overwhelming joy replaced dread and doubt, and Adelaide felt her arms spread wide to receive the girl. Catching her, she spun her around in a circle, feeling Tillie's little arms clinging to her tightly. "Oh, I've missed you, my girl!"

"I've missed you, too," Tillie beamed, snuggling closer.

Holding the little girl in her arms, Adelaide closed her eyes, savouring the moment. When she would see Tillie again, she did not know. Although her grandmother had urged them to simply speak to Adelaide's new husband about the girl, her mother had insisted they proceed cautiously.

As Tillie was a bit of a rambunctious child, they had always had trouble keeping her in line and out of the earl's way. Always had they feared that he would find himself annoyed with her and send her from his house.

"What man would want a bastard child living in his house," her mother had pointed out vehemently, "especially when it is not even his own? I doubt he would be welcoming to his brother-in-law's illegitimate daughter."

Adelaide had hung her head at her mother's undoubtedly correct reasoning. As kind as her husband seemed to be, there were certainly limits to his patience. Although Adelaide doubted that he would downright reject her, she wondered if he would not be bothered by her presence in his house. Would it not cast a bad light on his reputation? Especially after the scandal around his father's death?

As Tillie drew her toward the banks of the Serpentine, her little hand clinging to Adelaide's, Adelaide flinched when out of the corner of her eye she thought to see someone she had not seen in a long time.

Through the thicket of trees, her eyes widened as they stared, seeking to confirm whether or not her mind had played a trick on her. And yet, they could not. All she could determine through the branches and leaves was a group of people strolling down the path.

Had it truly been him?

Adelaide closed her eyes, praying that her mind had indeed merely conjured a ghost.

21

LONGING

All afternoon Matthew had found one reason or another to repeatedly stroll by the front entrance, his gaze drawn to the door, willing it to open and return his wife from her outing with Lady Elton. However, time passed—excruciatingly—slowly, and nothing happened.

Supper time drew near, and Matthew began to grow restless. Had something happened to her? Ought he to go after her?

Just when he was about to force his feet to return him to his study, the sound of wheels churning on cobblestone reach his ears. His head snapped up, and his heart skipped at least a beat—if not more. He had already taken two strides toward the door when he called himself to reason.

If he were to yank open the door on her, his wife would certainly be frightened. Would she believe him controlling? Displeased with her afternoon's excursion?

Gritting his teeth, Matthew stopped halfway across the hall. No, he had to be patient, or all their progress would have been for nothing.

A smile came to Matthew's face when he remembered their afternoon in the library. The fire in her eyes. The shock on her face. The tentative smile that had barely been there.

She was indeed radiant, and more than anything he wanted to see her fiery spirit and not her fearful timidity.

Hearing his butler open the door and greet his wife, Matthew took a deep breath before approaching the door. "I see you have returned," he greeted her, unable to keep his delight from his voice. "I hope you had a pleasant afternoon."

For a moment, a hint of fear crossed her face, and Matthew could have kicked himself. He ought to have returned to his study and not cornered her the moment she crossed the threshold.

"I'm sorry, my lord," she whispered, relinquishing her coat and bonnet to a footman. "I forgot the time. I promise it shall not happen again." All the while, her gaze barely met his, but seemed to find something utterly fascinating on the hall's floor.

Swallowing, Matthew waited until they were alone before he approached her. Slowly her gaze rose to meet his, and yet, he did not see courage or defiance there. No, it was as though she feared if she did not look at him, it would anger him more.

Nothing could be further from the truth. After all, he was far from angry. Quite on the contrary.

"There is no reason to bow your head, my lady," he whispered as he forced himself to keep his distance and merely smile at her in an encouraging way. "You have every right to see your friends and family, and I would never object to your going out."

His wife swallowed, then nodded her head almost imperceptibly.

"I admit," Matthew said, leaning forward as he glanced around the room in a fairly obvious way, "that I've been waiting by the door."

At his admission, her eyes widened—if in alarm or merely in surprise, he could not say.

Smiling, he held her gaze. "I missed your company this afternoon."

She seemed to grow rigid, and yet, there was doubt in her eyes.

"Do you doubt my words?" he challenged teasingly.

"No, of course not, my lord," she hastened to answer. "I simply…"

"But you do not believe me."

"I…" Swallowing, she wrung her hands, her gaze slowly finding his. "I apologise I'm late."

"Don't," Matthew insisted, feeling a hint of anger rise at the sight of what her father's influence had done to her. "I am not angry or upset or disappointed or anything like that because you are late. If at all, I'm angry that you would apologise."

Her brows drew down into a frown, and her eyes searched his face with a bit more determination.

Matthew sighed, "The way you apologise—in such a fearful way—only makes me wonder what I did wrong to instil such fear in you. I never wanted you to apologise. I only ever wanted you to come home and tell me about your day. Would you do that?"

Unable to make out all the many emotions that had flitted across her face at his explanation, Matthew breathed a sigh of relief when she finally nodded, the tension in her body receding. "I would."

"Good." Stepping forward, he offered her his hand. "Would you like to change, or shall we go in to supper?"

For a moment, she hesitated, clearly worried that he might disapprove if she sat down to supper in a dress with a dusty hem, but then she smiled—even if timidly—and said, "I admit I'm quite famished."

"Then let's eat," Matthew exclaimed, accepting her hand and guiding her toward the dining room. She still seemed tense, and yet, it was nothing compared to the terror he had seen in her in the beginning of their acquaintance.

Step by step, Matthew reminded himself as he escorted her to her chair. Catching his mother's watchful eye, he smiled at her before seating himself.

Unfortunately, a bit of an uncomfortable silence fell over the room as they began to eat, and Matthew racked his mind over how to put his wife at ease. Strangely enough, he felt a bit self-conscious at his mother's presence.

"How was your afternoon, my dear?" his mother finally asked, shooting him a knowing glance.

Rolling his eyes at himself, Matthew focused his attention on his wife as she glanced a bit nervously from his mother to him.

"We went to Hyde Park," she began. "Lady Elton and I."

"It was a beautiful day for a stroll, was it not?" his mother commented, an encouraging smile on her face, and Matthew wondered at the woman she had become since her father's passing. It was quite remarkable!

His wife nodded, and for a second he thought to see a hint of hesitation on her face as though she was contemplating what to share with them. "We met my mother and grandmother there," she finally said, her gaze meeting his mother's instead of his, and he wondered why. "They went for a walk with…Mathilda."

For a moment, his wife's gaze dropped to her plate, and Matthew could see that what she had just revealed to them was not only a matter of great importance but also of concern to her.

"Mathilda?" his mother asked. "I must say I'm not familiar with that name. Pray tell, who is she?"

"Tillie," Matthew whispered as a memory surfaced. A memory of his wife speaking to a little girl with black curls and a mischievous twinkle in her eyes.

At the sound of his voice, his wife's gaze jerked up and met his, her eyes wide as she drew in a deep breath. Her fingers tensed around the fork in her hand, and she swallowed. "Yes, Tillie."

"Tillie?" his mother enquired once more, a hint of an amused smile on her face. "I'm afraid I'm still lost."

Seeing the tension on his wife's face, Matthew said, "She's a little girl I met when I called on Lord Radcliff to inform him of my intention to marry his daughter." A slight blush came to his wife's face at the mention of their wedding. "You seemed close," he observed. "Who was she?"

His wife swallowed, then licked her lips. "She is…my brother's daughter."

"Your brother's?" Glancing to the side, Matthew saw a frown coming to his mother's face. "I thought your brother was still unmarried."

The very moment his wife blushed, once more lowering her head, his mother's eyes widened. "Oh! I see."

Finally understanding the nervousness that hung about his wife like a thick fog, Matthew sighed in relief. Certainly, it was far from commendable to have an illegitimate child. However, he knew from personal experience that children had no influence over their parents' actions. It would be wrong to blame little Tillie for her father's indiscretion.

"I remember her fondly," he said, smiling. "She had quite the spirit for such a young girl."

A deep smile claimed his wife's face at the thought of Tillie, and for a moment, Matthew could not help but envy the little girl. What he would not give to be the one to make his wife smile like that?

"Yes, she is rather headstrong," his wife admitted, her eyes glowing as she spoke, "but sweet and affectionate."

"You miss her," Matthew observed, realising that with no mother present—as far as he knew—his wife had probably been the one to take over Tillie's care. She was a born mother with her kind soul and gentle ways.

"I do," she whispered, bowing her head as the deep smile was chased away by a look of utter sadness.

Matthew's heart twisted painfully in his chest. "You must invite her over," he said, "so we can all meet her."

Slowly, his wife lifted her gaze to his, her own filled with fearful hope as she studied his face. "You would not mind?"

Matthew smiled. "Children are a delight, and this house has resembled a tomb for far too long. Please, bring her. Perhaps her presence will reawaken all of us."

"Thank you," his wife breathed, her voice barely audible as she blinked back tears. Her hand trembled as she moved the fork to her plate, and Matthew was awed by the deep emotions he saw on her face. He had only ever seen her in fear or behind a carefully maintained mask of indifference. Utter joy and relief that gripped her body in such a way that he would feel its effect even across the table made him speechless. What other passions slumbered in his wife's heart?

Sitting back, Matthew sighed. Out of the corner of his eye, he caught his mother smile at him, her own face speaking of the same stunned surprise he felt himself.

The next afternoon, Matthew invited his wife to have tea with him. Although she looked mildly surprised, she agreed without hesitation. That alone warmed his heart. As they sat together, he once more asked her about Tillie, remembering how deeply the little girl had touched her heart.

"My grandmother has agreed to bring her by in a few days," she said, a hint of a question in her tone of voice.

"Wonderful," Matthew beamed, watching her relax. "I cannot wait to meet her…for real this time. She sounds like an entertaining child."

His wife laughed. She laughed! Matthew watched her rather thunderstruck. "That she is, but she is a handful. My mother says she's never met a child with less inclination to learn."

Matthew chuckled. "I do not believe that can be true. After all, children are so adept at learning. Simply think of all the thousands of things they learn when so young. Never again are we capable of opening our mind to new things than we are at that age."

Sobering, his wife watched him. "That is true. I often envy her the innocent way with which she looks at the world. That and her courage."

Remembering how the little girl had held his gaze, Matthew nodded. "She did seem rather brave."

Pride shone in his wife's gaze as she nodded. "She does not…bow her head," Adelaide mumbled as though to herself. "She does what she pleases, and she learns what she deems worth learning. She does not allow anyone to change her."

"It sounds like you admire her," Matthew observed, carefully dipping the tip of his finger into his tea without his wife noticing in order to check the temperature.

"I do," she whispered. Blinking, she met his gaze. "I can only hope that growing up she can hold on to that strength—wherever she found it—for it's impossible to retrieve once it's lost."

"Not impossible," Matthew replied as he leaned forward, cup in hand, and then poured his tea over his wife's arm, soaking her sleeve and staining the pale blue fabric.

Adelaide sucked in a sharp breath and jerked back her arm, her eyes going wide before they returned to meet his. For a moment, she simply stared at him. But then her gaze hardened, chasing away the confusion that had been there before. "You did this on purpose?"

Somewhat disappointed with her lack of a reaction, Matthew sat back, grinning. "Are you certain?"

Her gaze narrowed as she fingered the wet fabric nervously. "Why would you do this?"

Still grinning, Matthew lifted his brows.

Instantly, her mouth fell open. "This is a game to you," she gasped. "You could have burnt me?" A touch of hurt came to her tone.

"I made certain the tea was not hot enough. I assure you, my lady, I would never do anything to harm you, to cause you pain," Matthew vowed, his gaze free of humour as he looked at her.

Her brows crinkled, and for a moment, he thought she would roll her eyes at him. "However, you do believe it right to pour your tea on me and ruin my dress?"

Delighted with the hint of annoyance in her voice, Matthew nodded. "Surely you must admit that it was a good plan. Few people enjoy being doused with tea." Grinning, he watched her, noting the slight crinkles that came to the corners of her mouth as though she wished to smile.

Not quite what he had hoped for, but perhaps humour was better than anger after all.

Inhaling a deep breath, she seemed to be striving to calm herself. "You planned this," she said, a bit of an accusing tone in her voice. "What kind of a husband would plan to pour tea on his wife?"

Matthew shrugged. "The kind that wishes to anger his wife, no doubt."

"Have you still not given up on this?"

"Why would I?" he demanded as her eyes lit up with something he had only once glimpsed there before. "It is most entertaining."

At his words, she truly did roll her eyes at him. "If you'll excuse me, my lord," she began, rising from the settee, "I'll have to change."

Pushing to his feet, Matthew stepped in her path, noting the way her eyes widened a fraction as she looked up at him in question. "I know that you have great control over your emotions," he whispered as though confessing a secret, "but will you at least admit that you felt something right then and there? Will you at least admit that it angered you that I did this?"

Her lips pressed into a thin line as she held his gaze.

"Did this annoy you?"

She swallowed. "Yes."

"Did it upset you?" he asked, his feet moving closer as he held her gaze, feeling a stronger connection to her than before.

"Yes."

"Did it anger you?"

Gritting her teeth, she stared up at him, and he could see that she was loathe to admit her true emotions. "Yes, it did anger me," she finally said, her voice harsh and without fear. "I am angry with you for toying with me. I'm angry because this is a game to you. I'm angry because…" Her voice trailed off, and she dropped her gaze.

"Because?" Matthew prompted, feeling his breath stuck in his throat as he prayed that she would answer.

His wife swallowed and inhaled a deep breath. Then she pushed back her shoulders and met his gaze anew, her own reluctant and yet unwavering. "Because you know me so well," she whispered. "How can you know me so well?"

"Do you mind?" Matthew asked, overwhelmed by the way she looked at him. Never before had she held his gaze quite like this.

"I don't know," his wife replied, doubt in her pale blue eyes. "Those who know us well are those who can hurt us the most."

Matthew nodded. "You're not wrong," he said, remembering the way his father had manipulated him with ease. "And yet, is it reason enough never to allow anyone to come close? Would you tell Tillie not to open her heart to anyone for fear of having it broken?"

Her jaw quivered as she drew in a deep breath, her eyes misting as they remained on his. "She deserves to be happy."

"As do you."

Her breath caught, and she dropped her gaze, stepping away. "I need to change," she hastened to say as her feet increased the distance between them.

"We're invited to a ball tonight," Matthew called out before she had reached the door.

Stopping in her tracks, she turned to look at him. "Tonight?"

He nodded.

"Why did you not tell me this bef–?" Her voice trailed off as she closed her eyes, shaking her head. "Will you ever stop?" she asked. "Or will you continue this game indefinitely?"

Smiling, Matthew stepped towards her. "I promise I will stop as soon as you claim your rightful place."

A slight frown came to her face as she stared at him, and yet, Matthew believed deep down that she understood him. "Go change," he urged teasingly, "or we'll be late."

Rolling her eyes, she turned away from him, mumbling something rather harsh under her breath.

Matthew laughed. She could not have pleased him more if she had kissed him.

At least not much.

22

TO FEEL SAFE

Later that evening, Matthew found himself seated across from his wife in their carriage on their way to…some ball. He could not have been less interested especially since all his attention was currently focused on the rather pale woman trying to blend into the corner of the carriage in order to avoid him.

Her eyes were downcast; her skin pale. Still, a rosy blush danced on her cheeks, proving that she was well aware of the way he was looking at her.

Although Matthew had seen her dressed up in her finest before, it had always been from a distance. Now, she merely sat an arm's length away so that he could still smell the faint rose scent of her midnight black tresses. Her pale blue eyes seemed darker in the dim light of the carriage, perfectly matching the soft glow of her azure gown.

Matthew smiled at her. "You look beautiful tonight," he whispered, surprised to find his voice rather hoarse. "Not that you're not always beautiful, but…" Grinning, he shook his head, peeking at her carefully. "I'm making a mess of things, aren't I? I've never been good at voicing compliments."

"Then don't," was all she said, her voice rather flat and displeased as she kept her gaze firmly averted, her hands clenched in her lap.

Matthew frowned. "Does it bother you that I would look at you? That I would tell you that you look beautiful?"

The muscles in her jaw tightened, and she turned her gaze out the window, her eyes focusing on the darkness passing them by.

"Why?" Matthew pressed, wanting nothing more than to understand the woman he had married. After all, she was beautiful, so why would that bother her? Did women not dress to their advantage in order to be seen as beautiful?

For a moment, her gaze shifted to his before darting back to the window, her chest rising and falling with a deep breath.

"Please," Matthew urged, hoping for another moment of honesty that had occurred here and there between them. A moment when he had felt closer to her, when he had felt as though she was coming to trust him.

Meeting his gaze, she swallowed. "It bothers me," she finally began, her voice barely a whisper, and yet, it was filled with such heartbreaking sadness that Matthew felt the urge to comfort her, "because that was all my father ever saw in me." Her hands clenched around one another, and she dropped her gaze. "All he ever cared about was what my *beauty* would buy him. He never saw me, only ever what I was worth to him. He saw me as something to pay his debts with, something he could sell off to the highest bidder." Anger and disappointment laced her voice. "He didn't care who I was so long as my face was pretty to look at." Her gaze rose to meet his, a hint of an accusation shining in their depths. "Whenever he called me beautiful, I knew that he only thought of that. Always."

Matthew nodded. "I understand." From the way she looked at him in that moment, the way she held his gaze, a hint of a question in them, Matthew knew what she wished to know, and his heart jumped at the thought that she might care so deeply about what he thought of her, about how he saw her.

A gentle smile came to his face as he leaned forward, holding her gaze lest she dare retreat again. "To me, you're the most beautiful when you speak of Tillie."

Her eyes widened, and all suspicion slowly fell from her face as she listened.

Matthew chuckled softly, "Whenever you speak of her, your whole face lights up. Your eyes glow with such love and delight that I cannot help but look at you."

A soft blush rose in her cheeks, and she dropped her gaze.

"You're also exceptionally beautiful," Matthew continued, relieved to see her head lifting once more when she heard the teasing tone in his voice, "when you roll your eyes at me."

An almost silent chuckle escaped her lips, and her eyes rolled as though of their own accord.

"Yes!" Matthew laughed. "Exactly like that. It gives you such a defiant, headstrong look, and I can see the fire that lives in your heart, the fire that you've kept buried for far too long." Gently, she smiled at her. "You'll be even more radiant once you finally unleash it and allow it to guide you. I cannot wait for that day. It'll be one to remember."

Blinking her lashes, she looked at him, her breath coming faster than before, and Matthew could tell how much his words had affected her. Had no one ever told her how much she was worth? Not with regard to monetary gain, but she as a person? Did she not know how exceptionally unique she was? There was no one like her. Not in all the world. And Matthew felt equally exceptionally blessed that she was his wife, and no one else's.

His alone.

If only she would dare open her heart to him.

As impatient as he felt, Matthew knew that he needed to wait. Even now he could see that she was relaxing in her seat. Her hands uncurled, and the line of her jaw was soft and not clenched with tension. Her eyes were gentle, even joyful, as she gazed at him from across the carriage, and Matthew knew that even small steps would eventually lead him to her heart.

It might take time.

But she was worth it.

Despite his own unease at these social events, Matthew felt like the most fortunate man in the world when he led his wife into the ballroom, her delicate hand resting on his arm, holding to him tightly as though she trusted no one but him to see her safe.

Smiling, he gazed down at her. "I admit I was never fond of these occasions," he whispered, feeling her lean in closer to hear. "My father often insisted I attend whenever the opportunity arose in order to cement my standing among the peers." He sighed, thinking it might have been a mistake to speak of his father as his own mood immediately fell. "If only I had known what had been on his mind."

Stopping, his wife looked at him, her eyes searching his. "No one can know what truly lives in another's heart. He was your father. Are we truly wrong not to expect our fathers to plan evil things for our future? Are we to blame to not have seen it coming?"

Matthew shook his head, his other hand coming to rest on hers. "We are not," he whispered. "However, knowing that does not hold at bay the guilt that I feel is inevitable. I cannot help but regret what happened, and I have found that regret and guilt often walk hand in hand."

Sighing, his wife nodded. "We always wonder what we could have done differently if we could have prevented the outcome if only we had been more attentive."

For a long moment, they stood in the middle of the large room. Couples moved around them, their voices rising to the tall ceiling as music filled the air, mingling with the aromas of tonight's supper. And yet, Matthew could have sworn they were alone in the world.

"There you are," a familiar voice exclaimed, jerking them from the place they had retreated to. "For a moment, I had thought my eyes were deceiving me."

Sighing, Matthew turned from his wife to greet his cousin. "Good evening, Tristan, Beth. How are you tonight?"

"Splendid," his cousin replied, exchanging a meaningful glance with his wife. Then he turned to greet Adelaide. "My lady, you look stunning tonight, which explains how you managed to lure my cousin away from the solitude of his home." He winked at Matthew good-naturedly. "It's been a while since we've seen you at an event like this."

Matthew sighed, avoiding his cousin's gaze. "I saw no need to attend."

"And you do now?"

Glaring at Tristan, Matthew inhaled a deep breath. "Everything is different now," he replied, unwilling to explain himself further. Not here. Not in public. "My wife deserves a night of dancing."

As Adelaide looked up at him, Matthew knew that she, too, would have preferred to stay home as these events only reminded her of her father's attempts to marry her off.

"I'm glad to hear it," Tristan commented before his eyes turned to the woman by his side. "We're here for the same reason."

Beth laughed, "Quite frankly, it was I who dragged him here tonight." Tristan rolled his eyes as she placed a gentle hand on his arm. "Tonight is a special occasion for us." She grinned at her husband with such longing delight that Matthew felt his heart stir with envy. "One year ago today," she said, smiling at him and Adelaide, "was the day we first met. The perfect reason to celebrate."

"That is wonderful," Adelaide said beside him, her gaze glowing with emotions as she looked at Beth and Tristan. "Congratulations."

Matthew wondered if she felt the same longing to find what they had already claimed as theirs. His hand squeezed hers gently, and when she looked up at him, Matthew could almost believe that in a year from now, they, too, would be equally happy as Tristan and Beth.

Would that day come? Would there be a time when Adelaide would look at him the way Beth looked at Tristan? When he, Matthew, was the one to make her look exceptionally beautiful—and not simply by annoying her? But by making her happy?

Watching Tristan and Beth walk away toward the dance floor arm in arm, Matthew inhaled a deep breath, then turned to his wife. "Would you like to dance?" he asked, noting the way her eyes seemed distant and focused on something across the room.

Following her line of sight, Matthew could not see anyone he knew. "Did you see someone you wish to speak to?" he asked, his eyes narrowing as he took note of the slight paleness that had come to her cheeks.

Her eyes were still distant as she shook her head. "No, no one," she mumbled before her gaze returned to his, but only for a moment. Then it dropped to her hand still resting on his arm and she drew in a shuddering breath.

"Are you all right?" Matthew asked, wishing he could see her eyes. "Are you unwell?"

"I'm fine," she replied, her voice weak and her gaze firmly fixed on the ground.

Not knowing what had brought on this sudden change in her, Matthew reached out to her before he could stop himself. His fingers grasped her chin gently, and he felt her tense, but not pull away. Lifting her gaze to his, he looked deep into her eyes, wishing he could read her mind, wishing he could know what had rattled her so. "You can tell me," he whispered, wishing she would believe him. "I will be there for you. Always. No matter what."

A soft smile came to her lips. A smile that warmed his heart, and yet, she said, "It's nothing."

Forcing himself to ignore the small barrier that had once more risen between them, Matthew renewed his invitation to dance, and this time, she accepted it without hesitation.

As they stood up together, Matthew remembered his promise to her, and as the dance led them together, he gently stepped on her toes.

His wife's mouth opened, and she stared at him. But only for a moment as her shock over his action no longer lasted as it had in the beginning. Only a moment passed before her eyes narrowed, shooting daggers at him. "Will you ever stop teasing me?"

The harshness in her voice brought a smile to Matthew's face, and he felt himself relax. "Give me a reason to, my lady. Get angry."

Her gaze studied his face for a moment. "What reason would I have to do so? After all, you've done nothing that would deserve my anger. What you do is merely…annoying."

"I see," Matthew mumbled as his steps led him closer to her. "If that is so, then I fear my endeavour is doomed to fail for I would not dare cross that line. I enjoy your company far too much to incite true anger."

"As do I, my lord," she said smiling and with such open honesty that for a moment Matthew forgot to move. Another gentleman bumped into him, jarring him from his stupor.

"Are you all right?" his wife asked, her pale blue eyes full of concern as she pulled him aside, away from the dancing couples. "You look pale."

Shaking his head in disbelief, Matthew smiled. "I am perfectly fine…now."

Understanding came to her eyes, and for a moment she dropped her gaze, her hands trembling. "I cannot remember," she whispered, her eyes still firmly fixed on the tips of her shoes, "ever having felt so much at peace as I do now," her gaze rose to meet his, "with you."

Staring down at her, Matthew swallowed.

"You would not hurt me, would you?" she whispered as though her words were not meant for him, but only to remind her of what she already knew but did not dare believe.

"Never," Matthew said, answering her nonetheless, hoping that she eventually would believe him if he promised her often enough. "You're safe with me."

Tears came to her eyes as she held his gaze. "I never knew what that meant," she whispered, her voice choked, "but I'm starting to learn."

Gently, Matthew took her hands in his, feeling her tremble as he held her close. "Do not rush yourself," he whispered, finding her hands chilled. "There is time. Take all the time you need. I will be patient."

A soft smile drew up the corners of her mouth. "I do not doubt you."

At her words, Matthew's heart soared into the sky, and he knew that as long as she would remain by his side, it would never fall.

23

A TRUTH REVEALED

The day after the ball, Lady Elton and her husband called on them at the house.

Adelaide was happy to see them as their marriage was becoming the one that she began to think of as *the marriage.* Certainly, there were all kinds of different marriages. As different as people were as different were the marriages they entered into. Still, all her life, Adelaide had looked to her parents to see how the world worked.

And it had frightened her.

Now, however, everything was changing. Never would she have thought to marry a man who was as kind and considerate as her new husband. Certainly, his insistence to annoy or even anger her was actually starting to annoy her, but she knew that it came from a good place. He was trying to help her, to make her see that she need not live in fear, that she could be herself and not be punished for it.

The only question was: who was she?

For so long, Adelaide had adapted her character to suit those around her that she hardly knew who she was deep inside. It was time to find out.

And so, she looked to Lady Elton and her husband for inspiration. The way they acted around one another was inspiring to say the least, and here and there, Adelaide rejoiced in seeing similarities between their marriage and her own.

"It is good to see you," her husband greeted his cousin as they sat down in the drawing room. His eyes narrowed as his gaze travelled back and forth between Lord and Lady Elton. "You two seem exceptionally happy," he observed, and Adelaide sat back to study their faces. Indeed, there was a new glow in Lady Elton's eyes, and the way husband and wife exchanged glances here and there spoke volumes.

"We are," Lord Elton intoned, his hand reaching for his wife's, squeezing it gently, "and as we are family and I am particularly fond of you, dear cousin, we have come to share our good news with you."

Matthew chuckled, and Adelaide smiled, feeling herself grow more and more comfortable with these people, people who now truly were her family. It was a comforting thought!

"Do not tease him," Lady Elton chided her husband. Then she inhaled a deep breath and said, "We are happy to say that come autumn we will be welcoming a new little life into our family." Wide grins hung on their faces as they looked from Adelaide to her husband.

"That is wonderful!" Matthew exclaimed, rising to his feet and hugging his cousin. "Congratulations! You'll be a great father. I have no doubt." Their faces sobered suddenly, and Adelaide thought to see a deeper meaning pass between them.

"Allow me to offer my congratulations as well," Adelaide said to Lady Elton as the men stood over to the side, speaking to each other in quiet tones. "You must be very happy indeed."

Lady Elton smiled, a deep sigh leaving her lips. "I'm deliriously happy, yes." She rose from the seat she had taken next to her husband and came to sit with Adelaide. "Only this morning we received a letter from Henrietta—my husband's sister—saying that she and her husband are expecting as well." Another sigh rose from Lady Elton's throat. "I think it will be wonderful to have our firstborns be of the same age."

"That is truly wonderful," Adelaide said, finding her gaze shift to her husband. Would they ever have children? She wondered, remembering his intention of asking her for a kiss. Her cheeks warmed at the thought, and she realised that the prospect of being intimate with her husband was no longer a duty, a threat even—as it once had been before she had learnt what a truly good man he was. No, it was slowly becoming a temptation, and she found herself wondering more often these days when he would finally ask for her kiss.

After all, she had no intention whatsoever of refusing him.

"You have come to care for him, have you not?" Lady Elton observed, a soft smile on her face as she watched Adelaide.

Unable to hide her smile, Adelaide sighed, "I'm afraid I could not help it. He is…" Again, she sighed, feeling her words would fall far short of what she was coming to know in her heart.

Lady Elton nodded knowingly. "I'm so relieved to hear you say so. I—"

"Shall we call for champagne?" Adelaide's husband asked as he and Lord Elton stepped closer. "To toast your wonderful news?"

Lady Elton's brows crinkled at the interruption. "Quite frankly, my dear," she said to her husband, "I find myself quite bored with your company at present and wish to speak to Lady Whitworth in peace. Would you mind…?" Grinning, she nodded toward the door.

Smiling, Lord Elton shook his head. "It is always good to know what you truly think of me, my dear."

Lady Elton rolled her eyes rather theatrically, and despite her usual constraint, Adelaide found herself laughing with the others. Her eyes met her husband's, and she returned his smile, feeling as though there truly were a certain intimacy between them. One that did not need words as she knew exactly that he, too, was reminded of their own teasing banter. Never would Adelaide have thought she would ever know what such a deep connection felt like.

And now, here she was, merely at the beginning of her journey, surprised how promising her future suddenly looked.

If only—

"Let's go, Matt," Lord Elton said, striding toward the door as he cast another meaningful glance at his wife over his shoulder. "The ladies have no need for us at present. Let's find someone else to celebrate with."

"What do you suggest?" Matthew asked as he followed his cousin, his own gaze gliding back to Adelaide one last time, a soft smile curling up his lips.

"White's?"

"Lead the way."

And then the door closed behind them, and Lady Elton sank back against the settee. "I love him dearly," she laughed, "but he does need to learn how to take a hint."

"You two look very happy," Adelaide observed as her gaze returned from the door through which her husband had just left.

A teasing grin played on Lady Elton's lips. "As do you, I must say." Patting Adelaide's hand, she asked, "How is everything between you and Matthew?"

Adelaide sighed, "I'm not sure I have the words…"

"You look like a different woman now," Lady Elton said in her usual direct way. "I've never seen you so much at ease, and yet, so daring. Is it because of him?"

Adelaide nodded, a chuckle rising from her throat. "He insists on teaching me how to be angry," she laughed. "He teases me in the most annoying way, and he—"

"But you love it," Lady Elton interrupted, a knowing look in her eyes.

Adelaide shrugged. "Is that wrong? I never used to get angry, not like others do. Certainly, there were many occurrences that would elicit that emotion; however, I never entertained it. What good would it have done? It would only have led to further problems."

"There is nothing wrong with being angry," Lady Elton stressed, her eyes knowing as they held Adelaide's. "Anger is a part of life, and you're perfectly right to express it. I'm glad you finally feel safe enough to do so. I've always wondered and worried about your lack of emotions. The way you always shrank into the background and tried to become invisible." Smiling, Lady Elton squeezed her hand. "It's no way to live, and that is—I believe—what Matthew is trying to teach you, to stand tall and not bow your head."

"I'm beginning to see that." A smile tugged on Adelaide's lips as she thought of her husband, of the many times he had teased her, urging her to feel. And he had succeeded. She did feel. More than just anger. What she was beginning to feel was something she had dreamed of as a little girl, but then abandoned as reality had taught her a harsh truth. Never would she have thought to be able to reclaim the hopes and dreams that had been hers before the harshness of the world had ripped them from her. But now she had hope again, and she was slowly coming to trust it…not fear it.

"You care for him deeply, do you not?"

Blinking, Adelaide found Lady Elton looking at her, her blue eyes gentle as she smiled. "I don't know when it happened," Adelaide whispered, shocked at the realisation that had so suddenly come to her in a moment when she had least expected it, "but it is true." A smile claimed her lips. "I cannot deny that it's true, nor do I want to." Grasping Lady Elton's hands, Adelaide sighed. "Thank you so much for everything you have done. You've always been there for me, protecting me."

Lady Elton grinned. "So, you don't mind my meddling?"

Laughing, Adelaide shook her head. "Not at all. You saved me from my father and brought Matthew into my life."

"Matthew? Do you call him by his given name?"

Adelaide shook her head. "I do not." Her gaze remained on Lady Elton's, asking for advice.

"I believe you should," the young woman said. "I cannot imagine that he would mind. In fact, I suspect he'd be overjoyed."

Adelaide sighed, a new warmth flooding her being, and she wished her husband were here so that she could call him by his given name right this minute. Instead of his kind, melodious voice, however, another one suddenly echoed through the closed doors of the drawing room. This one was far from kind, but rather harsh and filled with anger.

Lady Elton frowned. "Are you expecting anyone?" she asked, her blue eyes darting to the door before they narrowed, and a hint of suspicion came to her face.

Adelaide could not answer. Her body froze, and her voice remained locked in her throat as her being responded in the only way it had ever known to the threat that had always loomed over her life. Before her mind had even formed a conscious thought, her heart knew who had come to call.

Her father.

In that moment, all his threats came rushing back, and Adelaide could have slapped herself for ignoring them. Always had she known that her father was a man to be feared, and yet, she had allowed her husband to distract her, to draw her mind from the threat he presented to her new life. In the past fortnight, she had all but forgotten about him.

About his threat to reveal her secret.

About the fact that any happiness she might find with her new husband might be snatched away at any moment.

Oh, how could she have been so careless?!

A moment later, her father came barrelling through the door like a charging bull, shutting it behind himself with a kick of his boot—right in the butler's rather pale face.

Adelaide knew only too well how the poor man felt.

Out of the corner of her eye, Adelaide saw Lady Elton rise to her feet, her chin raised, and the look in her eyes unwavering. Oh, how Adelaide envied her courage!

All she herself could accomplish in that moment was to force her legs to still and hold her upright. Her heart hammered in her chest as she met her father's angry stare, reminding her that she was indeed all alone.

Her husband had left the house and would not come to her aid this time, and despite Lady Elton's courage, Adelaide doubted that the woman was a match for her father. In truth, now Adelaide did not only fear for herself but also for her friend. And she was with child! What would such a confrontation do to her? Would the stress harm the child?

Fresh panic welled up, and Adelaide felt her fingernails dig into her palms as she fought to keep it at bay.

"I expected to hear from you!" her father growled, his bloodshot eyes narrowed as he glared at her. "I expected—" His voice broke off when he finally realised that they were not alone.

His forehead crinkled, showing more frown lines, as his gaze turned to Lady Elton.

Adelaide knew she ought to interfere, but her body would not move. Fear held her immobile, and in that moment—like never before—she hated her own weakness. Disgust filled her heart, and she wished for nothing more than for the ground to open and swallow her whole.

"What are you doing here?" the earl snarled, fixing Lady Elton with a loathsome stare. "No matter where I turn, there you are, causing trouble." He stomped toward the young woman. "Stay out of this! This does not concern you, understood?"

Adelaide watched in amazement as Lady Elton held her ground, her blue eyes sparkling with a hint of mirth as she shook her head, a devious smile on her lips. "You're wrong," she replied, her voice hard and full of conviction as she took a step toward the earl. "I am wanted here. You are not." Her brows rose as she glanced at the door. "Leave. Now."

Awed by the young woman's courage, Adelaide saw her father's face lose some of its vehemence, replaced by a touch of confusion. Adelaide could not remember anyone ever having spoken out against him, not to his face, except for her grandmother. And yet, she had never challenged him in such a direct way. Still, she had always been the only one to hold any sway over him.

Was that the key to protecting herself from her father? To not let him see her fear? To stand tall and stare him down?

Was it not strength and courage that carried him? But instead dominance granted to him by those who trembled in fear whenever he approached? Once it was taken away, what would be left of him?

Once again, her father's eyes hardened. "You have no right to order me from this house." Then his gaze turned and met Adelaide's, and in that moment, she knew that he was like a predator going after the weak one in the herd.

While Lady Elton had proved herself to be a worthy adversary—someone her father could not handle—he sought out new prey.

Her.

Seeing her father stomping toward her, Adelaide felt her old instincts take over, urging her to bow her head and shrink into a corner. And yet, one look at Lady Elton's tall stature forbade her to do so.

Inhaling a deep breath, Adelaide willed her chin up and her hands to stop trembling. Her husband's voice echoed in her head as he had told her that no one had the right to treat her thus.

No one.

Not him.

And certainly not her father.

"Tell her to leave," her father ordered, his dark gaze finding Adelaide's, urging her to do what he could not.

It was a realisation that momentarily stole Adelaide's breath. He was weak! Insecure! At another's mercy as she had been all her life! There was no strength in him, no courage. It had only been pretence. A charade!

This simple truth almost brought Adelaide to her knees as she remembered all the years wasted, obeying her father out of fear. What would her life have been if she had simply stood up to him?

As though of their own accord, Adelaide felt her shoulders draw back and her back straighten. Her gaze rose with new purpose and conviction, and she could see the change she felt in her heart reflected in her father's eyes as he beheld his daughter. Still, before Adelaide could make up her mind to speak, Lady Elton stepped in front of her.

Blocking her father's path.

Protecting her once again.

"I demand that you leave this instant," Lady Elton snarled, her own voice now laced with threat, and once again, Adelaide was awed by the courage that lived in this woman's heart. How had she grown up to become such a strong person? "You are not welcome here."

Her father's gaze shifted from her to Lady Elton, and instead of anger, annoyance came to his face. The energy that had propelled him forward before seemed to be fading as he looked down at her, indecision in his eyes as to how to proceed. "Why do you care?" he demanded, puzzlement in his voice. "She is nothing to you. A mere acquaintance. Why can you not stay out of this?"

Adelaide was surprised to hear an almost pleading tone in her father's voice. And yet, it was when Lady Elton spoke again that the air was knocked from her lungs.

"It's what you do for family," the young woman hissed, anger lacing her words as she stepped toward the earl, who almost took a step back. "Do you truly not know? Do you truly not see it?" Pausing, she watched him, her jaw tense. "I have every right to be here. Always and forever will I be at her side because she is my sister."

For a moment, Adelaide thought she would faint, staring at the young woman before her, her blue eyes shining with defiance. Blue eyes just like her own. Just like her father's.

Blinking, Adelaide looked at her father, finding his own gaze fixed on Lady Elton's face, his own dangerously pale.

A snort rose from the young woman's lips. "Do you truly not see it?" she demanded. "After all, I take after my mother in most ways. Your mother saw it right away."

"Grandmother?" Adelaide gasped as another puzzle piece fell into place. Always had they seemed close. Closer than would have made sense under any circumstances.

Except these.

"It cannot be," the earl stammered, his pale blue eyes fixed on Lady Elton's face. "It cannot be. This can't be true. You died. You…" Swallowing, he licked his lips. "Beth," he whispered. "My little Beth."

The gentle endearment so misplaced in that moment brought a new tension to Lady Elton's body. "Leave!" she snarled. "You're not wanted here. Out! Now!"

As though he had been punched in the chest, Adelaide's father stumbled backwards until his back collided with the closed door. "It cannot be," he mumbled once again before he turned and fled, his hastened footsteps echoing on the marble floor in the foyer.

On trembling legs, Adelaide stepped forward, her eyes fixed on the young woman's face. "Is it true?" she breathed, her voice sounding too loud for the sudden silence that had fallen over the room.

After inhaling a slow breath, Lady Elton turned to her. Her face looked still strained, and yet, when their eyes met, Adelaide saw the same loving concern and devotion she had always seen there.

And never been able to understand.

Now, she did.

Smiling, Lady Elton nodded. "Yes, it is true. We are sisters."

Overwhelmed, Adelaide sank into her sister's arms, tears running freely down her cheeks as she clung to the woman she had never known, and yet, missed all her life.

24

SISTER'S AT LAST

Overwhelmed, Adelaide sank back onto the settee, her hands holding on tightly to her sister's. Sister! She had a sister!

"Are you all right?"

Blinking, Adelaide looked at Beth—for all of a sudden it seemed wrong to call her anything else but Beth. After all, they were sisters!

Swallowing, Adelaide nodded. "I'm fine. I'm simply…"

"Overwhelmed?" Beth asked with a smile, the look on her face somewhat fatigued. "When I found out, I felt the same."

"How *did* you find out? When?" Adelaide asked, her mind racing as she tried to make sense of everything. Certainly, she had known that her father had been married before, but to her knowledge, his first wife and child had died in an awful accident. Neither one of her parents, not even her grandmother, had been willing to say any more than that on the matter.

"I found out only a year ago," Beth said, sinking back against the settee, her hands still linked with Adelaide's. "I found a letter in my mother's things, and to learn the truth about her past as well as my own, I came to London. It was our grandmother who told me the whole story."

Our grandmother!

"She recognised you?"

Beth nodded, tears misting her eyes at the memory. "She took one look at me and knew."

Adelaide sighed, trying her best to understand. "But how did this happen? Where were you all this time? My father—our father clearly thought you had died. You and your mother. It's the story that everybody knows."

For a moment, Beth remained silent, her gaze directed inward as she chose her words. Then her blue eyes met Adelaide's. "Our father has always had a temper—it was never different—and he always went after those who could not defend themselves. After my mother. She was strong, but she…had too much to lose to stand up to him without fear."

Adelaide nodded, knowing exactly how it felt to be trapped in a life with no options. How desperate Beth's mother had to have felt. The same as her own. Adelaide could not recall a day in her life when her mother had not been afraid. Fear had been always there, even if only in the background.

"One day," Beth continued, "when I was about two years old, he discovered me in his study and raised his hand to me."

Adelaide gasped. Never had her father struck her, and yet, she had always wondered if he would have had she given him a reason to. It would seem only her submissive character had saved her from that fate.

"My mother was shocked. Grandmother told me that she had always bore his anger but could not do so in good conscience where I was concerned." Beth inhaled a deep breath. "And so, she decided to leave…to protect me. Grandmother helped us start anew somewhere far away."

"Then why did he think you dead?"

Beth shrugged. "I cannot say. I suppose when we could not be discovered, he simply assumed. After all, he had to continue his line, and he could not very well do so with an absent wife, could he?"

"My brother," Adelaide mumbled, remembering that John was the only one her father seemed to care about. Not necessarily because he loved him, but because he was his heir. A status symbol. A man's pride.

Beth nodded. "Yes, Father married again, and we were safe. It was all my mother had hoped for."

"And you've been away all this time?" Adelaide asked, thinking of her own close ties to her family. The thought of leaving them behind to never see again tightened her chest. "You never came back to London? To see us? Not even Grandmother?"

Beth shook her head. "My mother did not dare, and I do believe she was right. She could not risk us being discovered."

Adelaide's eyes filled with tears. "It must have been hard on your mother and Grandmother."

"I was too young to remember," Beth explained, her gaze distant as she remembered her childhood, "but I often saw my mother sit by the window, her eyes seeing something only she could see, and tears would stream down her face. Now, I know why she was sad sometimes." Inhaling a shaking breath, Beth squeezed Adelaide's hands. "Grandmother, too, was overwhelmed when she saw me. It must have been hard for her not to know for certain where we had ended up and if we were all right."

Watching Beth carefully, Adelaide felt herself tense as she asked, "Where is your mother now?"

Like a wave crashing onto the beach, sadness filled Beth's eyes, and Adelaide knew the answer even before her sister spoke. "She died," Beth whispered. "That's how I found out. I went through her things after the funeral and found an old letter she had written to

Grandmother but never sent. It brought me to London, to Grandmother, to you," smiling, Beth squeezed her hands, "and to my husband. I cannot regret what happened, but I do wish she had lived."

Wrapping her arms around her sister, Adelaide felt tears of her own fall. "I cannot imagine what you must have gone through. Being all alone. On your own. With no one to turn to."

"But I found you," Beth said sniffling. "I found you again, and I'm grateful for it. Although a part of me wishes I could have grown up here with all of you, I know that that would never have worked. If my mother hadn't left, neither you nor John would ever have been born."

Adelaide sucked in a sharp breath when a sudden realisation slapped her hard in the face. "My mother's marriage is void," she gasped, cold fear and dread crawling over her skin, raising goose bumps in their wake. "They're not married. We're not…" Turning, she looked at Beth. "We're bastards."

"That is why Grandmother asked me not to tell anyone," Beth explained. "She was worried about the two of you and did not wish for any harm to come to you."

"But why didn't you tell me?" Adelaide asked, knowing in her heart that her grandmother would never deceive her, and yet, she had chosen to keep Adelaide in the dark. "Why?"

"She did not wish to concern you," Beth said, a gentle smile on her face. Still, her gaze would not quite meet Adelaide's.

"You didn't trust me to keep this a secret?"

"Oh, no. Don't be silly," Beth replied, shaking her head. "We simply did not wish to burden you. You always seemed so fragile, and we didn't want you to have to lie. We didn't want to put that on you."

Although Adelaide knew that her family had acted out of concern, out of the desire to protect her, she realised that it was her own weakness that had convinced them to do so. And although she had known herself to be weak all her life, now it bothered her.

Misreading the look on Adelaide's face, Beth said, "Believe me, I would never do anything to harm you. I did not come back here to cause trouble or to reveal that your parents' marriage is not valid. I only came to know the truth, and I stayed because I found my family here." She grasped Adelaide's hands more tightly. "I will always look out for you. You're my sister."

Smiling, Adelaide nodded. "And you're mine." Blinking back tears, she said, "That is why you came to my rescue at the ball and discouraged Lord Arlton from proposing to me and why you helped when my father lost my hand to Mr. Hawkin."

Beth nodded. "Of course. Whether we grew up together or not, you're my sister. And although I've never had one, I'm fairly certain that's what sisters do, isn't it?"

Unable not to, Adelaide surged into her sister's arms, clinging to her tightly as though she had always done so. As though they had known each other all their lives. As though she had always lived under her big sister's protective hand. "Your mother was a very strong woman," Adelaide said, wiping at her eyes as she sat back, "for having done what she did. It takes great courage to leave everything behind and start anew. I see the same strength in you."

Fresh tears spilled down Beth's cheeks.

"You still miss her, don't you?"

Beth nodded, pressing the tips of her fingers to her reddened eyes. "She ought to be here," she whispered, hiccoughing as she spoke. "She ought to see her grandchild." Looking up at Adelaide, she placed a gentle hand on her belly.

"What was her name?"

Beth inhaled a deep breath, and a soft smile came to her face. "Ellen."

Whispering a silent thank-you to the woman who gave her this wonderful sister, a sister who would come to her aid without a moment of hesitation, Adelaide smiled. "She was a wonderful woman, just like you. You're right, Father should have seen it. He must have been blind not to. So much of her lives in you, and I'm certain her legacy will live on in your children. She made a great sacrifice for you, and it was worth it."

"I'll be forever grateful to her," Beth whispered, "but I still wish she were here."

"I do, too." Again, Adelaide drew her sister into her arms, now being the one to give comfort instead of receiving it. It was an empowering feeling to be able to do this for her sister, and Adelaide vowed that she would never bow her head again.

No, she would fight down her fear and stand tall. She would honour the sacrifice Beth's mother had made. She would be a woman her own children could be proud of.

25

OPEN WORDS

The moment he and his cousin stepped across the threshold to his townhouse, Matthew was informed of his father-in-law's visit. Wringing his hands, his butler told him that he had done his utmost to dissuade the earl but had been unsuccessful.

Matthew's blood ran cold. "Where is he now?"

"He left about an hour ago."

"Where is my wife?"

"And mine?" Tristan added from behind Matthew's shoulder, his voice a bit strained, but not nearly as tense as Matthew's. Perhaps he was not aware of the earl's lack of restraint whenever he was inebriated, which was most of the time.

"Lady Whitworth and Lady Elton are in the drawing room."

Without another word, Matthew left his butler standing in the foyer and hastened on, Tristan's footsteps echoing behind him. He all but threw open the doors to the drawing room, not knowing what to expect but fearing the worst, only to find two women with tear-streaked, but smiling faces embracing one another.

Dumbfounded, he stopped in his tracks, staring.

Tristan stepped up beside him, and out of the corner of his eye, Matthew took note of the grin that slowly stretched over his cousin's face. "I suppose the secret is out, eh?"

Beth nodded, wiping her hand over her face. "As observant as always, my dear."

"What secret?" Matthew all but croaked, his throat suddenly dry as the little hairs on the back of his neck rose. After all, *secret* was simply a harmless sounding word for *lie*, and lies never led to anything good.

At least not in his experience.

Beside him, Tristan chuckled, clasping a hand onto Matthew's shoulder. "That our wives are sisters," he said without preamble. "Well, half-sisters. But I suppose that does not matter."

Smiling, Beth rose to her feet, brushing her hands down her dress. "It does not," she confirmed, holding out her hand to Adelaide, who took it, a deep smile on her face, and came to stand next to her…sister?

Thunderstruck, Matthew stared at his cousin, then at Beth before his gaze travelled to his own wife, her face reddened and yet filled with joy. "I don't understand," he mumbled.

Smiling rather indulgently, Beth patted him on the arm. "You will. Talk to your wife." Then she turned to her husband. "Shall we? I admit I'm rather tired."

"You do look tired," Tristan agreed, a hint of a teasing note in his voice.

"Thank you, my dear. Every woman loves to hear that."

Chuckling, Tristan led his wife from the room. However, before they left, Beth once more turned and looked at Adelaide, deep emotions in her eyes. "Always and forever," she whispered, a promise shining on her face.

Adelaide nodded, her lower lip quivering as fresh tears threatened. "Always and forever."

And then they were alone. Matthew wondered about the emotional woman he suddenly found himself facing. All her barriers seemed to have come down, and her eyes shone with all the longing and love she had held at bay for too long.

Turning from the door, she looked at him, a soft warmth about her features. Her eyes shone brightly as she smiled at him, and Matthew wished he knew what she was thinking in that moment.

"Are you all right?" he asked, stepping toward her. "I heard your father was here. Did he…?"

"He was angry, yes," his wife confirmed, her voice portraying a new strength. "He yelled at me, and then Beth…she stepped into his path. She protected me. Again." Sighing, she shook her head in disbelief. "She is such a strong woman. She stood up to my father—our father—without flinching. I've never seen anyone do this. Not even my grandmother. Even she has a touch of concern in her eyes whenever she speaks to him." Again, a smile claimed Adelaide's lips. "She was magnificent."

"And she's your sister?" Matthew asked, searching his wife's face. It was as though he had never truly seen her before today.

"She is," Adelaide confirmed. "She's my sister. My sister!" Shaking her head yet again, she clasped her hands together. "I keep saying it, and yet, I cannot believe that it is true. I'm so…so overwhelmed."

Matthew knew exactly how she felt. "How did this happen?"

Inhaling a deep breath, his wife looked at him, her mouth opening, and yet, no sound came out. Then she stepped toward him and, to his utter surprise, took his hand, pulling him down onto the settee next to her.

Matthew held his breath as she began to tell him her story, all the while holding his hand in hers as though it belonged there. Occasionally, he caught himself sinking into her eyes, his ears unaware of the words that left her mouth. And yet, he saw every emotion that clung to her beautiful face.

"When I grew up," she said, the words flowing from her mouth as though a dam had broken, "I was always afraid of my father's temper. I always saw how my mother cowered before him, and so I quickly learnt what to do to try and appease him. At the same time, I saw my mother hold her head high when out in society. The way she spoke to friends and acquaintances painted such a different picture of her. It made me realise that people are rarely who they seem to be. I began to look at each and every one I met, wondering who he or she truly was in the security of their home. I wondered what secrets they strove to keep hidden, doing their utmost to appear different than they truly were. No one seemed true and honest." Pain and regret and utter sadness filled her voice, and yet, the strength he had heard there before remained. "It is something we all do. Something we are all guilty of. And yet, can we truly be blamed for wishing to keep a part of ourselves hidden? Secret? Only sharing it with those we love and trust?" Slowly, she shook her head. "Yet, there are different kinds of secrets, are there not? Those that lie, and those that simply conceal."

Matthew nodded, her words finding a spot deep inside him that ached with more vehemence now than it had ever before. "My father was the same," he said when her eyes lingered on his as though she expected him to answer. "No one ever knew how consumed with greed and envy he truly was. Everyone always saw him as the responsible younger brother, who strove to undo his elder brother's mistakes, who looked out for family and took in his niece and nephew when his brother finally killed himself." Shaking his head, Matthew held her gaze even though he wanted nothing more but to avert it in shame. "I believed it, too."

"You didn't know," his wife said softly, her hand tightening on his. "You didn't know."

"I should have known!" The vehemence in his voice surprised even him. "I should have seen the truth. Instead, I followed in my father's footsteps, blindly accusing my own cousin of seeking to destroy this family when in truth it had been my father all along." Sighing, he hung his head. "I cannot remember a time when I did not try to prove myself to him. All I ever wanted was to be seen and seen as worthy. Still, the only time my father would bestow his respect and approval on me was when I gave up who I was and became an echo of him, repeating his thoughts as though they were my own. I even turned against Tristan in my blind attempt to please my father, to gain his admiration and respect. I will never forgive myself for that."

On a soft chuckle, Adelaide released a rushed breath. "Beth told me," she began, her blue eyes holding his own, "that you're the only one thinking of yourself thus. No one blames you. Everyone understands how this happened. She said that you're a good man and that the fact that you doubt yourself only proves that you truly are." The corners of her mouth curled upward, lighting up her face in the most endearing way. "You made a mistake as did we all, but in the end—when it mattered—you did the right thing. You did not hesitate to stand by what you deemed right…even against your own father. Ever since then, there has been no doubt in anyone's mind about who you truly are."

Frowning, Matthew stared at his wife. "How do you know this?"

"It is in the way your cousin looks at you," she replied, a soft smile on her face as she held his gaze. "I can see the respect he has for you, and the love, and…I am proud of you." A soft chuckle escaped her at the intimate nature of their words. "I'm proud of you."

Touched by her words and overwhelmed by the effect they had on him, Matthew gazed into her eyes, realising how much her opinion mattered to him.

"To stand up for oneself is far from easy," his wife said, a hint of regret coming to her eyes. "I, too, have regrets. I, too, wish that things had gone differently, that I would have done things differently. But the past is the past." She inhaled a deep breath. "Now, I will look to the future, and I want to learn." Nodding, she smiled at him. "Will you help me?"

"Of course," he said, almost tripping over the words in his eagerness. "I do believe, though, that you've taken a first step today. There's something different about you. Something…" He shook his head. "I can't quite say."

Adelaide sighed, "I do feel different," she whispered. "I feel more optimistic, not as though bad things are inevitable. I want to be more like my sister. Stronger. Willing to fight for those I love."

"Family has that effect on one, does it not?" Matthew said with a smile. "There is nothing else more worth fighting for, is there?" Squeezing his wife's hand, Matthew felt his heart beating a little faster at the gentle, trusting look in her eyes. Never in his life had he felt closer to another.

In that moment, a knock sounded on the door and their butler stepped inside, holding out a silver platter. "This was just delivered for my lady."

A shy smile crossed Adelaide's face as she slowly drew her hands from his. Then she rose and retrieved the letter. As her eyes flew over the words, her whole face lit up, and Matthew felt his heart beating even faster. She was radiant in her joy, and the way she carried it in her whole body. It was in the way she looked at him, the way she smiled, but also in the way she walked, the way she moved her hands, in the tilt of her head and the skip in her step. It was as though she had finally reconnected with the little girl she had once been…before life had destroyed her dreams and hopes for a bright future.

"I assume it is good news," Matthew said as he stepped closer, unable to tear his gaze from the joy on her face.

"It is!" she exclaimed, her blue eyes finding his. "Grandmother writes that she will bring Tillie over tomorrow," she whispered, a hint of awe and disbelief in her voice, before a frown descended on her face, chasing away the joy that had seemed so indestructible a moment earlier. Apprehension took over her features as she tensed. "You don't mind, do you?"

Surprised by her sudden doubt, Matthew shook his head. "Why would I?"

She sighed as though realising that she had returned to old habits. "My father always did. After all, she was only a girl and not even legitimate. He never wanted her around, and we always did our best to keep her away from him." Sadness came to her deep, round eyes. "It was like pretending she didn't exist, and it always seemed wrong. And yet, what would we have done if he had sent her from the house?"

Matthew frowned. "You fear for her," he observed, his heart constricting at the sight of her misery, her fear, her pain. "You truly fear for her."

"I do," she whispered, and Matthew finally realised how much that little girl meant to her.

In the darkness of her life, Tillie had been a ray of hope for Adelaide, and whether his wife knew it or not, she had even before today stood tall to protect one she loved. With the constant fear and pain in her family, she had dived into loving her brother's daughter, giving her everything she had, everything she could give…

…until the day Matthew had taken her away, separating them.

Silently cursing himself, Matthew could not believe he had not seen it before. Certainly, he had realised that being apart from her family would be a painful transition, but one that could not be avoided if they wanted to see Adelaide safe. And yet, little Tillie was a different matter entirely. Especially now, with Adelaide gone, was she still safe at the earl's house?

"Then she should live with us," Matthew heard himself saying, belatedly realising that he truly meant it with all his heart.

His wife's eyes opened wide, and for a long moment, she simply stared at him. "Do you truly…? No, you cannot mean…Please don't say this if you don't–"

"I'm certain," Matthew interrupted her, pulling her left hand back into his own. "You clearly love her, and although I have not seen much of her so far, I'm certain she is a very special little girl. I can tell only by the way your face lights up whenever you speak of her." Tears began to pool in his wife's eyes. "Every child should have a home, a real home, where they feel safe and loved. No one knows that better than we do. If your father does not want her, then that is his loss and our gain. Bring her here, and we will take care of her together."

Blinking her eyes rapidly, his wife briefly averted her gaze, tears running freely down her cheeks. "What if…what if we have…children?" Shyly, she raised her gaze to his once more.

Matthew smiled. "*When* we have children, then they'll have someone to play with, someone to teach them the ropes, someone to look up to because I know beyond the shadow of a doubt that Tillie is an amazing person. After all, you've raised her. How could she not be?"

Slowly, ever so slowly, joy reclaimed his wife's features. The sadness and doubt receded, and she smiled at him with the same abundance that he had seen earlier.

"All will be well," Matthew whispered, holding her gaze. "Trust me."

Swallowing, his wife nodded. "I do."

Never in his life had Matthew heard more wonderful words.

In a single afternoon, everything had changed. Certainly, they had made progress in their relationship even before. However, now it seemed as though that which had kept them apart had finally been overcome. The fear that had always been present in his wife's eyes was no more, only a mild echo of a life lived under unfortunate circumstances remained. Her earlier fear had been replaced by determination and a new sense of worth as though she had finally come to realise that she deserved more.

Perhaps she had always known but never dared to believe it.

Matthew knew how that felt.

His mind had always known that while he had made a mistake, he had not been at fault for his father's deeds. And yet, his heart had still harboured doubts. Doubts that were now whispering their poisonous words with less strength, less vehemence, less conviction.

Had he been able to alleviate them simply by sharing them with his wife? Had he merely needed to open up and confide in another in order to rob them of their power?

Whatever the reason, Matthew realised that he felt a thousand times lighter and—as his wife had said—more optimistic. The future was a bright place, and he could not wait.

Now, all they needed was Tillie.

Tomorrow could not come soon enough.

26

A CHILD COMES HOME

aiting was torture! Nothing in the world ever compared to one pacing up and down and staring at a door that would not open.

"You'll wear a hole in the floor," her husband laughed, his eyes glinting with mischief as he smiled at her.

Adelaide felt a touch of anger bubbling up at his teasing and was still surprised that she now felt it so clearly where before it had only been a mild echo. "I cannot help it," she replied, a certain harshness to her voice that had her husband raise his brows at her…in surprise as well as with pride.

"She'll be here soon."

"I know," Adelaide replied, her gaze travelling to the door yet again. Certainly, all the servants thought her daft by now. How long had she been here, pacing up and down? Five minutes? An hour? Adelaide honestly could not tell. It seemed like an eternity.

Then a knock sounded on the door, and out of nowhere their butler appeared to receive their caller.

Staring, Adelaide swallowed, her gaze fixed on the door as she wondered if she was only seeing things or if they were real. A part of her was afraid to believe that Tillie was actually coming, fearing the disappointment and heartbreak if it was indeed not true.

"Don't be foolish," Adelaide chastised herself, reminding herself that these fears belonged in the past. However, to abandon them altogether was easier said than done.

"Are you all right?" her husband asked, his gentle green eyes looking into hers. "You seem tense."

Inhaling a deep breath, Adelaide shook her head. "I'm not. I'm happy." His face lit up when she smiled at him, and Adelaide felt her heart skip a beat.

Then her attention was drawn back to the door where her grandmother stepped over the threshold…with Tillie by her side.

The moment the little girl's eyes fell on Adelaide, joy lit up her beautiful face. Her mouth dropped open and her eyes widened. "Addy!" Her little voice echoed through the tall foyer as Tillie lunged forward, her little feet carrying her speedily across the floor before she flung herself into Adelaide's arms.

Embracing the child's small body, Adelaide felt Tillie's arms encircle her tightly, and she closed her eyes, savouring the moment. A lone tear ran down her cheek, and yet, Adelaide knew that it was one of joy, of relief.

Dimly, Adelaide heard her husband speak to her grandmother. However, all her attention was focused on the little girl, who was looking up at her with bright eyes.

"I have a new doll," Tillie confided, a sparkle in her blue gaze. "She is so pretty. Can I bring her next time? Please?"

"Of course, you can, my sweet." Smiling, Adelaide brushed a dark curl behind the girl's left ear, her eyes lingering on Tillie's soft features, taking note of all the small changes that had happened since she'd last seen her. Oh, how she had missed her!

A sigh left Adelaide's lips as she listened to the little girl prattle on about her dolls and then about a robin she kept seeing in the gardens. "Tomorrow I'll put out food for it. It'll be my new friend."

"That is a wonderful idea," Adelaide replied, hoping that nothing would delay their plan to have Tillie come live with them. However, before she could speak to the girl, she would need to speak to her grandmother. Adelaide could only hope that her grandmother would not consider it too risky. Her mother certainly would. Fortunately, she had not accompanied them today.

After introducing the girl to her husband, they all stepped into the drawing room, where Adelaide took note of a rather large trunk sitting right next to the coffee table. A frown descended upon her face as she tried to recall if she had ever seen it before.

"Tillie, would you help me with this?" her husband called out to the little girl, waving her over. He stopped right beside the trunk, his gaze darting from Tillie to the heavy-looking lid. "I'm not sure I'll manage to open it on my own. I think I'll need your help."

Bouncing up and down, Tillie stepped closer. "I'll help. I'm strong."

"I'm glad you are," her husband replied with a sidelong glance at Adelaide. The moment their eyes met, a deep smile lit up his face, and Adelaide felt her insides quiver.

"What's in it?" Tillie asked, drawing his attention back to her.

"Oh, I'm hoping we'll find a few dolls and perhaps an old tea set. You see this trunk belonged to my cousin."

"Your cousin?" Tillie asked, running a hand over the lid. "What's her name?"

"Henrietta."

"That's a pretty name."

Adelaide's husband nodded. "It is, and so is Tillie."

With bright eyes, the little girl beamed up at him, and Adelaide felt her heart warm at this peaceful scene. It was exactly the life she had always dreamed of. Nothing spectacular. Nothing noteworthy by society's standards. Just a simple life with people she loved and who loved her.

Silent joy.

Together, her husband and Tillie pushed open the heavy lid, and the little girl squealed with joy when she beheld the dolls. "Oh, they're so pretty," she exclaimed, setting them side by side onto the settee. "Can we have a tea party?" she asked Adelaide's husband when she spotted the old porcelain cups.

"Of course, that's the very reason I had this brought down. It's just…" His face crinkled as though in embarrassment. "I don't know how to make tea. Do you?"

Eagerly, Tillie nodded. "I'll show you."

Absorbed in the scene before her, Adelaide almost flinched when her grandmother placed a hand on her arm. She sucked in a sharp breath, and her arm flew to her chest. "I'm sorry," Adelaide gasped. "I seem to have been lost in thought."

Her grandmother grinned. "So, it would seem." Her gaze drifted to the two setting up the tea set on the coffee table. "He is a good man."

Adelaide nodded, touched by her husband's tender ways and attention toward Tillie. "He is indeed."

Her grandmother's face sobered. "Did you tell him?"

A shiver went down Adelaide's spine at the question, and for a moment, she closed her eyes. "I can't," she whispered, seeing understanding, and yet, also disapproval in her grandmother's gaze. "I'm afraid."

"I know you are," her grandmother said, gently drawing Adelaide from the peaceful scene beside them and farther away to the other side of the room. "But lies are like poison for a marriage, and secrets are no better."

Adelaide nodded, remembering her husband's words from the day before. He had lived with lies and secrets far too long and had come to loathe them for they brought nothing but pain. How would he react if he found out that she had been keeping something from him all this time? "I'm afraid he'll reject me once I tell him." Shaking her head, Adelaide turned to the window. "I admit in the beginning I only worried about him getting angry at me, the way Father gets angry. But now," a deep sigh left her lips, "now it's different."

"You've come to care for him," her grandmother observed, a pleased tone in her voice. "I had hoped you would."

"Yes," Adelaide replied with sudden vehemence as she turned to meet her grandmother's eyes. "Yes, I care for him. I care for him deeply. I'm afraid I…" Swallowing, she drew in a deep breath. "I'm afraid I might be losing my heart to him."

"Would that be so bad?"

Adelaide shrugged. "If he rejects me once he knows, then yes." Tears began to sting her eyes, and Adelaide quickly blinked them away. "Losing him will be worse if he holds my heart."

Placing a gentle hand on Adelaide's shoulder, her grandmother looked at her as one would look at a child who has not yet come to see reason. "I understand your fears, my dear. But I do believe that living this lie, keeping this secret from someone you feel so deeply for, will not bring you happiness. The longer you wait the harder it will be to reveal the truth and the more he might feel betrayed by someone he trusted."

Adelaide nodded, knowing her grandmother's words to be true, and yet, fear held her back. "I'll think about it."

"Do so," her grandmother urged. "But don't wait too long. I swear you will regret it if you do."

Nodding once more, Adelaide tried to focus her thoughts as there was something else she needed to discuss with her grandmother. "He suggested Tillie come live with us," she said without preamble, unable to wait any longer for her grandmother's verdict.

The old woman's gaze widened ever so slightly, and yet, her head bobbed up and down as though she had expected this to happen. As though to prove Adelaide's assessment, her grandmother smiled. "I cannot say I'm surprised." Her gaze travelled to Adelaide's husband, currently sitting in line with Tillie's dolls on the settee, sipping tea. "He looks like a man starved for a family he can dote upon." Sighing, she turned her attention back to Adelaide, her eyes full of meaning. "He will be a wonderful father."

"I do believe so, too," Adelaide whispered, warmth flooding her heart at the thought of having a happy little family all her own. "Do you think we can simply bring her here?" she asked, all but holding her breath. "Do you think there would be…consequences if we did so? Whispers? Rumours? Would–?"

"I do not believe so," her grandmother replied instantly. "Your father will not miss her, and although society often pretends to turn a blind eye, everyone is well aware who has been raising the girl these past two years. Your brother's rather immature and somewhat reckless character is well known, and people will most likely speak highly of you for taking in Tillie."

"Good," Adelaide mumbled, unable to ignore the nagging feeling that she ought to speak to her husband–tell him the truth–before bringing Tillie into their family. If he truly were to reject her, the little girl would suffer, too.

"I heard you spoke to Beth."

Adelaide's head snapped up, her eyes finding her grandmother's face a trifle tense. "I did," she said, wondering if her grandmother was worried she would be angry for being excluded from their secret. "I understand." Placing a hand on her grandmother's arm, Adelaide smiled, feeling the older woman's muscles relax. "I mean I wish I had known, but I understand that some secrets are necessary." Her gaze shifted to Tillie.

"I'm glad," her grandmother replied, a deep smile on her face as she placed her own hand on Adelaide's. "I've always wanted you two to know each other as sisters. Beth is a remarkable, young woman just like you, and although you've both suffered in the past, you've grown stronger because of it. It's good to know that you have each other now." She glanced at Tillie. "I shall speak to your father, but I doubt that he will even take notice. Ever since he's learnt of Beth's true identity, he's locked himself away in his study, drinking even more than before."

Sadness came to her grandmother's eyes as she spoke of her son, and Adelaide wondered what kind of a person her father had been as a child, as a young man. He could not possibly have been born the man he was today. What had changed him? Made him unfeeling? Would they ever know?

Adelaide doubted it. Still, she wondered, if he truly did not care about any one of them, why did this news about his firstborn daughter seem to affect him so?

"Give me two days," her grandmother said, interrupting Adelaide's thoughts, "and then come for Tillie. I promise everything will be ready by then." A soft smile came to her face as she looked at the little girl. "She deserves to live in a happy family, a happy home. You'll be good for each other."

"Thank you, Grandmother. A part of me wishes you and mother could come live with us as well."

Her grandmother chuckled. "Oh, you don't mean that, my dear. Enjoy your own little family, but I promise I shall call on you frequently."

Adelaide smiled. "Any time you feel like it. You'll always be welcome."

"Thank you, my dear," her grandmother whispered, pulling Adelaide into an embrace. "I'm proud of you. You've done well."

After bidding her grandmother and Tillie farewell—at least temporarily—Adelaide turned to her husband. "It was such a delight to see you with Tillie. I had no idea you were so good with children."

Her husband chuckled. "Neither did I. She truly is a sweet girl, and a clever one. In the end, she had me cleaning up the dishes while she and the dolls lounged around on the settee."

Adelaide laughed. "You need to be careful or you'll lose your heart to her. I know. I'm speaking from experience."

Her husband smiled. "I fear it is already too late for that…Addy."

Adelaide froze at hearing Tillie's nickname for her leave his lips. For a moment, she simply stared at him, seeing the teasing grin on his face and the mischievous twinkle in his eyes. "Don't call me that. It makes me feel like a little girl."

"But *she* is allowed?" her husband asked in mock outrage.

Adelaide grinned. "She *is* a little girl."

"Fine," he relented. "What may I call you then?"

Feeling heat creep up her cheeks, Adelaide averted her gaze. "If you wish, call me Adelaide."

A gentle hand settled under her chin, lifting her head until she met her husband's gaze. "I do wish," he whispered, smiling at her.

"Good," Adelaide replied, feeling a sudden urge to tease him. "May I call you Mattie?"

As expected, her husband's eyes went wide, and he laughed loudly. "If you insist," he finally said. "However, I, too, would prefer you call me Matthew."

"Then I shall."

For a long while, they stood there, looking at one another, and Adelaide could feel the air around them grow heavy with meaning. Excitement seized her, and yet, goose bumps rose on her flesh. When the weight of his gaze grew too heavy for her to hold, she dropped her eyes to the floor. "Are you certain? About Tillie?" Taking a step back, she looked up at him once more. "She can be quite noisy, and once she settles in she can be difficult to handle. You need to be certain."

"I am," her husband assured her before his gaze swept over their surroundings. "The hushed silence has lingered in this house for far too long. We could do with a little laughter."

Adelaide smiled. "You'll be getting a lot."

"The more the better." He grinned. "I have no doubts."

Adelaide sighed, wishing she could say the same.

If only she could trust that her secret would not destroy the fragile bond that was slowly developing between them.

If only.

27

RETURN TO AN OLD LIFE

Two days later, Matthew found himself seated across from his wife in the carriage on their way to her father's townhouse. Her gaze was distant, and her hands kept fidgeting with her skirts or the hem of her sleeve. Occasionally, she would draw in a long, shuddering breath as though she had all but forgotten to breathe. Her face was tense, her jaw clenched, and now and then she would sink her teeth into her lower lip as though fighting for control, desperately trying to maintain her composure.

"Scream if you want," Matthew suggested, a mild grin on his face as she turned wide eyes to him.

"Excuse me?"

"You seem unbearably uncomfortable," he observed, trying his best to sound mildly cheerful, adding a bit of a teasing note to his voice. "Perhaps it would help. I find it tension-relieving."

Her eyes widened even more. "You scream when you're tense?"

Matthew sighed, "Not always," he admitted. "I try not to in public, and yet, can you imagine what it would be like to stand in the middle of a ballroom and start screaming at the top of your lungs?"

A soft chuckle escaped his wife's lips as she shook her head at him. "You're teasing me."

Matthew shrugged. "Perhaps. Perhaps not."

A soft smile hung on her lips as she inhaled a deep, strengthening breath. "Thank you," she whispered, her blue eyes shining like the clear blue afternoon sky.

"Any time," Matthew replied, feeling himself getting lost in the gentleness of her beautiful features. Before he lost all hold on reality though, he cleared his throat, trying to focus his thoughts. "All will be well," he said, regretting the doubt that immediately came to his wife's gaze. "If your father is truly bothered by the girl, then why would he insist she stay? No, I do not believe he will." A grin came to his face at the thought of his wife's grandmother and the stern look she had given him on their wedding day. "I'm certain your grandmother took care of everything. She seems like a very capable woman to me. Do you not agree?"

Another sigh left his wife's lips, and Matthew took note of the slight relaxation that came to her shoulders. "That she is," Adelaide agreed, a warm smile playing on her lips. "She always seems greater than life, like nothing can stop her, as though she can accomplish anything. She has an iron will."

Matthew held her gaze. "So, you have that from her?"

His wife's mouth opened…and then closed as she stared at him, clearly taken aback.

"You do," Matthew stated, conviction strong in his voice. He did not want there to be any doubt in her mind about how he saw her. "You don't give yourself enough credit, Adelaide. You are strong, and you know what you want, and you see it through…in a very gentle and compassionate way. It's who you are."

Tears misted her eyes, and she quickly blinked them away. Her eyes met his, and she was about to say something when the carriage jarred to a halt. Her eyes drifted out the window, and she inhaled a deep breath as she beheld her father's townhouse, a place she had not seen since their wedding.

Stepping outside, Matthew held out his hand to her. "Are you ready?"

Again, she inhaled a deep breath before her blue eyes hardened, a note of determination in them. "I am," she said, sliding her delicate hand into his.

The way she leaned on him as she stepped out of the carriage made Matthew wish that she trusted he would always be at her side, always holding her hand, always ready to catch her. He could only hope she knew that.

After stepping across the threshold, they were received by his wife's mother and grandmother. While the dowager countess welcomed them warmly, Lady Radcliff looked tense, whispering something under her breath as she hugged her daughter.

Tension hung in the air, and as Matthew glanced around, he felt reminded of his father's house. The same gloom he had always considered normal while growing up lingered everywhere in the earl's home as well. It spoke of the influence of a hardened man, a man incapable of love and devotion, a man lost in an obsession, disinterested in the well-being of those under his care.

Only his own father's passing had been able to lift the gloom from his home. Matthew was certain of it as he thought of his wife's gentle smiles, the strength he saw in his mother's eyes these days as well as the echo of Tillie's childish giggles echoing through the hall. Indeed, his house was becoming a true home, a place where a family would feel safe and loved. A place where he felt at ease. A place where he felt welcome.

The earl's house, however, had not undergone such a change, and it probably never would. Not as long as the source of that gloom still lived under its roof. It was sad to think of how one man could affect an entire family, robbing them of their happiness.

"Do not look so concerned," the dowager countess chided her granddaughter. "Everything is in place. As expected, your father barely blinked when I informed him, and he hasn't set foot outside of his study in the past two days."

Matthew noticed the hint of sadness that hung on the old woman's face, and he felt awed by the silent strength with which she pushed it aside, unwilling to yield to it.

Adelaide's face relaxed, and a soft smile came to her lips. "I'm glad. I admit I had doubts."

Her grandmother chuckled, "Have you learnt nothing growing up with me? There is nothing I cannot do if I put my mind to it." She took a step toward Adelaide, her eyes intent as she looked at her. "And you are my granddaughter. Don't ever think yourself incapable of something. Those who succeed are not better equipped to handle life. They are simply more determined than those who fail. Never forget that."

Sighing, Adelaide embraced her grandmother. "Thank you…for everything."

"Perhaps we should hurry this along," Lady Radcliff suggested, casting a concerned glance down the corridor that Matthew knew led to the earl's study. He could see the tension on her face, the same tension he had seen countless times on his mother's and knew exactly the kind of life the lady of the house lived.

Matthew's heart went out to her, and he wished there was something he could do to bring the earl to his senses and help him realise how fortunate he was to have such a loving and devoted family.

Still, Matthew knew that any attempt would be one in futility.

In the sudden silence, footsteps echoed to their ears from the upper floor and then down the stairs. Stepping out of the drawing room, Matthew saw a young woman in uniform hasten toward them, her face pale and her eyes wide. "She's gone," she all but yelled, her hands gesturing wildly. "I was packing the last of her things and when I turned around, she was gone."

"She's probably hiding somewhere in the house," Matthew suggested with a chuckle, which died on his lips when he took note of the women around him. All their faces had gone pale to match that of the child's nurse, alarm in their eyes as they glanced around themselves as though hoping Tillie would simply materialise out of thin air.

"We need to find her," Lady Radcliff all but whispered, her gaze once more darting down the corridor which led to the earl's study. "But quietly. Do not disturb him."

Everybody nodded, and the women broke off, each heading into a different part of the house.

Following his wife, Matthew reached for her arm. "Wait." Meeting Adelaide's eyes, he could see the worry that held her in its clutches. Her hands trembled, and she seemed reluctant to turn back to him. "Think," he urged. "Where would she go? This is a big house. I doubt it would make sense to simply go from room to room. Does she have any hiding places she prefers? I doubt this is the first time she's disappeared."

The ghost of a smile flashed over his wife's face, and Matthew knew his suspicion confirmed. "No, it's not the first time."

"Then where does she go? Where have you discovered her before?"

Adelaide's forehead crinkled into a frown as her eyes became distant. "Nowhere in particular," she said, a hint of discouragement in her voice. "She simply goes off exploring."

"What does she explore?"

An unexpected snort left Adelaide's throat. "Places we tell her to stay away from."

Matthew smiled. "Such as?"

"The ballroom, the drawing rooms, the…" Adelaide shook her head. "She is supposed to stay in the nursery because we are afraid she might cross my father's path."

Matthew felt the little hairs in the back of his neck stand on edge as a sense of foreboding came over him. "Has she ever gone to your father's study?"

His wife's eyes widened. "She tried once," she whispered, her voice hoarse. "In fact, it was the day you came to…"

"Inform your father of our wedding?"

Swallowing, Adelaide nodded. "I found her before she could…" Turning her head, her gaze drifted down the corridor that led to her father's study. "She wouldn't," she whispered rather like someone desperately trying to convince herself instead of someone who already believed her own words. "She wouldn't."

"Does she know she will be leaving here?" Matthew asked carefully, seeing the fear in his wife's eyes. His stomach clenched at the sight.

"I believe so," Adelaide whispered. "Grandmother would not send her away without giving her the chance to say her goodbyes."

"Perhaps that's what she's doing," Matthew replied, feeling his anger rise as his wife turned fearful eyes to him.

"She's saying goodbye to my father," Adelaide stammered before her jaw clenched and her eyes hardened. In the next instant, she was off, striding toward her father's study at a brisk pace.

Matthew rushed to catch up with her, fighting the urge to offer his help. Certainly, he would be at her side, but although he wished he could do this for her, take this burden from her shoulders, he knew it was important that she handle this herself.

The moment she had stormed off, he had seen something in her blue eyes. Something that he had rarely seen in his life. Something that reminded him of his cousin Henrietta.

As Tristan's older sister, she had always seen to him, always protected him, but not until recently had Matthew learnt that she had in fact saved her little brother's life numerous times, protecting him from Matthew's father.

Her eyes had always held the same determination, the same loyalty and conviction, the same devotion and love that Matthew had glimpsed in Adelaide's eyes only a moment ago. It made him think of the purest form of selfless love. The kind of love a mother had for her child.

A mother who would risk everything to keep pain from her child, who knew that nothing would be worse than seeing that precious little life come to harm and who could put aside her own fears in order to do so.

Although Adelaide was not Tillie's mother—like Henrietta had not been Tristan's—she had raised the girl, had taken over that role when her brother's child had turned up on the earl's doorstep. In her heart, it probably did not matter that she had not been the one to give birth to Tillie, and Matthew could kick himself for not realising this sooner.

He should never have allowed mother and child to be separated like this.

"I don't know why," Adelaide said as she hastened along the corridor, "but my father's study seems to hold an almost magical attraction for her. I've told her countless times not to go there, but I could see that no matter what I said, she was completely unimpressed."

"Are you truly surprised?" Matthew asked. "Are not all children drawn to what is forbidden? Is it not that specific allure that draws them near? Curiosity? The need to know? To understand?"

"I suppose you're right, but—" Her voice broke off as they stepped around the corner and came face to face with the door to her father's study only a few steps farther down. Only now it stood ajar.

Judging from the way his wife's face paled, Matthew supposed that it never stood ajar. "She is in there, isn't she?"

Swallowing, Adelaide nodded. For a moment, she seemed hesitant, but then the muscles in her jaw tensed, and he could see her draw back her shoulders. The moment she made to approach the door, a loud, booming voice echoed to their ears, "Out! Out with you!"

Adelaide flinched, and for a moment, she closed her eyes as though old memories had returned to torture her. Still, instead of shrinking back or turning to him for help, Matthew watched her face harden. Her hands curled into fists as she stormed forward, her eyes unblinking as she focused on what lay ahead.

Never had Matthew felt prouder of her.

Not halting in her step, Adelaide pushed open the door and crossed the threshold. Matthew followed a step behind, his gaze falling on little Tillie standing in front of the earl's large desk as the man leaned forward, his hands braced on the desk's top, glaring at the girl. "I said out with you! Or I will throw you out myself! Bastard that you are!"

Anger boiled in Matthew's veins as he saw Tillie's wide fearful eyes and the slight quiver in her bottom lip. Still, she held herself upright, meeting the earl's ferocious stare with an innocent one of her own. "I only came to bid you farewell," she stammered, her voice feeble, and yet, there was a silent strength in the way she stood her ground that reminded Matthew of his wife.

Looking up, Matthew saw Adelaide's eyes light up with fire as her anger broke free. Fuelled by the instinct to protect the helpless girl before her, Adelaide was at Tillie's side in one large stride, sweeping the girl into her arms. "All will be well, my sweet," she said in a gentle and reassuring voice. "Do not worry. I will look after you."

A grateful smile crossed Tillie's face as she hugged Adelaide tightly.

"Out! All of you!" the earl yelled, his face bright red and his eyes blood-shot as always. "How dare you come in here? How dare you—?"

Turning away from her father, Adelaide stepped toward Matthew. "Here, take her," she said, her voice quivering with something held in check.

Matthew nodded, his eyes filling with the radiant sight that was his wife as he held out his arms to receive the trembling child.

With her shoulders back and her chin raised, Adelaide stood tall. The moment she knew Tillie to be safe with him, she turned to face her father. Her eyes shone clear and pale like the sky on a chilled winter morning, and yet, a deep fire burned in them that spoke to the courage that had lain buried far too long. Finally, it was unleashed, and Matthew could see that in this moment Adelaide knew no fear.

Perhaps for the first time in her life.

As he watched his wife step toward her father's desk, Matthew took note of the way the earl's eyes narrowed as he tried to make sense of the change he detected in his daughter despite his level of inebriation. His gaze swept her face, and for a moment, he was silent.

"This," Adelaide said, her voice strong and controlled, but laced with the disappointment of almost twenty years, "is precisely why Beth's mother left you."

Matthew was stunned to see the earl turn white as though the air had just been knocked from his lungs. Did he truly care? Had his daughter's return somehow affected him after all?

"You are an awful man," Adelaide continued, one last step bringing her to the edge of the desk, "and you do not deserve our company, our love. I want you to know that we—your family—would have left you years ago if we'd had a choice. All you've ever given us is fear." Gritting her teeth, she shook her head. "It might surprise you to hear that fear does not create loyalty, but it is the truth. Only respect can, and that has to be earned." Again, she shook her head, and Matthew could see a lone tear roll down her cheek. "You've never done anything to earn my respect, Father. I never felt safe with you or protected or cared for. Never. You have always been the monster that not only lived in my nightmares but also in my home." She lifted her chin a fraction, her eyes turning to steel. "But you will not do the same to Tillie. I will not allow that. This house is not a home. It is no place for a young child. She deserves more as I deserved more." She took a step back, and Matthew could see her shoulders relax as though she had just found peace. "Goodbye, Father. I doubt we shall ever see each other again." Then she turned on her heel, took Tillie from his arms and marched out of her father's study, her body trembling with the aftermath of the confrontation.

With a last glance at the earl, Matthew followed his wife, wondering about the tears he saw in the man's eyes.

Despite the man's anger, it would seem that his deeds were finally catching up with him. If Matthew was not mistaken, he would think that Lord Radcliff was slowly coming to realise the wrongs he had committed against his family. Perhaps his daughter's return as well as her rejection had cracked open the shell he had been hiding under, and now, bit by bit, all his atrocities found their way back to him.

If only he had seen it sooner. After all, some mistakes could not be corrected. Matthew knew that only too well.

28

A MAN FROM HER PAST

ith Tillie under the same roof with them, everything was different.

Every morning, Adelaide woke with a smile on her face, looking forward to the day ahead with utter joy in her heart. Tillie had settled into her new home as though she had been born there, as though she had never lived anywhere else. Adelaide often found herself looking at the bright, happy child in awe, wondering about the ease with which young children adapted to new circumstances. Her laughter and smiles quickly turned their house into a home for Adelaide. Finally, she felt like she belonged, like this was the place she was meant to be.

Her husband seemed to feel the same way.

Doting on the little girl as only a father would, he often took her outside into the gardens to track birds as Tillie seemed especially fond of them. They set up little feeding grounds and even tried their hands at building a nest. Once they were finished, Adelaide stood on the ground, looking up at the tall oak tree, her husband sitting on a tall branch with Tillie in his arms. Together, they set the finished nest onto a fork in the branch ensuring that it was secure.

"Now, we have to wait and see," her husband told little Tillie after they had managed to return to the ground without falling. "Only a bird mother can tell us if we've done a good job with this nest."

Tillie beamed up at him. "I think she'll love it."

Matthew winked at her. "I think so, too."

Adelaide was speechless, too stunned by the little family that she had found so unexpectedly. Even her mother-in-law seemed more cheerful these days as she spent many of her waking hours having tea parties with Tillie and discussing new dresses for the girl's countless dolls. They would sit together in the drawing room, looking over different kinds of fabric as though preparing for a London season. It was a sight to behold.

"Tillie seems happy," Matthew commented rather unexpectedly as they sat in the carriage one night on their way to a ball.

Adelaide sighed, "She does, doesn't she?"

Her husband nodded, a wide grin on his face. "So, do you."

"I am," Adelaide beamed, her heart so full of happiness that she felt certain it would burst. "I mean Tillie has always made me happy, but now…that happiness is no longer overshadowed. It is pure and peaceful. I've never felt like this before."

Walking into the ballroom on her husband's arm, Adelaide realised that the smile from the carriage was still on her face. Although she had never particularly enjoyed large crowds, things were different now. She felt different. She was different.

To have someone at her side, who had proved more than once that he would stand with her no matter what, that he would help her if needed, that he would stand back all the same, made Adelaide feel completely safe and at peace.

It was an utterly new feeling, and one she hoped she would never again have to live without.

Half the night, they spent dancing and talking about Tillie, about their new life, about what other changes to make to the house. Matthew's eyes were bright and smiling whenever they met hers, and Adelaide could not ignore the silent flip in her stomach she felt whenever he drew near.

As she watched him walk away to procure a drink for them, Adelaide once more remembered his words about asking her for a kiss once he could be certain she would refuse him if she wished so.

"When?" she whispered to herself, realising that her heart was getting impatient.

Once her husband was lost from sight, Adelaide turned away and toward the large windows opening up to the gardens. The silver moon cast a magical glow over the dark oasis, and Adelaide found herself quietly humming along to the music.

Could life get any better?

Footsteps echoed to her ears then, drawing closer, and Adelaide turned back to her husband, a smile on her face, determined to show him how much he had come to mean to her.

However, when Adelaide's gaze fell on the man approaching, the smile slid off her face and her eyes grew round with shock. Her heart began to hammer in her chest, and panic slowly crept into every fibre of her being, stealing the voice from her throat.

"Hello Addy," he said in that deep, familiar voice, his dark brown eyes meeting hers with frank intimacy. "It's been a long time."

No! No! No! No! The silent voice in Adelaide's head kept repeating over and over as though it could will him to disappear. And yet, he did not.

Right there in front of her, perhaps two arm lengths away stood her brother's childhood friend, Joseph Bartholomew, second son to the Earl of Rundike.

"I had heard you were on the continent," Adelaide heard herself say as though the reminder would make him realise his mistake and disappear. However, it did not.

"I was," he merely said, shrugging his shoulders before he stepped closer, his brown eyes looking into hers. "Now, I'm back."

Adelaide felt her insides twist and turn at his approach, her mind still repeating its mantra. *No! No! No! He could not be back in England! He absolutely could not!*

And yet, it seemed he was, looking at her with the same knowing smile she had seen on his face countless times.

In that moment the music stopped, and the murmurs that drifted through the crowd around her finally drew Adelaide back to the here and now. Reminding herself of her position, she forced a polite smile on her face and said, "Good evening, Mr. Bartholomew."

It was the best she could do.

Unfortunately, it was not good enough for him for he chuckled at her formal greeting. "Call me Bart," he urged her, leaning in confidently. "After all, we know each other well enough I should think." Then he winked at her, and Adelaide felt as though she might faint.

In the very moment when she found herself happy, found herself falling for her new husband, a ghost from her past had to reappear, had to return to torment her. What on earth could he want?

"I heard congratulations are in order," Bart commented, his smile still in place as though he did not have a care in the world…which he probably did not.

She, on the other hand, …

Adelaide nodded in confirmation to his statement, her tongue feeling dry like sandpaper. "And you? I mean, are you married?"

As though she had made a joke, he laughed, shaking his head at the absurdity of her question. "I'm not the marrying type, Addy. You of all people should know that. Marriage is for old men. I like to enjoy myself." Again, he winked at her.

Adelaide felt a cold shiver run down her back as her eyes drifted past the ghost before her, trying to determine where her husband was. If he was to come upon them…?

Oh, she did not dare imagine what he would think! What he would do!

Her eyes snapped back from the crowd on the other side of the room when Bart suddenly stepped closer, invading her private space, his dark eyes finding hers. "I've missed you, Addy."

Adelaide's breath lodged in her throat as she stared up at him, unable to form a coherent thought. However, it was not until a moment later that she felt like sinking into a hole in the ground.

"Excuse me," came her husband's voice from merely a step or two away. Only now it did not hold the gentle, often teasing tone she had come to love, but instead rang of a darker quality, one she had feared in the very beginning of her marriage.

Now, it once more sent cold shivers down her back…but for a very different reason.

Jerking a step backward, Adelaide put some room between the man of her past and the man of her present, her heart hammering wildly as fear consumed her anew.

Then Bart turned to greet her husband, and she stared at Matthew with the same shock she had felt ever since first seeing her past materialise before her.

His gaze was narrowed as he glanced back and forth between her and Bart, suspicion written only too clearly on his face.

"Allow me to offer my congratulations," Bart said, apparently completely unimpressed by the tension that hung in the air.

"Thank you," Matthew replied rather curtly, stepping in-between the two of them and drawing Adelaide to his side. Then he handed her one of the drinks he held in his hands. "I do not believe we've met before."

Clutching the glass tightly, Adelaide scarcely dared breathe as she watched the moment unfold as though it did not concern her in the least.

Bart chuckled, and Adelaide could not keep herself from rolling her eyes at him. "Oh, we've known each other all our lives. We practically grew up together. I was close friends with her brother, but the two of us spent much time together as well." Again, he winked at her—that blasted man!

Adelaide could all but feel the tension in her husband's body as he stood beside her, rigid as a stone column. His jaw was clenched, and his hands seemed as tight on his glass as her own were.

"If you'll excuse me," Bart suddenly said, respectfully inclining his head, "I have another old acquaintance to greet." Yet again, the man winked at her—was this some kind of affliction? "See you around, Addy." And then he strode away as though nothing had happened, perhaps completely unaware of the damage he had done.

Clearing his throat, Matthew downed his drink in one gulp. "I suggest we return home," he said, his gaze never once meeting hers. "It is late, and I cannot say I'm enjoying myself at present."

Unable to discover her voice, Adelaide merely nodded before she slipped her hand through the crook of his arm and allowed him to escort her to their carriage. The entire drive home, her husband did not say a word, only mumbled something unintelligible to her rather desperate attempts to return the ease that had existed between them only a few hours ago.

Politely, he helped her up the stoop into their home and then up the steps to the upper floor. All the while, he did not say a single word, and yet, Adelaide could feel his emotions burning under the surface like a volcano about to erupt. To Adelaide's surprise, she realised that she did not fear him.

Certainly, she feared what he might make of the events of this evening, what he might think of her and how their relationship might change. But she was not afraid of *him*. No matter how angry he might be, he would never raise his hand to her. He would not hurt her, and the knowledge of that put Adelaide at ease.

Escorting her to her chamber, her husband held open the door for her, and Adelaide felt her heart sink at the distant look on his face. However, she turned to him in astonishment when instead of bidding her a good night, he followed her into the room, entering her chamber for the first time since their wedding night.

Then he closed the door.

For a long moment, Matthew simply looked at her, his gaze gliding over her face, hesitation in his eyes as he seemed to be deciding whether or not to ask the question clearly torturing him. Running a nervous hand through his dark hair, he gritted his teeth. Then his eyes met hers for the first time since Bart had returned to her life. "How well do you know Mr. Bartholomew?"

Adelaide swallowed. "He is my brother's friend." Of course, Adelaide understood the hidden meaning behind such a simple question, and the little voice in her mind urged her to take this opportunity to share her secret, to finally tell the truth and heed her grandmother's words.

And yet, Adelaide could not for her memories brought forth an image of Tillie laughing and playing, her husband by her side, his own face showing the same happiness as hers. What would happen if she told him? Would Tillie be robbed of the only happy family she had ever known?

"Is he your friend as well?" her husband asked, his brows drawn as he fixed her with watchful eyes, doubt shining only too clearly in them.

Adelaide shook her head. That much at least was true. Bart had never been her friend.

Still, her answer did not seem to satisfy him or put him at ease. Instead, Matthew began pacing, once more running his hands through his hair. "I felt like an outsider tonight," he confided, pain in his voice that felt like a stab to Adelaide's heart. "The way you spoke to each other, the way he looked at you…" Shaking his head, he all but glared at her. "It seemed he knew you in a way I never would. What did you share with him that you won't share with me?"

Stopping, he inhaled a deep breath, then crossed the small distance between them. "I've known for a while that there is something you're keeping from me, and I've told myself to be patient. I've told myself that you would share it once I'd proved myself trustworthy to you." Looking defeated, he sighed. "I've done what I could, and yet, you've never said a word. Was it not enough? What could be so bad that you cannot tell me?" His gaze hardened. "Does *he* know? Bartholomew? Did you confide in him? Does he…?"

Adelaide felt her heart hammer in her chest as she looked up at her husband's pained face. His gaze held hers, urging her to confide in him now. "What are you asking?" Adelaide mumbled, needing him to say it, unable to find the courage to do so on her own.

Matthew swallowed, then gritted his teeth as though in pain. "Are you…are you having an affair with him? With Bartholomew?"

Adelaide felt her jaw drop at his accusation. "Do you truly believe I would be unfaithful to you?" she stammered, feeling her head begin to spin. Never would she have expected him to think this. She had only ever feared he would discover her secret. Her mind had been so focused on it that she had not seen this coming.

"How can I not?" Matthew snapped, his hands balling into fists as he once more began to stride around the room. "There is clearly something between you. Some kind of…confidence. Something you won't share with me." Halting in his step, he suddenly froze, his eyes widening before he closed them in resignation. Shaking his head, he mumbled, "I'm such a fool. I should never have…"

Inhaling a deep breath, he looked at her once more. "I know our marriage was not a love match, and I should not put any expectations on you that you cannot fulfil. You married me to be safe from your father. We both knew that," he said as though to remind himself. "I cannot blame you if you lost your heart to another. After all, you never promised it to me." His head sank, and the misery he felt was so clearly written on his face that Adelaide could no longer bear the distance between them.

Her feet carried her closer, and her hands gently cupped his cheeks, lifting his head so that he would look at her. "I promise I am not having an affair with Bart or anyone else. Please believe me."

Although she detected a hint of relief in her husband's gaze, she could feel his muscles harden under the tips of her fingers. "Bart?" he repeated, jerking his head away. "He called you Addy! You asked me not to call you that, but when he does it, it's fine?"

Adelaide drew in a sharp breath. "He did know me as a child," she tried to explain, feeling her pulse thudding in her neck. "Back then, I was Addy. And no, I do not care for him calling me that now. However, he did not ask, and I was too shocked at seeing him. I—"

"Do you care for him?" her husband demanded, suddenly stepping toward her and cutting off her words.

Adelaide flinched, and yet, she held her ground, her gaze not dropping from her husband's. "I do not," she said calmly, enunciating each word.

Matthew exhaled sharply, the tension on his face dissipating. "But you're keeping something from me."

Adelaide sighed, then nodded. "I am, but I'm not having an affair. Neither have I lost my heart to Bartholomew or anyone other than y—" Her voice broke off when she realised what she was about to say, her gaze dropping to the floor as heat flooded her cheeks.

Barely an arm's length away, she heard her husband inhale a deep breath, his body trembling with deep emotions. Then his arm moved, and she could feel his fingertips gently grasping her chin. As he began tilting her head upward, Adelaide closed her eyes, unable to meet his.

"Look at me," her husband whispered, his voice practically pleading, and she found herself unable to deny him anything. "Do you care for me?" he asked gently, almost fearfully as his green eyes held hers.

Adelaide inhaled a slow breath, feeling her skin tingle where his fingers rested on her chin. "I do," she whispered, afraid to grant him such power over her, and yet, unable not to. Whether he knew how she felt about him or not did not matter. All that mattered was that she did feel for him, and that alone gave him the power to hurt her. She could only hope that he would not, that her trust in him would be rewarded.

A soft smile came to his face at her words. "I care for you as well," he whispered back. "I have for a long time." Then his gaze drifted lower, touching her lips.

Adelaide found herself holding her breath as his words brushed over her like a warm summer breeze, and yet, it was the look in his eyes that made her stomach flip and sent heat through her body.

"Will you grant me a kiss?" he asked finally! —as his other arm came around her middle pulling her closer into his embrace.

Adelaide sighed, feeling herself shiver with anticipation, and yet, she heard herself ask, "Why now? I've wondered when you would ask me, but why now?" A part of her deep down berated her for ruining the moment and postponing—if not preventing—the kiss. Had she not waited long enough?

A teasing grin came to her husband's face, the kind that riled her, and yet, made her feel safe. "Because just now, you openly defied me," he said, a touch of pride in his voice despite the accusation she knew his words to be. "You stood your ground and answered me without bowing your head." He sighed, "You did not look at me with fear in your eyes as you did before. Reject me now if you do not want me to kiss you. I have no doubt that you would do so…should you wish to."

Adelaide swallowed, feeling a tentative smile claiming her lips. "I do not."

Her husband's eyes narrowed. "You do not what?"

"I do not wish to reject you," she clarified, heat once more rising to her cheeks. Still, never in her life had Adelaide felt more daring, more in control.

Her husband smiled, and she could see the joy and relief over her answer plainly on his face.

Her body yearned to be closer, and when Matthew's arm around her tightened, pulling her toward him, she went gladly. Her lips began to tingle with anticipation, and she closed her eyes as he lowered his head to hers.

His kiss was gentle, but full of passion. Still, beyond all, it made her feel safe and whole and at ease. In that moment, Adelaide knew that her heart now belonged to him and that there was nothing she could do to get it back…even should she wish to.

And to say so would be a lie.

And Adelaide did not want to add that to the secret she already kept from him.

One day, he would find out. That was inevitable, but what then?

Oh, if only she was not such a coward!

29

A THREAT

The following morning, Matthew woke with a smile on his face.

Try as he might, he could not remember the last time that had happened. Not merely the absence of dread and loneliness, but true joy and the urge to jump out of bed to be with the people in this house. Although he had always loved his mother dearly even as a child, Matthew had seen her misery and had felt restrained in his ways towards her. His little cousins had been great playmates at first, but his father had soon found ways to drive a wedge between them, stoking Matthew's displeasure about how much attention Tristan received...even when it was in the form of reprieves and lectures.

There had always been a dark cloud.

And there was one even now.

As wonderful as Matthew felt that morning remembering the previous night when he had shared a most wonderful kiss with his wife, he could not deny that there was still something standing between them. After all, she had flat-out admitted that to him, confirming that there was a secret she did not dare share with him.

Matthew had been tempted to take things further the previous night, loving the way she had responded to his touch, to his words, how she had reciprocated, the way she had held his gaze, proud and honest. Still, after their kiss, he had bid her a good night and retired to his own room, knowing that they still had a little way to go before all between them was resolved. He had been patient this long. He could be patient a little longer.

After all, she was worth it.

He did not doubt that.

Not for a second.

And yet, he wondered. What could be so awful a secret that she did not dare share it with him? Not after the way they had gotten closer over the past few weeks?

Matthew had believed her when she had sworn she was not having an affair with Bartholomew, and yet, he could not shake the feeling that there was more to the story than his wife had chosen to share. If she was not having an affair with the man, then what had happened between them?

Unlike her father and brother, Adelaide had always had a sparkling clean reputation. Not even the escapades of the men in her family had been able to taint the way people looked at her. Could she truly have a dark secret? If so, how had she managed to keep whatever it was hidden? Or was her secret of only minor consequence, but considering the woman Adelaide was, she still believed it to be of shocking nature?

After tossing and turning in bed for a while longer, Matthew finally rose and headed downstairs to breakfast. Even before he strode through the door, he could hear Tillie's sweet little voice, prattling on in the way she usually did when she was excited.

The moment he stepped through the door, Matthew felt his heart jump at the sight that met him. His family—his mother, wife and…child, for all intents and purposes—sat around the breakfast table, their eyes shining and laughter spilling out of their mouths as the two women listened with rapt attention to the little girl's narration of how she planned to catch the robin she had spotted in their garden the previous day.

It was a sight Matthew had always longed for growing up. A sight he had always hoped for once he had begun thinking of his own future and family. A sight he had feared he would never find in his own home.

He was a fortunate man indeed, and he would have been perfectly happy…if it were not for his wife's secret.

Still, the moment his wife looked up and their eyes met, Matthew did not feel reminded of the gulf between them or the secrets that kept them apart. No, he felt reminded of the previous night when he had drawn her into his arms and kissed her, when they had admitted that they cared for each other.

The slight blush that came to her cheeks and the way she momentarily averted her gaze told him that she, too, thought only of what connected them. Nothing else.

It gave Matthew hope that in time they would put even her secret behind them.

Meeting his gaze once more, Adelaide smiled, "Please join us. I'm afraid we've already begun. Someone was quite famished this morning." Her gaze slid to Tillie, who grinned at him with a mischievous sparkle in her eyes.

"You're late," the girl commented. "But I saved you some bacon."

Sighing with joy, Matthew slid onto his chair. "That is very sweet of you, Tillie. And you're right. I was late. I couldn't bring myself to get out of bed this morning."

"Did you dream something nice?" Tillie enquired excitedly, hoping for a good story.

For a second his gaze darted to his wife as she had been the only one on his mind last night. The way her jaw dropped ever so slightly, and she quickly turned her attention back to her plate told him that she had become very much aware of that. Still, the way her eyes kept returning to meet his suggested that she did not mind.

"I'm afraid not," Matthew told Tillie. "I slept like a log. But what about you? Any fascinating dreams?"

A large grin came to the girl's face. "I dreamed of a large doll. She was as tall as Addy." Her blue eyes drifted to Adelaide. "She looked like her, too."

Matthew laughed, "I bet such a large doll would be difficult to carry around, wouldn't she? And to take out on strolls?"

Thoughtful, Tillie put a little finger to her mouth. "That's true," she decided. "I guess I don't need such a large doll." A grin came to her face. "I've got Addy, and she can walk on her own and hug me and laugh and tickle me and even carry me."

Matthew smiled. "I agree. Adelaide is much better than any doll."

A serious look on her young face, Tillie nodded. "Much better."

Shaking his head, Matthew looked at the little girl, taken with the simple joy children brought to one's life, and judging from the silent smirks on the two women's faces, they were thinking the same thing.

It was a wonderful morning. Pleasant and simple, and yet, extraordinary.

The next few days passed in the same manner, and Matthew could feel them all slipping into more and more of a family routine, chatting over meals, spending time in the gardens, reading in the library before supper and going for strolls in the afternoons. Mostly, they were all together, even his mother loved to accompany them whenever Tillie decided it was time to take one of her dolls outdoors for a little fresh air. The little girl's happiness was contagious, and soon Matthew began to wonder how he could have ever lived without her. He finally understood—with his heart, not his mind—how his wife had to have felt when she had been separated from Tillie upon their marriage.

Adelaide, too, seemed to be more at ease these days. Although it had been a while since he had seen actual fear in her eyes, she still seemed at odds every now and then as though she was not quite certain what to make of the happiness that had found them so unexpectedly. And Matthew had no doubt that she was happy. The way she smiled and laughed often took his breath away, and he realised how much he had come to depend on his wife being by his side.

The moment she stepped into a room, he felt her presence like a warm breeze. When she smiled at him, her eyes aglow like two stars in the night sky, his insides quivered with excitement, and Matthew no longer had any doubt that they had been meant to find each other. It was as though they completed each other, the people they were; the lives they had lived had made them more than simply suitable for one another. It felt to Matthew as though they were two halves of a whole, and only when she was near, did he feel complete.

It was a strange sensation. One he had never felt before.

One afternoon, they all sat together having tea with Tillie and her dolls. Matthew had been granted the seat of honour next to Tillie's favourite doll, a dark-haired girl that Tillie swore resembled Adelaide…although he could not see it.

His mother had voiced her surprise that Matthew—after arriving late—had been granted that seat, but Tillie had insisted her doll liked him best. They had all laughed, and yet, Matthew had detected a slight blush come to his wife's cheeks as she had turned her gaze from his and back to her niece.

His mother had chuckled as well, answering Tillie's question if Matthew wished for more tea when he had been completely oblivious that the girl had even spoken, his gaze focused on his wife.

It was in that moment that their butler entered, announcing Lord Radcliff was here to see his daughter.

Matthew immediately turned his gaze to his wife but was distracted when Tillie suddenly dove under the coffee table.

In a flash, they all were on their feet before kneeling down beside the low table, trying to peer underneath. "Sweet one, what is it?" Adelaide asked the wide-eyed girl.

Nervously, Tillie glanced at the door. "Did he come to take me back?"

Matthew gritted his teeth at the sight of the girl's fear, wishing someone so young had not already learnt what it meant to be afraid.

"Of course not," his wife said, her voice strong and without doubt as she held out her hand to Tillie. After a while, the girl took it and allowed Adelaide to pull her out and into her arms. "I don't know why he's here, but I would never allow him to take you back. Do you believe me?"

Tillie nodded, then hugged Adelaide tightly.

"You stay here with Clara," his wife said, exchanging a meaningful glance with Matthew's mother that made him wonder how close these two women had become. "I'll see what he wants and then I'll come back, all right?"

The little girl nodded. "Promise?"

"Promise."

Then Tillie stepped into his mother's embrace who skilfully turned the girl's attention back to her dolls. Within moments, they were serving tea once more.

"What shall I tell Lord Radcliff?" the butler asked, doing his best to keep a straight face.

Matthew glanced at his wife. "Have him wait in my study. We shall be there shortly."

Bowing, the butler left to do as he was bid.

With a last glance over her shoulder, Adelaide straightened her back and then strode toward the door with quick steps. Matthew hurried to catch up with her, closing the door to the drawing room behind him before he reached out to stop her progress. "Wait, Adelaide!" His hand wrapped around her delicate arm and pulled her back to him. Gently, he placed one hand on each of her shoulders and looked down at her. "Are you sure you want to speak to him? The last time you said you didn't expect that that would ever happen."

Inhaling a deep breath, she looked up at him. "I will not be afraid," she stated calmly. "I will not allow him to intimidate me any longer. Standing up to him felt good…liberating." She sighed. "However, it took all the strength I had to fight my instincts that day and not cower in a corner of the room."

Matthew swallowed. From the stern look in her eyes that day, he would never have suspected such a turmoil had filled her heart. Now that he knew, he felt even prouder of her.

"I need to do this," Adelaide told him, her blue eyes shining with conviction. "I need to…practise, for lack of a better word."

Pure and utter pride surged through Matthew's heart, and a deep smile claimed his face. Then, before he knew what he was doing, his arms pulled her closer and his mouth closed over hers.

For a split second, she tensed in surprise. Then, however, her lips yielded. More than that, she returned his kiss with the same passion that had so suddenly flared up in his own veins.

There was no doubt left in Matthew's mind; they fit well together.

Exceedingly well.

Reluctantly, he released her, his hands sliding down her arms until they reached hers, pulling them into his own. "I'm very proud of you," he whispered, looking down into her blue eyes, now shining with new vibrancy. Matthew liked to think that he had something to do with it.

Returning his smile, Adelaide briefly dropped her gaze, her cheeks flushing a becoming red. "You have an interesting way of expressing your opinion."

"Do you dislike it?" Matthew asked, a teasing note in his voice. Still, he held his breath, wondering if he had overstepped a line without realising it.

Adelaide's smile deepened, and her blue gaze glowed brightly as it held his. "Not at all," she whispered. "I admit I rather care for it."

Matthew inhaled a deep breath, feeling his insides dance at her words. "I do as well," he said with equal frankness, once more tempted to pull her deeper into his arms. Before he could though, he dimly recalled that they had a visitor.

Clearing his throat, Matthew blinked, his gaze drifting to the door in her back. "We should go. Do you have any idea why he came?"

The smile vanished from Adelaide's face, and Matthew could have kicked himself. "I cannot say," she mumbled, her forehead in a frown. Then, for a short moment, her eyes seemed to widen in shock before she closed them, almost imperceptibly shaking her head.

"What is it?" Matthew asked, fresh concern coursing through his veins. What else might lie ahead?

A rather forced smile returned to his wife's face as she lifted her gaze to his. "Nothing. I'm fine. Let's go."

In order to keep her arm looped through his own, Matthew took a large step after her, wondering what it was she did not feel comfortable sharing with him. Was it connected to the secret she had admitted she kept? Did her father know? Was he somehow connected to it all? Had it nothing to do with Bartholomew after all?

Outside his study, Adelaide halted and took a deep breath.

"Are you ready?" Matthew asked, and when she nodded, he opened the door, allowing her to step inside first. Following close on her heel though, he took note of the dark scowl that came to the earl's face when he perceived him.

"I wished to speak to my daughter alone!" the man snapped, his tufts of hair sticking up from his head and his clothes dishevelled. His eyes were red-rimmed, and yet, he seemed—for lack of a better word—sober. There was a clearness in his eyes that Matthew had not seen before, and he wondered about the subtle changes in the man's appearance. What had happened since they had last seen him?

Meeting the earl's gaze, Matthew scoffed, "Did you truly think I would allow you in my wife's presence without protection for her?" Matthew shook his head. "No, I do not dare trust you where her well-being is concerned."

At his words, Lord Radcliff seemed to cringe as though he had been dealt a painful blow, and yet again, Matthew wondered why he seemed suddenly bothered by such honesty.

Beside him, Adelaide stepped forward, her hands linked casually as though she did not have a care in the world. In truth, Matthew knew the courage it took for her to address her father. He could see the almost imperceptible tremble in her hands and the slight paleness of her cheeks. Indeed, it took great courage to do what she did.

And yet, she hid it well.

Was that how she had kept her secret hidden for so long? Because she had learnt to hide her emotions and appear indifferent and unaffected? Had life with her father taught her to lie?

"Why did you come here today?" she asked, her voice strong as her gaze met her father's, her own unflinching. "What do you want?"

Sighing, the earl turned to look at his daughter, the look in his eyes suddenly showing nothing but regret and exhaustion. Tears clung to the corners of his eyes, and he cleared his throat to regain his composure. In a tone quite unlike any Matthew had ever heard from him, he said, "I came to apologise."

Matthew was thunderstruck.

And from the looks of it, so was his wife.

30

AMENDS

Staring at her father, Adelaide could not help but think that she had to have misunderstood. For a long moment, she was unable to form a coherent thought and simply stood and stared at him. Never would she have expected to hear him utter these words.

Never.

A part of her had feared that his visit would be about her secret. That he had come to threaten her yet again and demand money. That he wanted to reveal all to her husband and forever ensure that she would not find happiness.

Could he truly mean what he said?

Beside her, Adelaide felt her husband move, his hand coming to rest in the small of her back. Slowly, the warmth of his nearness began to ease the tension resting in her limbs and the daze retreated.

"Please take a seat," Matthew said to her father, gesturing to the armchair in the corner. Then he gently urged her to sit down as well—next to him and at a safe distance from her father.

Looking at her husband, Adelaide smiled, touched by his concern for her safety. Never would she have thought to ever feel safe in her father's presence, and although he acted less threatening today, it was her husband's nearness that put her at ease. Because he was here with her. Because he would not leave her alone to face her father. Because she trusted him.

Completely.

Safely seated beside her husband, Adelaide stared across the small table at her father.

A long sigh left his lips before he leaned forward, resting his elbows on top of his knees. He looked older than Adelaide had ever seen him, his face haggard and his eyes almost hollow. Sadness and regret clung to his features, and for a brief moment, Adelaide felt sorry for him.

Then her father inhaled a deep breath and lifted his head, his eyes finally meeting hers. For the space of a breath, father and daughter looked at one another before he once again averted his gaze, shame clouding his eyes.

Again, Adelaide felt thunderstruck. This was not the man she had grown up with. This was not the man who had intimidated her at nearly every turn of her life. This was not the man who had lost her hand in a card game. What on earth had happened to make him seem so different? Was it a ruse? Or had he truly come to understand the wrongs of his ways?

"I tried to…," he began, his gaze fixed on his hands which he held linked in front of him, "speak to…your sister." A long sigh left his lips before he lifted his head. "But she refuses to see me."

"Does this truly surprise you?" Adelaide asked, a hint of regret claiming her heart at the harshness in her voice. Of course, she had reason to mistrust him, and yet, she could not help but feel that his regret was genuine.

Her father shook his head. "No. I cannot blame her. I merely…" His eyes held hers for a moment. "I do not want to hurt her or her mother, I assure you that. Neither will I ask for their forgiveness. I only want to know what happened."

Overwhelmed by the sudden changes in her father's behaviour, Adelaide felt her mind spin. Forgiveness? Did that mean he had finally come to realise that he had done something wrong? That he ought to plead for forgiveness even though he did not deserve it?

Belatedly, Adelaide realised that her father had not only referred to Beth, but also to her mother, his first wife. Did he not know that she was dead? Perhaps not. After all, both had vanished twenty years ago and had not been heard from again.

Not until Beth had come to town after her mother's death, trying to uncover the secrets of her past.

Watching her father, Adelaide frowned when she failed to detect the usual odour of spirits on him. Even over the distance between them, she ought to have been able to smell him. But there was nothing. His eyes were reddened, and his face pale, almost greyish, but he looked more weary than inebriated. Was he sober? When was the last time that had happened?

A silent plea lay in her father's eyes, and Adelaide felt her heart respond despite her arguments to the contrary. She wondered if she would be betraying Beth's trust by telling her father what he wished to know. However, her sister had never asked her to keep her story confidential—at least not from their father—and a part of Adelaide needed to know if her father would truly show regret for what had happened, for what his actions had caused.

Sighing, Adelaide looked at her husband, grateful when he placed his hand on hers, squeezing it gently. Silent words passed between them, and Adelaide knew that he would support her no matter which path she chose.

After all, she could trust him.

If only she dared trust him with her own secret.

"Grandmother and Beth's mother planned their escape for weeks," she began, her voice hard, and yet, the eyes that looked back at her held only sorrow. "They knew the only chance they had was to put as much distance between them and you as possible. So, they chose a time when you allowed them to retreat to Beechworth Manor while remaining in town yourself…on business." An accusatory note slipped into her voice. "We both know what you were doing."

Sighing, her father nodded, his lips pressed together.

"They left everything behind," Adelaide continued, imagining what it had to have been like for Beth's mother to leave in the middle of the night, all on her own, with no one to support her, no one to help her, no one to lean on. "Her mother knew that she could not be weighed down. They had to cover as much ground as possible. She had to make certain that they would not be caught. She had to ensure that Beth would be safe from you, that she would grow up in a house without fear and pain."

Hanging his head, her father rubbed his hands over his face. Then he pushed to his feet and walked over to the window, his gaze focused on something outside.

Feeling her husband gently squeeze her hand, Adelaide inhaled a deep breath. "Luckily, they made it to a small village with good people where they were received with kindness. They found a home there, and Beth's mother managed to support them by working as a seamstress and using the money Grandmother had given them."

Her father's shoulders tensed, and his head fell forward until his chin seemed to rest on his chest. "She never said a word."

"Of course not," Adelaide snapped, unable to let go of her anger and disappointment. "Grandmother had to ensure that they would remain safe." Swallowing, she drew in a long breath. "As far as I know, they were happy there, and Beth grew up safe and sound, surrounded by people who cared about her. She was happy…at least until the day her mother died."

Spinning around, her father stared at her with wide eyes, shock stealing the last remnants of colour from his face. "Ellen is dead?"

Adelaide nodded.

"How?" he breathed, his voice barely audible as he slumped back against the window.

"Pneumonia."

Adelaide watched as her father closed his eyes, his hands gripping the backrest of the chair in front of him. The muscles in his jaw tensed to the point of breaking, and he seemed to have no strength left to hold himself upright.

"Do you truly care?" Adelaide could not help but ask. "After all, you had them declared dead with the utmost haste, so you could remarry. If you had cared, I would have expected you to look for them harder. Longer." Adelaide shook her head. "But you didn't."

Silence fell over the room, and for a long moment, the only thing that could be heard was her father's laboured breath as he fought to control the emotions that had seized him so unexpectedly. Then he finally lifted his head and looked at her. "A part of me had hoped that they were living somewhere. Safe. Every once in a while, I would picture them." Swallowing, he shook his head. "I never expected this. I knew they had gone. I never believed they had been taken. I always knew that she had left me, taking my daughter along."

Adelaide sat up straighter, her eyes not wavering from her father's. "If you cared about them, why did you treat them thus? Why did you force her to leave? You left her no other choice if she wanted to ensure her daughter's well-being."

Gritting his teeth, her father momentarily shifted his gaze to Matthew before bowing his head once more.

Adelaide knew that speaking so openly about his shortcomings was difficult for him, but if he had truly come to regret his ways, he needed to admit to what he had done wrong. Only if he was willing to feel the pain would he ever truly have a chance to change. If that was what he wanted!

Despite a small flame of hope, doubts still remained in Adelaide's heart.

"All my life," her father began, his eyes distant as he recalled his own past, "I felt such…anger in me, and I never knew how to restrain it. I fought it down, but the more I did that, the greater the outburst once I lost control." He swallowed hard. "My father died when I was very young, and I felt left alone without him, not knowing how to become the man everyone expected me to be. I did not know what to do."

For a moment, he grew quiet, thoughtful, before he blinked, and his gaze returned to Adelaide. "Is she happy?"

For a moment, Adelaide was at a loss, but then she nodded. "She is," she whispered. "She married the man she loved, and she will be a mother soon."

Her father's eyes widened slightly at the news, but then he nodded, the ghost of a smile flickering over his face. "That's good. She deserves nothing less." He inhaled a deep breath. "And you?" he asked, his gaze focusing on Adelaide's with more intensity. "Are you happy?" His eyes darted to Matthew. "In your marriage?"

Her husband's hand, which was still tightly wrapped around hers, tensed as though he was holding his breath, waiting for her answer. Adelaide sighed, allowing her father's question to wash over her. Was she happy?

Turning her head, Adelaide looked at her husband. She saw his deep green eyes looking back into hers, open and honest. She felt his hand on hers, protective but not restraining. And she remembered the many moments he had stood by her, and yet, always given her the freedom to choose.

A heartfelt smile claimed Adelaide's face, and she saw its effect reflected in her husband's eyes. "I am," she whispered, feeling his hand close more tightly around hers. Then she looked at her father. "I am happy."

Relief came to his eyes, and he nodded. "I'm glad to hear it," he replied, his voice sounding more and more strained. "I'm glad you managed to find a way to…escape my influence." His lips pressed into a thin line, and his hands tightened on the backrest in front of him.

Moments ticked by as her father fought to regain control. Then he swallowed, the hint of a smile on his face as he looked down at her. "I'm proud of you," he whispered. "You deserve to be happy." Overwhelmed, Adelaide watched as her father stepped around the chair. "I promise I will not bother you again. My presence is like poison to everyone around me, and so I will keep my distance. You have my word." He nodded to her, utter sincerity in his eyes, before he stepped toward the door without a look back.

Adelaide kept staring at the empty spot where her father had stood a moment earlier as she listened to the door open and close and then the sound of his receding footsteps. Had he truly meant what he had said? Would she now be safe from him? Was he truly relieved she had defied him?

Beside her, Matthew cleared his throat. "Are you all right?"

Absentmindedly, Adelaide nodded. "I never would have expected him to say this," she whispered, feeling as though she had strayed into a dream. Blinking, she turned to her husband. "You heard him, too, didn't you? It wasn't my imagination, was it?"

A soft smile on his face, he looked at her. "I heard him, too," he assured her, brushing a curl behind her ear. Then she felt the tips of his fingers travel down the slope of her ear before they traced along the line of her jaw. Finally, he gently grasped her chin, his green eyes meeting hers. "I'm proud of you," he whispered, a mischievous twinkle in his gaze.

Adelaide chuckled, feeling all tension fall from her. "Is that so?"

Her husband nodded, his gaze studying her face. Then he leaned closer and placed a gentle kiss on her lips.

Looking up at him, Adelaide smiled. "I must admit you seemed prouder before."

At her teasing, he laughed and then pulled her into his arms, kissing her soundly.

Surrendering to his warm embrace, Adelaide wondered what had brought on her father's change of heart. What had made him face his past? Admit his wrongdoings?

And more than before, Adelaide wondered if she ought to confront her own past as well. Speak truthfully and accept the consequences…however much they would cost her.

Was not that the right thing to do?

The only way to find peace?

31

PAST DEMONS

Over the next two days, Matthew watched his wife wander the house with a blank expression on her face. Almost like a ghost. He knew that the encounter with her father had left its mark, and it would take time for Adelaide to think everything through and make her peace with it.

Still, Matthew worried.

"Are you all right?" he asked as they sat together in the library, each a book in their hands. Still, his wife's gaze had been unfocused, blindly staring into the distance, and she had not turned a page in a long while.

Then again, neither had he…as he had been too busy watching his wife.

Blinking, she turned her pale blue eyes to him. "Pardon?"

"Are you all right?" he asked, closing his book and putting it aside. Then he leaned forward in his chair and placed a hand on hers. "Is it your father?"

A long sigh left her lips. "I've never seen him like that. Never have I heard him utter regret about how he treated us or even acknowledge that he did." Shaking her head, she set her book on the small table next to her. "Was it my sister's return that brought forth this change?"

"Possibly," Matthew said, nodding to her. "However, do not discount the way you spoke to him. It was all too visible on his face how shocked he was to hear what you had to say, to hear you speak to him so honestly. Now, he finally knows—beyond the shadow of a doubt—how his actions affected you and the rest of your family, how they made you feel. Perhaps he truly had not been aware of or had ignored that realisation because deep down he knew how it would affect him."

Adelaide swallowed. "He looked almost devastated," she mumbled, her eyes distant as she recalled the scene in his study two days prior. "As though he was ready to give up."

Squeezing his wife's hand, Matthew smiled at her when she turned to look at him. "How do you feel about all this?"

Shrugging, she sighed. "I cannot say. Mostly, I feel drained, exhausted…and sad. All this is so sad."

Matthew nodded. "It is." Inhaling a deep breath, he swallowed. "It's not easy facing one's parent, but you stood your ground, and I'm proud of you."

A gentle smile danced across her face; however, her tone remained serious. "How did you feel when you realised the truth about your father, about his nature?"

Despite having expected this question, Matthew felt himself returned to the darkest moments of his life. It seemed like an eternity had passed since then, and as he glanced around the room, his wife by his side as they sat comfortably by the large window front, sunlight spilling inside and birds singing outside, Matthew wondered if it had all been a mere nightmare. Nothing remained of that dark place that had once been his life. From the moment his wife had set foot over the threshold to this house, everything had changed. Life and happiness had returned.

"To tell you the truth," he finally said, "I was devastated. My world was turned upside down, and yet, a part of me felt that I should have known. I felt regret and guilt, and, yes, sadness, grief…utter grief." He shook his head. "All my life I dreamed of having a family to feel safe in and be able to rely on." He scoffed, "Don't we all? Well, I wanted it so much that it…it blinded me to the truth. Only when my father revealed his true nature, only when there was no longer any chance of explaining his actions in a rational way, only then was I able to accept that he was not the man I had wanted him to be."

"You're right," his wife whispered, her eyes gentle as she placed her other hand on his. "We all want a family. We want to feel safe and be loved. There is no shame in that longing. No one can blame you for wanting to see the good in him."

Matthew inhaled a shuddering breath. In a strange way, her words of comfort brought on even more guilt. "I don't know if that is true," he admitted, head bowed. "My unwillingness to see him for who he truly was almost got my cousin killed. His life was at stake, and still I was willing to follow my father's lead."

Her hand squeezed his, and he looked up, meeting her pale blue eyes. "From what I heard," Adelaide said, "both of your lives were at stake, and the moment you realised that your father was serious about risking the both of you, you stepped in his way." A proud smile came to her lovely face. "You risked your life to protect your cousin. You proved yourself to be the kind of family we all dream of. You're a man who stands by his family no matter what. You'd risk your life to save…them. There is no shame in that. You should be proud."

Matthew's heart swelled with warmth at her words, at the way she looked at him, at the slight pause before she had uttered the word *them* as though asking whether or not he thought of her as family as well. How could she not know? How could she not see that she was everything to him? "You're right," Matthew whispered, unable to look anywhere but into her gentle eyes. "I would give my life to protect my family. You, Tillie, my mother, Tristan and Beth. We belong together, and we look after one another as it should be."

Tears came to her eyes as she nodded her head. "As it should be."

"Indeed," Matthew agreed, awed by the silent bond that grew between them. "My only regret is that my father never came to see the error of his ways. A part of me still wishes he had come to realise the truth before he died. Still, I cannot mourn his loss for I know now how poisonous his presence has been to this family. Ever since he's been gone, our family seems to be reawakening, and joy has finally returned to this house. It was a tomb for so long, too long, but now it is no longer. You and Tillie have brought life back into this place, and for that alone, I will forever be grateful to you."

A shy smile flashed across her face, and she briefly averted her gaze. "Do you think I ought to have spoken to my father sooner? Do you think it would have made a difference?" Her blue eyes found his once more. "I keep thinking if I had said something sooner, perhaps the past few years could have been avoided."

Matthew shook his head. "The one thing my father taught me is that you cannot change people if they don't want to change. He was never willing, not even at the very end. Even then he'd rather cling to his anger than admit that he might have been wrong." Inhaling a deep breath, Matthew held her gaze, hoping she would believe him and not blame herself. He knew only too well how painful that was. "Things unfold in their own time. I don't believe that you could have swayed him before he was ready. Only now when everything came together—your sister's return, the circumstances of your wedding, Tillie's removal from the household—was it enough for him to finally see through the haze he had been hiding behind. He seems to slowly come to see the truth behind it all."

Holding his wife's gaze, Matthew allowed silence to fall over them as he reminded himself that there was still something left unspoken between them. Everything had turned out so promising if only she would tell him her secret. Then they could finally move forward.

For good.

"We are family," Matthew finally said, "and that will never change. No matter what."

Her gaze narrowed slightly, and he could see that she was taking note of the underlying meaning of his words. Then she suddenly stilled, and her eyes widened. Her hands tensed, and almost imperceptibly she leaned back…away from him.

"Why can you not tell me?" Matthew asked, trying to put as much reassurance in his voice as he could. "I promise there is nothing that would make me turn from you. For years, I've watched you from afar, dreaming of…of…this. And now that I have you here with me, I will not do anything that might risk what we have. I have made mistakes in the past, yes, but I'm not a fool."

Tears began misting her eyes as she looked at him, the hint of a smile playing on her lips as though his words pleased her. Her mouth opened, and Matthew could see the desire to speak in her eyes. Still, a moment later, she shot to her feet and rushed from the library.

Closing his eyes, Matthew fell back in his seat. For the millionth time, he wondered what could be so awful that she even now felt the need to hide it? Did she truly doubt him? Doubt his love for her?

Sitting up, Matthew suddenly realised that in truth he had never once spoken of love, had he? In his heart, he had known for a while although it had taken him some time to even admit it to himself. He had been too afraid to have his heart broken should she not return his feelings. But she did, did she not? Was it not all in the way she sometimes looked at him, the way she now finally stood tall and held his gaze, the way she had responded to his kiss? Or could he be mistaken? Did her heart belong to another—to Bartholomew! —and she did not dare share this with him?

Indeed, if that was the case, then she was right. It was a truth, he could not live with. And yet, he would have to. After all, he had married her, and there was no changing that. He had given his word, and he would not break it. No matter what, he would always protect her. Still, if she loved another, he could not continue living here with her. It would eat him up inside until there was nothing left of him but pain and regret.

And yet, was not knowing better? Was it less painful? Or more, as now there was still hope? After all, was not disappointed hope the worst pain there was? When something seemed to be within one's grasp only to have it snatched away?

A knock sounded on the half-open door, and Matthew flinched.

"Do you mind if I come in?" his mother asked, stepping inside, her eyes watchful as they flew over his face. "Are you all right?"

Clearing his throat, Matthew rose to his feet, forcing a polite mask on his face. "I'm fine, Mother. What can I do for you?"

Her brows rose. "A moment ago, your wife rushed up the stairs and headed straight for her chamber. She seemed rather out of sorts, to say the least."

Matthew swallowed, willing his shoulders not to slump. "It's nothing. She'll be fine."

Taking a step closer, his mother put a hand on his arm, her pale eyes holding his. "I can see that you're lying," she said, a touch of humour in her voice. "Don't look so shocked. I'm your mother. I've known you your whole life. Now, tell me what's going on!"

For a moment, Matthew stared at his mother. Never had she spoken to him thus. Always had she been so quiet and inconspicuous. She truly had changed since his father's passing. Life had reclaimed her, and it did her good, judging from the strength that shone in her eyes.

"Perhaps I can help," she urged when he continued to remain silent.

"I doubt it."

"Please."

Sighing, Matthew nodded. "All right, even though there isn't much I can tell you as I don't know myself." A slight frown came to his mother's face. "She has a secret, and she refuses to share it with me."

"A secret?" his mother repeated, her gaze veering from his for a split second. "How do you know if she never told you?"

"I don't know what it is, but she admitted that she has one." The last words sounded like a strangled growl, and Matthew drew in a deep breath, trying to hold his frustration at bay. Strangely enough, he realised that it had been a while since he had been out boxing. Life had changed, and he had rarely felt the need to relieve tension through physical exhaustion.

Life was good.

Almost perfect.

Almost.

"You need to be patient with her," his mother counselled. "Like yourself, your wife has past demons to battle with, and you need to let her do so in her own time…as difficult as it may be for you."

Balling his hands into fists, Matthew nodded. He knew his mother to be right, and yet, he felt his own strength slipping away as doubt ate at it. Not knowing–but imagining! –slowly drove him mad!

"Take strength from knowing that she loves you," his mother said gently, her eyes shining as she looked at him.

Matthew felt as though she had punched him in the stomach. The air rushed from his lungs, and all he could do was stammer, "D-did she t-tell you so?"

Smiling, his mother shook her head. "Of course not. In my experience, the two people most concerned in these matters are generally the last to know." Chuckling, she patted his arm. "Be patient, my son. Everything will be well."

Listening to the sound of his mother's receding footsteps and then the door closing quietly, Matthew stood staring at something on the opposite wall.

She loved him!

Could this be true? Or was his mother wrong? If Adelaide had not said so herself, then his mother could not be certain. And yet, she had seemed certain.

Inhaling a shuddering breath, Matthew sank back into the armchair he had vacated upon his mother's entrance. If only he knew!

32

DAUGHTER MINE

acing the length of her bedchamber, all Adelaide could see in her mind were her husband's kind eyes as they had looked into hers, pleading with her to speak honestly, to confide in him, to share her secret.

Adelaide knew she ought to have told him. And yet, she had not. Fear had all but paralysed her, making it impossible for her to utter a single word.

Fear had always been such a big part of her life that it felt almost natural to allow it to make decisions for her. All her life, Adelaide had done her best to avoid things that made her fearful as they generally proved devastating. All her life, she had done her best to avoid her father, to avoid angering him, to avoid even being noticed for fear of what the consequences might have been. For whenever there had been consequences, they had never been good.

Always had they been devastating.

Always.

Sighing, Adelaide sank onto her bed, her heart aching with such acuteness that she feared it might stop beating. Her husband's kind smile once more drifted before her inner eye, and the sight almost made her topple over in pain.

Always had he been there to protect her—even when they had not yet known each other. Always had he been patient and kind. Always had he urged her to speak her mind. More than anyone else he deserved her trust. But if she gave it, would such a risk be rewarded? Would he forgive her, and would their relationship grow ever closer? Or would he be unable to forget what she had done? Would she and Tillie lose the little family they had only just found?

Perhaps he would send her away to the country, unwilling to lay eyes on her ever again. Once, that would have seemed like a desirable outcome. Away from her husband. Alone. Safe.

Now, however, Adelaide could not imagine being without him. His presence had become essential to her happiness. She no longer feared *him*. What she now feared was losing him.

What if he divorced her? Never had she known anyone to suffer such consequences, but one never knew!

Out of habit, Adelaide's mind conjured the worst consequences it could find in order to prepare her for what might lie ahead. She had done so all her life, and her imagination had rarely fallen short of the truth. Was there truly a limit to the consequences that could be thrust upon one?

A soft knock sounded on the door, and before Adelaide could utter a word, the door opened, and her mother-in-law stepped inside.

Almost jumping off the bed, Adelaide stepped toward the window, her back to her husband's mother, and quickly brushed the tears off her cheeks. Then she drew in a deep breath and tried to smile as she turned back to face her mother-in-law.

"I can see that you are upset, dear," Clara said, a gentle smile on her face as she crossed the room. "I just spoke to my son, and he looked about as miserable as you do."

A sob escaped Adelaide's lips, and she clamped her mouth shut. "I'm sorry," she whispered, no strength in her voice, as fresh tears began to fall. "I never meant to hurt him. He has always been so good to me and deserves better."

"He does," his mother confirmed, but her eyes held humour, "but so do you." Placing a hand on Adelaide's arm, she looked at her. "He told me that you have a secret that you refuse to share with him."

Overwhelmed, Adelaide closed her eyes. "He's right. I…I'm afraid if I tell him, it will destroy us, destroy what is between us." Turning pleading eyes to her mother-in-law, Adelaide grasped the woman's hands. "I cannot lose him. I cannot."

Smiling, Clara brushed a tear from Adelaide's cheek. "My son loves you, and there is very little you can do to change that. You're a wonderful wife to him, and I'm grateful that he married you. You're good for each other."

Warmth flooded Adelaide's heart as she looked at Clara through a curtain of tears. "Do you truly believe so? But…I…" Wiping her hands over her face, Adelaide stepped around her mother-in-law, certain the woman would not have said what she had if she knew her secret. In all likelihood, Clara would curse the day her son had married her, no longer thinking her worthy of him.

"It's Tillie, isn't it?" her mother-in-law asked from behind her.

Adelaide froze, cold sweat breaking out on her forehead.

"She's yours, isn't she?"

Spinning around, Adelaide stared at her mother-in-law as panic crawled up her spine. "How…? How do you…? Who told…?"

Smiling, Clara stepped toward her, her warm hands wrapping gently around Adelaide's chilled ones. "No one told me," she whispered, her eyes still gentle, far from what Adelaide had expected. "You look at that precious little girl as only a mother would. Perhaps it is something only a mother can recognise. It's a bond. A bond that only exists if a woman sees herself as a child's mother." Smiling, she squeezed Adelaide's hands. "You've always been careful not to act as

Tillie's mother as though if you did, others might see the truth. She's yours."

With tears streaming down her face, Adelaide nodded. "She is. She's mine." A jolt of triumph went through her heart at that proclamation, and Adelaide realised how painful it had been to pretend to merely be Tillie's aunt and not claim the girl as her own daughter. "But I cannot tell him. He…he would never forgive me. He would send Tillie away, and I cannot be without her…or without him."

"Of course, you can't," Clara scoffed as though such a notion was ridiculous. "She's your daughter. She belongs with you." Inhaling a deep breath, Clara once more wiped the tears from Adelaide's face. "Listen to me. My son is a good man, and he loves you. He loves Tillie. What you fear he might do does not stem from your knowledge of him but is born out of fear alone." A cloud seemed to descend on Clara's face. "Believe me, I know how you feel, always expecting the worst, always preparing yourself for it. It's a way of thinking that has helped you in the past, but your life is different now. Now, such thinking will only hurt you, will keep you from being happy. You need to find a way to let it go and begin anew."

Adelaide looked at her mother-in-law, and for a moment, she saw herself. A woman who had spent her life in fear, always bowing her head and cowering in a corner. But now, here, in this moment, Clara stood tall, her eyes were bright and her voice strong. She had returned from the shadows, reclaiming her place in the sun.

"My son loves you," Clara said with vehemence, "and although he might not be overjoyed to hear the truth, he would not allow it to stand in the way to your happiness." She sighed. "Does Tillie's father—whoever he is—still holds your heart?"

As though struck, Adelaide shook her head. "No. He never did. It was just…"

"Then you have nothing to fear. All will be well…as soon as you tell my son the truth. He would be a fool to let you go, and I swear to you he is not. Have faith."

Earlier that day, her husband had spoken those same words to her, and Adelaide wondered if indeed they could be true. Was it only her fear holding her back? Her fear that clouded her judgement?

"Think about it," Clara urged. "But not too long. Don't waste time in fear, not when you have such a wonderful family waiting for you."

"Thank you, Clara," Adelaide sighed. "Thank you for everything."

"Of course, dear. Any mother would see to her child's happiness no matter how old they are." A soft chuckle left her lips. "You'll see that soon enough. Whether Tillie is two or two-and-twenty, she'll always be your little girl. That never changes."

Squeezing Adelaide's hand one last time, Clara left her to her thoughts.

For a moment, Adelaide continued to pace the room before she came to stand by the window, gazing out at the garden where Tillie and her husband were watching a little robin hopping from branch to branch.

Her family, Adelaide thought.

All she needed was the courage to claim it.

33

CHILDHOOD FRIENDS

ays passed, and Matthew felt as though his wife was trying to work up the courage to speak to him. He suspected his mother had spoken to her—although she refused to provide him with any details on the matter, insisting he be patient and listen with his heart and not his ego once his wife was ready to confide in him. What on earth did that even mean?

Still, as much as Matthew tried to be patient, he could feel his heart thudding wildly in his chest and his hands ball into fists when he spotted no other than Joseph Bartholomew the next night at a society ball. The almost desperate need to punch him was overwhelming…and yet, Matthew did not even know for sure whether or not the man had anything to do with his wife's secret.

What was undoubtedly clear was the interest Bartholomew had in Adelaide.

The moment the man stepped into the ballroom, his gaze found her almost unerringly, and he continued to watch her for the next hour. Then he ventured over to greet them and asked Adelaide for a dance. Nervously, she glanced at Matthew before Bartholomew drew her onto the dance floor without bothering to wait for her answer.

Forcing his feet to remain where they were, Matthew seethed in silence, once again battling the overwhelming need to strike the man down. Never before in his life had he felt anything akin to the jealousy that now burnt in his heart.

But he held himself back.

If she refused to share her secret with him, then perhaps he could glean an insight by observing her, observing them.

When the dance came to an end, Bartholomew directed her not back to Matthew but toward the refreshment table, offering her a drink. All the while, his gaze never strayed from her, lingering in places that had Matthew's head red-hot in moments.

The only thing that held him in place was the clear fact that his wife looked rather ill at ease. She did not encourage Bartholomew's attention and seemed rather uncomfortable by his insistence to remain by her side.

After a few more words were spoken, she finally took her leave and strode across the ballroom back to Matthew's side. Still, her gaze barely dared meet his.

"Are you all right?" Matthew asked through gritted teeth, reminding himself that whatever might have been between her and Bartholomew once, it was now clear that that was of the past. At least as far as his wife was concerned.

Before she could answer his question though, Bartholomew stepped up to them, once more greeting Matthew as though they were the greatest of friends. "It is good to see you here tonight," he observed, glancing around the room. "I admit these events no longer hold such fascination for me." Then he cleared his throat and turned his gaze back to Adelaide. "Have you spoken to your brother recently? How is he?"

Adelaide swallowed. "He is well," was all she said.

Matthew frowned. Had he not spotted Adelaide's brother among the guests earlier tonight?

Scanning the crowd, Matthew found him standing across the room, a drink in his hand and his eyes narrowed into slits as he stared at them. There was something dark in the man's eyes, and Matthew got the distinct feeling that the hatred he saw there was directed at Bartholomew.

"He is right over there," Matthew offered, nodding in the direction of his brother-in-law. "Perhaps you should ask him yourself. I suppose he should have the answers you seek."

Not even bothering to look over his shoulder, Bartholomew nodded. "I might do that," he mumbled, then took his leave and walked away…

…in the opposite direction to where John stood glaring at him.

"Their relationship seems to be strained," Matthew observed glancing from his brother-in-law to his wife. "Did he not say they were childhood friends?"

Averting her eyes, Adelaide nodded. "He did. However, I think they haven't seen each other in a while."

"All the more reason to catch up," Matthew suggested, noting the way his wife's fingers played with the edge of her glove. She seemed uncomfortable once more, and Matthew got the distinct feeling that not only her father but also her brother knew what had happened between her and Bartholomew. Was this the secret she kept from him? An affair? Not ongoing, but of the past? Had Bartholomew ruined Adelaide? If so, why had they not married? Would her father and brother not have insisted upon it?

With his mind still reeling, Matthew suddenly realised that the spot where his brother-in-law had been standing until only moments ago was now empty. Instead, John was striding toward them, his eyes hard and glaring, fixed on his sister.

Instantly, Matthew's feelings toward his wife softened, and he gently pulled her hand through the crook of his arm. "Good to see you tonight," he greeted his brother-in-law, his tone polite but insistent, hoping to discourage the man from displaying the emotions that rested in his eyes openly.

John merely nodded to him before his glare turned to Adelaide. "What have you done?" he demanded. "Are you seeking to destroy him?"

Frowning, Adelaide shook her head. "I don't know what you mean." Her gaze darted to the direction in which Bartholomew had left.

"Don't play dumb!" her brother hissed under his breath, the liquid in his glass sloshing up the sides as he gestured wildly.

Taking a step forward, Matthew fixed his brother-in-law with a warning glare. "I suggest you watch your manners!"

For a moment, John glared at him before he inhaled a deep breath and his demeanour changed, became less threatening. "Ever since he called on you, Father has locked himself in his study. He's not himself. It's gotten worse in the past sennight." Brows drawn down, John shook his head, confusion and something akin to concern in his eyes. "He keeps sending letters—to whom I cannot say—which return unopened and unanswered. This—whatever it is—will send him into a depression."

Adelaide inhaled a deep breath before her eyes rose to meet Matthew's. "He is writing to Beth," she whispered, her hand tightening on his arm for comfort.

Matthew nodded, feeling his heart jump at the familiarity between them. As much as he did not know about her, there were some things—personal things—she had shared with him, trusted him with. He was not an outsider to her life as he sometimes feared when her secret loomed in front of him, large and threatening.

No, there was something between them. It had not merely been his imagination.

"Who is Beth?" John demanded, eyes narrowed into slits. "His mistress? I thought I knew them all."

Adelaide's lips thinned, and her eyes narrowed as she took a step toward her brother, her posture more self-assured than a moment before. John seemed to notice it as well as his gaze narrowed further, and his eyes swept over her face as though looking for answers.

"She is not his mistress," Adelaide said, her voice low but firm. "We should talk about this in private. Will you call on me tomorrow?"

Taking a step back, her brother shook his head. "I don't care what you have to say at this point. Simply go and speak to Father and apologise for whatever you did." For a weighted moment, his gaze held hers. "It's the least you owe me." Then he turned around and walked away.

Beside him, Adelaide sighed, and her shoulders slumped. "He will not come," she mumbled, regret heavy in her voice.

"Then you should go see him," Matthew suggested, hoping that once she had sorted everything out with her family, she might find the peace of mind she needed to speak to him. "I will accompany you to ensure your safety."

A small smile came to Adelaide's lips as she looked up at him, and from one moment to the next, Matthew felt reminded of the day her father had called on her, the day he had pulled her into his arms for a kiss, the day she had kissed him back. "I'm not afraid of him," she said, not only relief but also certainty in her voice. "I need to do this alone, but I thank you for your kindness. You always look out for me. Always." Tears misted her eyes as she held his gaze and her right hand came to rest on his chest, covering his thudding heart. "I feel safe with you."

Returning her smile, Matthew closed his own hand over hers. If only they could always be this close.

34

ONCE UPON A TIME

tepping out of the carriage, Adelaide looked up at the tall townhouse that had been her home for as long as she could remember. Now, as she climbed the stairs to the front door, she could not imagine ever coming back here. Nothing drew her to her past. Nothing but the family inside.

As though they had known of her arrival, the door opened, and her mother and grandmother stepped out, opening their umbrellas to shield themselves from the bright morning sun.

"Adelaide!" they exclaimed, drawing her into their arms. "How wonderful to see you!"

"Is everything all right?" her mother asked, a touch of concern in her eyes as she glanced behind her daughter at the waiting carriage. "Is your husband here as well?"

"No, I came alone," Adelaide replied, feeling a stab of guilt. While her own marriage had freed Adelaide, her mother's had put her in chains, tying her to this house and the man inside.

"Will you accompany us?" her grandmother asked, gesturing down the street. "It is such a beautiful day, and we haven't seen you in quite some time."

Adelaide smiled, seeing the teasing joy in her grandmother's eyes. While her mother was governed by the same fear that had ruled Adelaide's life for so long, her grandmother did not miss the signs of peace on her granddaughter's face, in the way she spoke and move, the way she held her head and met their eyes.

Much had changed, and Adelaide realised it only now when it was as though a mirror was held up in front of her. Indeed, she was no longer the young woman who had once lived here.

"I wish I could, but I've come to see John. Is he in?"

The women's faces darkened. "He is still abed at this hour," her mother replied, "which is nothing unusual as you know."

Adelaide nodded.

"Go and knock some sense into him," her grandmother urged, a touch of triumph in her voice as she all but grinned at Adelaide. "It'll do him some good."

Squeezing her grandmother's hand, Adelaide smiled. "Thank you for everything." Then she stepped aside and allowed them to pass, waving at them once they had reached the pavement. "Enjoy yourselves."

For a moment, Adelaide remained where she was, breathing in the fresh morning air, no longer chilled but already warmed by the sun. Then she turned and braced herself for what lay ahead. She stepped over the threshold without a moment of hesitation and fought to shake off the sense of old familiarity that clawed at her, threatening to rob her of the ease she generally felt these days.

Holding her head high, Adelaide made for the large staircase, determined not to let anything get in her way. Her feet carried her higher and higher until she turned down the corridor that led to her brother's chamber. Stopping in front of the door, she inhaled a deep breath, squared her shoulders and knocked.

After her fourth, more vehement knock, a clearly ill-tempered voice called through the door, "Go away!"

Unimpressed, Adelaide pushed down the handle and strode forward, the stale, liquor-filled air assaulting her senses the moment she stepped over the threshold. Clearing her throat, she pulled back the curtains and threw open a window. "John, how can you sleep here? The air is suffocating!"

A tortured groan rose from the bed as her brother yanked the blanket over his head. "What's gotten into you? Are you mad? Close the curtains!"

"It's almost noon."

"Why should I care?"

"Get up!"

Pulling the blanket down, he sat up, squinting his eyes at the bright light flooding his room. "You're not acting like yourself," he grumbled, rubbing a hand over his face. "What's wrong with you?"

Adelaide chuckled. She actually chuckled! "Nothing is wrong. I'd say it was about time things changed, about time I changed." Sighing, she smiled, feeling more at ease than she ever had in this house. Then she stepped toward the bed. "I'm here to talk to you."

"Fine," John snapped. "Then talk!" Finally, rising from the bed, he pulled on a robe.

"Last night, you asked me who Beth is," Adelaide began, her eyes trained on her brother as she wondered how he would react to such news. "Well, as I said she is not Father's mistress." Inhaling a deep breath, she said, "She's his daughter."

For a moment, John simply stared at her before his jaw dropped open. "What? Daughter?" Shaking his head, he staggered toward her but halted his steps when he began to sway more. "I didn't know any of his mistresses ever had a child."

"She is not the child of a mistress," Adelaide corrected. "You know that Father was married once before."

Her brother nodded, his gaze narrowing. "But they died."

"They did not," Adelaide corrected once more. "They ran away because her mother wanted to see her safe."

"Safe?" John croaked. "Safe from what?" Raking his hands through his hair, he stared at her. "What you say makes no sense!"

"Safe from Father," Adelaide said, reminding herself that her brother had a right to be shocked. Such news was not easily received as she knew from personal experience. "Her mother feared that he would strike Beth, and so they fled…with grandmother's help."

"She knew?" John all but bellowed. Sinking back onto the bed, he heaved one long breath after another into his body as he stared at the floor. Then he blinked, and his eyes rose to meet hers. "We're illegitimate," he whispered, all colour draining from his face. "Bastards. The title, the fortune…everything. I…I cannot inherit."

Stepping forward, Adelaide knelt by her brother, drawing his trembling hands into her own as she looked up to meet his eyes. "No one knows," she whispered, "and no one will know." A soft chuckle rose from her throat. "Unless you cannot keep your mouth shut."

Again, John blinked, looking at her as though she had grown another head. "You've changed, Addy," he whispered. "I haven't seen you like this in a long time."

Adelaide sighed, "You haven't called me that in a long time, either."

"It didn't seem fitting any longer."

Adelaide nodded. "I know." Remembering how close they had been during their early childhood, Adelaide held his hands tighter. "Beth did not come here because she wants to reveal who she is or to claim her inheritance. She came to find her family. It's something we've lost sight of over the years. We've only been concerned about money and connections, marrying well and upholding our family's reputation." Blinking back tears, she scoffed, "And what good has it done us? Are we happy? Are you?"

For a moment, she thought to see a slight quiver in his jaw, and her heart had hope. But then his face hardened, and he pushed to his feet, yanking his hands from hers. "I know what you're saying," he hissed, pain and accusation in his voice, "but Father and I are not the only ones who've made mistakes. What makes you different is not that you've made none yourself, but simply that you've managed to hold on to your reputation while making them." He spun to look at her. "You're no better than we are. You might recall that I was the one who helped you when you didn't know what to do. It was me who protected you."

Feeling the pull of her past, Adelaide knew that she could not ask her brother to face his mistakes if she was not willing to do the same. "You're right," she whispered, slowly rising to her feet and meeting his gaze. "You saved me, protected me. Me and Tillie. You were there when I needed you." She inhaled a deep breath. "That one time you were."

Pain stood in his blue eyes as he looked at her. Pain and regret, and for a moment, Adelaide felt reminded of the little boy he had once been.

"We've grown apart," she said, stepping toward him, "and it is as much my fault as it is yours. You are my big brother, but not by much. I expected too much from you, and I'm sorry. Father affected you as much as he affected me, and so we've become the people we are today." Reaching for his hands, she pulled them back into her own. "But we don't have to be them anymore. We can make our own decisions. That's what I came to talk to you about." A small smile came to her face. "Father knows."

John's face paled even further. "About Beth?"

Adelaide nodded. "I believe her return and the truth about why her mother took her away is the reason for the changes in his behaviour. I never thought I'd ever see this day, but I believe he might actually be realising the wrongs of his past, how his actions have ruined our family…not our reputation, but our happiness. I believe that's what's on his mind lately. I believe that's why he is so different now. He is filled with regret and shame."

Clearing his throat, John dropped his gaze, trying to step back, but Adelaide held on.

"Don't run from me," she told him, looking back into his wide eyes. "I'm your sister, and I will help you as you've helped me. All your life, you've followed in Father's footsteps, wrongly believing that that was the way to become a man to be reckoned with. But you were wrong, and I think a part of you already knows that. This path is not leading you anywhere good. If you continue to follow it, you'll end up like Father. For him, I believe it is too late to make amends. He has done too much to us to regain our love and trust. Our respect." She sighed, her gaze holding her brother's, willing him to truly hear what she was saying. "Some things cannot be fixed."

This time, John did not look away. His gaze held pain, but it was thoughtful, and Adelaide had hope that her words would find a way into his heart and mind. That he would listen. That he would heed her advice. For the thought of him ending like their father broke her heart. "Ask yourself," she continued when it seemed that he would not run from her, "what kind of man you are and what kind of man you want to be."

Her brother blinked, and then he swallowed hard, his features slackening.

Adelaide placed a gentle hand on his arm. "What do you want? Do you want to be feared? Do you want to be loved? Ask yourself that. Love and devotion and loyalty are never born out of fear." She swallowed, forcing the next words from her lips. "I've seen the way you treat the servants, the way you chase after women, the way you believe you are entitled to do whatever you wish. You completely disregard everyone's feelings, only looking after yourself."

The arm under her hand tensed, and John's jaw clenched. Still, he stayed where he was, his gaze never leaving hers. And yet, there was a new pain in his blue gaze, confirming her words.

"I know who you are, who you used to be," Adelaide told him, "and I know who you could be. But the question is, what do you want? Who do you want to be? For if you choose this path, you'll find yourself alone…like Father now. Only for you, it is not too late yet. You can still turn back and choose a different path, and I will help you. Do not become a man like him. Please! I know how hard it is. I always thought I'd live a life like mother's. But now," she sighed, feeling a gentle smile curling up the corners of her lips, "everything is different. I'm no longer the woman I was, the woman I feared I'd be. I am happy, and you can be, too."

For a moment, he returned her smile, and she could see in his eyes that he was pleased to see her happy. Then his features sobered, and he rubbed his hands over his face, his eyes darting about the room as though he did not know where to begin.

Adelaide was surprised to see him so calm. She would have expected him to yell at her, to shout as he had always done, just like their father. Perhaps a part of him had already suspected the error of his ways and was now urging him to listen.

Adelaide could only hope that he would comply.

Looking up, John met her eyes. "I saw Bart following you," he said, and Adelaide sucked in a sharp breath. "He's watching you, always near you. What does he want?"

Sighing, Adelaide shrugged. "I do not know. He is always polite, and yet, his words hint at…" Her voice trailed off, and she met her brother's eyes.

John nodded. "I see." His voice sounded strained, laced with anger. "Has he threatened you?"

Adelaide shook her head. "No, not at all. He's simply always around, seeking me out. I don't know what his intentions are, or if he even knows about Tillie."

"You never told him?"

"Of course not."

"Good." Inhaling a deep breath, her brother reached for her hands. "Does your husband know?"

Tears came to Adelaide's eyes. "I know I should tell him, but I'm afraid." A tear rolled down her cheek, and she felt her voice choking up. "I love him, and I love the life we've made for ourselves. I wake up happy in the morning, and the thought of losing that, of losing him is devastating to me." Sniffling, Adelaide hung her head. "I know I should tell him, but every time I try I…"

Gently, John pulled her into his arms. "I know," he mumbled into her hair, his hand rubbing small circles over her back. "I know you're afraid, but you must tell him. You'll never be free of your past if you don't." Stepping back, he lifted her chin and looked at her, the hint of a smirk on his face. "I promise that if he should decide to act like a fool, I'll set him straight."

Returning his smile, Adelaide hugged her brother tightly, unable to remember when they had last held each other like this.

35

A REVELATION LONG AWAITED

Unable to sleep, Adelaide rose early the next morning.

All night, her thoughts had been occupied with only one question: how to tell her husband the truth. Still, even after hours of lying awake, turning and tossing and screaming into her pillow, Adelaide was no closer to a solution, a way that would make him understand how much he meant to her and how truly sorry she was.

Rising before the sun did, Adelaide dressed and wandered the house, hoping the silence would settle her nerves. On her way downstairs, she stopped by the nursery and looked in on Tillie. The little girl's wild curls lay strewn about her pillow, her little mouth slightly open as she slept peacefully.

Adelaide could only hope that Tillie would not have to suffer.

She could only hope that—

"Are you all right?"

Spinning around, Adelaide stared at her husband.

Leisurely dressed, he stood in the door frame, his green eyes shining in the dim light of her candle as he looked at her with concern on his face. For a moment, his gaze shifted to Tillie, and a soft smile drew up the corners of his mouth. Then his attention shifted back to her. "Are you all right?" he asked once more as he stepped into the room and towards her.

Adelaide drew in a shuddering breath, her insides twisting and turning painfully. This was it! "I'm surprised to see you up," she whispered, trying to find her voice.

"I heard you stir." His eyes roamed her face as though trying to see into her mind. "It seems you had a sleepless night."

"You heard that?" Adelaide asked, momentarily taken aback by how much attention he paid her.

A small smile danced over his face. "Your chamber is right next to mine," he whispered, a hint of mischief in his eyes.

Adelaide inhaled a slow breath, remembering the two times he had crossed the threshold into her chamber. "I…I need to…tell you something. I couldn't sleep. I…"

For a moment, he held her gaze. Then he nodded and reached for her hand. "Come," he whispered and gently led her from the room, closing the door quietly. In silence, they walked down the stairs and into the drawing room. Once again, he closed the door behind them. Then he took the candle from her and lit others around the room, casting a warm glow over them.

Setting the candle on the mantle, he then turned to look at her, his green eyes sparkling in the dim light. "No matter what your secret is," he whispered, striding toward her, his gaze never leaving hers, "I promise you that it will not be the end of us."

Blinking back tears, Adelaide tried to smile, tried to honour his effort to put her at ease. "It is very noble of you to say that. However, you cannot promise how you will feel once you know. I wish you could, and I need you to be honest. Even if…" Her voice hitched, and she had to draw in a calming breath. "Even if you find yourself unable to care for me any longer. Please never lie to me. Not about that."

Sighing, her husband nodded; yet, the look in his gaze spoke of a determined mind. His green eyes grew in intensity as they held hers, and then the muscles in his jaw tightened as though he had just come to a decision.

In the next instant, he shot forward. His arms reached for her, pulling her against him, and his mouth claimed hers in a passionate kiss.

Adelaide gasped in surprise, and yet, her body immediately responded to his caress. She sank into his arms, welcoming the promise that lay in his touch, and her heart rejoiced.

Perhaps…

"I love you," her husband whispered against her lips, "and I want you to believe me when I say that nothing can change that." Again, he kissed her, proving his point, urging her to trust him. "Whatever you have to tell me, we will find a way." Gazing down into her eyes, he nodded, his arms still holding her as though he was the one afraid to lose what they had.

Smiling, Adelaide sighed, feeling hope budding in her chest.

Taking her hands, Matthew led her to the settee, and they sat down together, his hands still linked with hers. "Tell me," he whispered, and despite his brave face, Adelaide could see the tension that rested in his eyes.

Having concluded that there was no way of telling him that would cushion the blow, Adelaide straightened, lifted her gaze to his and then simply said, "It's Tillie. She's mine."

For a moment, her husband's eyes simply remained on hers. Then he blinked, and a slight frown came to his face. "She's yours?" he mumbled before his eyes suddenly widened. "Your daughter?"

Feeling his muscles stiffen, Adelaide gritted her teeth as panic welled up in her heart. "Yes, she's my daughter."

"But…?" Confusion clouded his eyes as he sought to make sense of what she had just shared with him. "But I thought she was your brother's child. How…?" He swallowed.

"He claimed her as his," Adelaide rushed to explain, fearing the direction his thoughts might travel if she hesitated, "so that I wouldn't have to give her away."

Swallowing, he nodded, his gaze distant. Silence fell over them, and Adelaide clenched her teeth even harder, dreading the moment when he would release her hands, when he would rise and step away. Put distance between them. Turn from her.

For good.

"How?" he suddenly whispered as his gaze returned to meet hers. "How did this happen?"

Surprised that he could remain so calm, Adelaide swallowed, returning her thoughts to the time of her past that had changed her life. "It…happened the holiday season," she began, turning her gaze to their linked hands, suddenly unable to look at him, "when Bart stayed with us at Beechworth Manor. I was lonely and afraid, and he was kind and treated me as though I were special." Inhaling a shuddering sigh, Adelaide wished she had the courage to look up at him. "When I found out, I confided in my grandmother and she…took care of everything. I was only sixteen and not out in society yet, so it was fairly simple to hide me away for the duration of my pregnancy."

When his hands tightened on hers, Adelaide finally looked up, her heart thudding painfully with what she feared she would see in his eyes. However, instead of the pain and anger and betrayal she expected to see, she saw only regret and compassion. "Only your grandmother knew?"

Adelaide swallowed, still overwhelmed by his lack of anger. Surely, he had to despise her for it! What husband would not hold it against his wife when he found out that she had given herself to another man…even if it had been before their marriage. "My mother, too," she whispered, her eyes searching his. "And then later, John found out as well." She sighed. "He was so angry at me for ruining the family."

Again, her husband's hands tensed, and this time, anger did come to his face. "Your brother ought to have protected you from Bartholomew," he growled, "ensuring that that man would have had no opportunity to seduce you. He was the one to fail you."

Surprised by the direction of his anger, Adelaide shook her head. "No, he didn't fail me. It was my decision, and I cannot blame another for what I did. I knew what I was doing. Only in that moment, I didn't care." Closing her eyes, Adelaide drew in a slow breath, wondering if sharing all this with her husband would finally destroy his faith in her. "My life has always been one of planning ahead, of anticipating how things would turn out, how pain could be avoided." Shrugging, she lifted her gaze to meet his. "And then for one moment, I didn't want to be afraid anymore. I didn't want to be cautious. I didn't want to weigh every word I spoke or step I took. I wanted to let go if only for a moment. One moment." She sighed. "And so, I made a mistake, but it was *my* mistake. Not his. Not John's. I know that now."

"Even though he was angry with me," Adelaide continued, unable to stop, wanting to have it all out in the open now with nothing held back, "he could see that I was miserable. My mother said that we needed to give the baby away if I was to have any chance of entering society and making a good match. I could see how frightened she was, terrified that my father would find out. I was, too, but at the same time I was heartbroken." Tears slowly rolled down Adelaide's face as she remembered the many moments she had cried into her pillows at the thought of losing her child. It had not mattered who the baby's father had been, whether she had loved him or not. All that had mattered was that she had loved her child.

Blinking back her tears, Adelaide met her husband's gaze, seeing his own shine with compassion as his hands closed more tightly around hers. "In the end, it was John who suggested he could claim the child as his, a bastard daughter from a tavern maid left on his doorstep. He said that even as young as he was no one would ask any questions, not with the reputation he had. After all, men were allowed freedoms that were denied to women. He said this way the child could stay with us and I could raise her. Not as her mother, but at least as her aunt." A sob shook her body. "I wanted her so much. I didn't think about what this would mean for her. I was selfish. I only thought of myself and not of how being known as a bastard would affect Tillie's life. I made another mistake by not letting her go. I'm certain my grandmother would have found a good family for her. She would have been safe and loved." Sobs shook her body violently, and Adelaide feared she might sink to the floor into a puddle of misery.

But then strong arms wrapped around her, pulling her against her husband's warm body, holding her close. Gently, he stroked her back and brushed stray curls from her face, and all the while, he mumbled soothing words of comfort into her hair, his warm breath brushing over her cheek.

It was only then, only when Adelaide began to feel the pain in her heart ease that she realised that she lay in her husband's arms. He had not pulled away. He had not run from her, disgusted with her betrayal. Instead, he held her, his voice warm and comforting. "We all make mistakes, but if you hadn't made yours, there'd be no Tillie. I cannot bring myself to regret it," he whispered, gently brushing the tears from her face. "She is ours now, and she is not alone. She is part of our family, and I promise you that I will do everything within my power to ensure that she will have every opportunity, that she'll always feel loved and wanted and cherished. She deserves no less, and neither do you."

Drawing back a little, Adelaide lifted her head, her gaze studying her husband's face. "Are you not…angry with me?" she whispered, afraid to trust that he truly did not hold her past against her. "I expected you to–"

"Have you been with him since…?"

Swallowing, Adelaide shook her head, her eyes open as they looked into her husband's. "No, never."

Matthew nodded. "Did he hold your heart?"

"I liked him," Adelaide admitted, wanting no secrets between them, "but I did not love him. Not the way I love you."

A deep smile suddenly claimed her husband's face. "You do?"

Blinking back fresh tears, Adelaide nodded. "I should have told you long ago, but I was so afraid to lose you. I still can't believe..." Her voice trailed off as she averted her gaze.

"What?" he asked, gently lifting her chin. "Tell me."

"A part of me cannot believe that...that you're truly not angry with me," she said, trying to choose her words carefully. "The fact that my brother could simply claim a bastard child and did not suffer for it while I would have been ruined had I done the same proves how strict rules in our society are...at least for women. No one would have wanted me if they had known. My father would not have been able to bargain with my hand if the truth had been revealed." A slight blush came to her cheeks, and yet, she held her husband's gaze. "I gave myself to another man. I bore his child. Does this not bother you? I need to know the truth. I need to know how you truly feel."

Holding her gaze, her husband drew in a slow breath. A hint of anger rested in his eyes, and yet, Adelaide did not feel afraid. Instead, she welcomed his honesty. "I cannot deny," he forced out through gritted teeth, "that the thought of you...with him turns my stomach. A part of me wants to rip him limb from limb, but I can accept your past with him if indeed it is only your past. It belongs to a time when we had not yet met, when we did not feel bound to one another. I understand...why it happened, and as I said, for Tillie's sake, I cannot truly regret it."

Sighing with relief, Adelaide smiled at him. "It is of the past, I swear it."

As his pulse hammered in his neck, his hands on her tightened possessively. "You're only mine now."

"I am," Adelaide whispered, joy claiming her heart like never before. "Only yours."

"Then what does he want?" her husband asked unexpectedly, his eyes hardening. "Why does he seek you out?"

Tensing, Adelaide shook her head. "I don't know."

Her husband's jaw tightened. "Perhaps he seeks to repeat what happened between you," he growled. "Some men have no honour. They compromise innocents and seduce other men's wives." He inhaled a long breath. "Does he know about Tillie?"

"No one knows, except for my grandmother, my mother and my brother."

"Good. Then I will–"

In that moment, footsteps echoed to their ears shortly before the door was flung open. Adelaide's brother stormed in, his face flushed and deep concern resting in his eyes. "I'm glad you're up," he remarked, holding up a letter. "Father left the house late last night and then again early this morning." Gritting his teeth, he shook his head. "I cannot say why but I feel that something is very wrong. He left this for you." Lifting his hand, he held out the letter to her, and Adelaide could see her own name written there in her father's hand.

Rising from the settee, she stepped toward her brother, a dark sense of foreboding coming over her. She could only hope that her father was not in the process of making another monumental mistake.

With trembling hands, she reached for the letter.

36

A RETURN TO HYDE PARK

Still feeling the pulse thudding in his neck from his wife's revelations, Matthew wished he could have a moment of peace and quiet to sort through the chaos in his head. Many questions still remained, but he could not deny that he felt a sense of relief not only because his wife had finally confided in him, but also because his worst fears had not turned out to be true. Yes, she had slept with Bartholomew—curse the man! —but it had not been out of love. She had never given him her heart. Bartholomew had not possessed it then, and he certainly did not possess it now.

Her heart belonged to Matthew.

Again, he recalled how she had whispered that she loved him, and his whole being warmed, finally content and at peace.

She loved him!

"What is it?"

His brother-in-law's concerned voice jarred Matthew from his thoughts, and he directed his attention back to his wife.

Her eyes had widened as they flew over the parchment in her hands. Her skin had turned pale, and her body began to tremble ever so slightly as she read on. Then she sighed and for a brief moment closed her eyes, inhaling a shuddering breath that sent chills down Matthew's spine.

John fared no better. "What does he write?"

Swallowing, Adelaide met her brother's gaze. "He…he wrote to apologise," she began, "for everything he did, for ruining my life, my happiness."

Matthew stepped forward, his arm coming around her, pulling her closer. Welcoming his support, Adelaide leaned into him, and again—despite the seriousness of the situation—his heart rejoiced at the knowledge that she was his.

His to comfort.

His to protect.

His to love.

"He also writes," Adelaide continued, her gaze fixed on her brother's, "to say that he will ensure that my new happiness will not be ripped from my hands. He promises to protect me." She swallowed hard, tears coming to her eyes. "What does this mean, John? This letter, it sounds as though he…he…"

Clearing his throat, John took a step back, his face paling as he raked his hands through his hair. His eyes grew distant as they flitted around the room, his thoughts racing to make sense of what he had just learnt.

In that moment, Matthew saw his new brother-in-law in a new light. He saw his vulnerability, his doubt and regret. He recognised him as a young man, who had made mistakes and was finally coming to realise the severity of his actions. Despite his mostly reckless and egotistical behaviour of the past, John Cartwright was a decent young man, who simply needed someone to believe in him in order to find his way.

After all, had he not done what he could to protect his sister when she had needed him?

"Bart!"

That single word on his brother-in-law's tongue whipped Matthew's head around in the very moment he felt his wife in his arms tense. "What?"

After glancing at Matthew, John immediately turned his attention to Adelaide. "Father must have heard us talking yesterday. From what we said, it is not unreasonable to assume that he concluded that Bart is a threat to you."

Adelaide's eyes widened. "What are you saying, John? Even if he heard us, even if he believes Bart is a threat to me, what could he do? Why would he–?" Clasping a hand over her mouth, Adelaide stared at her brother.

John's gaze had widened in shock as well before he gritted his teeth. "He called him out," he growled, his hands balling into fists. "It makes perfect sense. That's where he went last night, and that's why he left the house before the break of dawn this morning."

"A duel," Matthew whispered, feeling the blood in his veins run cold as his mind unbidden conjured another morning that had ended in a tragedy.

"Hyde Park," John exclaimed, then spun on his heel and strode toward the door. "We need to hurry."

Shaking off his paralysis, Matthew hastened after his brother-in-law, his wife by his side. "I'll call for the carriage."

"No need," John replied, crossing the front hall in large strides. "Mine is waiting at the kerb."

Without bothering to don coats and hat, the three of them rushed down the steps and into the waiting carriage. John yelled instructions to his driver, and they were off without delay. The wheels churned on the cobblestone as the carriage flew along toward its destination. Luckily, at this time of day, few people were on the street, not hindering their progress.

Holding his wife tightly in his arms, Matthew looked across at his brother-in-law. "In what way does your father think Bartholomew could be a threat to Adelaide?"

For a moment, John did not answer before his eyes travelled to his sister, a question in them that Matthew understood as well.

"He knows," Adelaide whispered, and Matthew felt a new warmth engulf him now that he was no longer an outsider. He knew. He was one of them. He no longer stood alone.

John nodded, then turned to look at Matthew. "Bart has been following her around."

Matthew nodded. "I've noticed that," he growled. "Do you know why?"

John cleared his throat, his gaze darting to the window before it returned to meet his. "I cannot say for sure. I have not spoken to him since he's returned to England."

"Then what does your father know that we don't know?" he asked, watching his brother-in-law carefully, certain that there was more to the story than he was willing to share. "Why would he think him a threat to her?"

"I believe," John said, his gaze travelling to Adelaide, a gentle smile coming to his features, "that Father does not believe Bart to be a…a threat to her in the way that he would harm her…physically." He sighed, running a hand over his face. "With everything that's happened lately and now considering the letter he wrote to you," he looked at his sister, a silent apology in his eyes, "I believe the threat he sees is the one Bart poses to your marriage."

"My marriage?" Adelaide exclaimed. "But if he believes Bart a threat to my marriage then he must know…" Her voice trailed off, and Matthew felt a shiver shake her body.

Instantly, his arms tightened on her.

"About Tillie," John finished for her.

Drawing in a shaking breath, Adelaide stared at her brother. "But how could he? In all those years, he never said a word. Did you tell him?"

John's jaw tightened, and pain came to his gaze. "I did not," he forced out through gritted teeth, and Matthew could tell that his sister's question, her doubt had wounded him deeply. "I spoke of this to no one, but despite his reputation as a gambler and drunkard, Father is not a fool. If he was, he would never have been able to survive this long. Our fortune is all but gone, and yet, he continues to gamble. He still finds funds. He finds people who provide him with funds because he knows things. Things others would rather not see revealed and so they pay."

Matthew scoffed. "He threatens them, blackmails them."

John shrugged. "He does what he has to in order to survive."

"You sound like you're proud of him," Matthew accused, his voice hard.

Sighing, John met his gaze. "I am not," he said, honesty ringing in his voice, "and yet, I understand how hard it is to abandon a path once chosen." He dropped his gaze for a moment before shifting it back to his sister. "It seems all Father is concerned with right now is your happiness." Matthew thought a touch of envy rested in his brother-in-law's eyes. "And so, he sees Bart as a threat. A threat from which he wants to protect you."

Adelaide hung her head, and she turned to him, leaning closer. "I cannot believe he would do this," she whispered, tears clinging to her lashes. "Always has he been the one I feared. How am I supposed to think of him now?"

"Do not worry," Matthew whispered to her. "We will find a way to deal with this. He is your father, and yet, he did wrong by you all your life. One good deed–if you want to call it that–does not redeem him from a lifetime of neglect and abuse." He held her gaze, praying she would not take this upon her own shoulders. "This is not your burden. You're not responsible for what he does."

Swallowing, Adelaide nodded. "I hope we'll get there in time."

As they passed through the gates of Hyde Park, a part of Matthew could not help but hope that the earl would kill Bartholomew. It was a primal, territorial and slightly vindictive part of him that never failed to frighten Matthew, making him wonder if given the right circumstances he could become a man like his father.

Still, deep down, he knew he had no grounds for this fear. It was not rational.

Certainly, he despised Bartholomew. The man had no honour, no decency, and thought that he had every right to prey upon innocent young women for sport. After all, the man had not cared for Adelaide. If he had, he would have married her back then. No, Matthew was certain that Bartholomew had seduced Adelaide for purely selfish reasons, and as he glanced across the carriage at his brother-in-law, he was certain John knew what those were.

Still, Bartholomew's character flaws were not a good enough reason to condemn a man to death. Perhaps a lesson would do him good and help him see that he, too, had made mistakes. Perhaps it was not too late for him to become a better man.

Turning his gaze out the window, Matthew swallowed as the scene drew him back to an early morning about a year ago. The sky was awakening with streaks of light blue and violet dancing across the lofty canvas. Beyond the horizon a soft glow rose as though out of the ground as the sun began its ascent. Morning dew still hung in the air, and he could smell the sweet scent of the world awakening, fresh and clear and invigorating.

And yet, the reason that had brought them there this morning was nothing short of devastating.

A year ago, Matthew had entered the park to confront his cousin, Tristan. He remembered only too well how his father had seemed that day, consumed by greed, madness shining in his eyes, willing to sacrifice his brother's son in order to steal his title and fortune.

It had been the day Matthew had finally realised the truth.

What would today bring?

Would the clearing at the edge of the park see another death this morning? Or would no blood stain its fresh grass?

"It's up ahead," Matthew said, pointing out the window the very moment the grove of trees grew sparser, no longer obstructing his view. His breath caught as his eyes detected movement between the trees.

"There they are!" his brother-in-law called, surging toward the window. Then he banged on the roof to draw the driver's attention. "Faster!"

In Matthew's arms, Adelaide shivered like a leaf, her eyes wide as she stared out the window. "Oh, no! It has begun."

Holding her tightly, Matthew knew there was nothing he could do, and so he simply looked at the few lone figures standing in the clearing. Two stood back to back and a moment later started to march in the opposite direction of one another.

"We're too late," John growled, his hand already on the door handle. "Faster!"

The carriage bounced on the uneven terrain as it left the path behind and surged through a gap in the tree line. Matthew held on to his wife, his eyes fixed on the two figures slowly approaching their final position.

For a moment, time seemed to slow down before the world exploded and everything seemed to happen at once.

One second, the two men were still walking away from one another. The next they spun around, raised their weapons and fired.

Two shots rang loud and clear through the morning air, tearing a scream from Adelaide's lips.

37

A FATHER'S GOODBYE

imly, Adelaide heard a scream ring from her own lips as she watched the two figures go down. From the distance, she could not tell who was who, and her eyes darted back and forth between them.

In the next moment—as though it had been a shot starting a race—John pushed open the door and leapt from the moving carriage. He landed on his feet, and then rolled sideways to break his fall. Instantly, he jumped back up and surged toward the clearing.

"Halt!" her husband called, and the carriage slowed down. Once it had stopped, he opened the door and helped her to the ground. Then they ran, following in her brother's wake.

As they drew closer, Adelaide could spot her father down on the ground, not moving. Bart, too, was lying in the grass; however, she could see his head moving as his second knelt beside him, tending to his arm.

Her father, however, was alone.

Moments later, John reached his side, dropping into the grass beside him. His face went ash-white as his eyes darted over their father's form. Then his arms flew forward, and he pressed his hands onto his chest. Sighing, John lifted his head, and the moment, Adelaide met his eyes, she knew that their father would not walk away from this.

Running, Adelaide held on to her husband, allowing him to pull her forward until they finally reached the clearing. She stumbled onward and then sank down onto her knees beside her father, her eyes drawn to her brother's hands, blood seeping through his fingers, staining her father's shirt and coat, her brother's hands and the grass below a bright red.

The wound in the upper left corner of his chest bled profusely, and his skin was already turning a bluish grey. His eyes were closed, but when she called him, they began to flutter open and he turned this head to look at her.

His gaze found hers, and Adelaide thought to see a small smile play on his lips. "For once I wanted to be the one to protect you," he whispered, his voice almost strangled as he spoke, and yet, his eyes shone clearer than she had ever seen them. He drew in another ragged breath…and then stilled.

Completely.

"Damn you!" John cursed beside her, his face drawn as he stared down at their father. Then he sank back, his hands leaving their father's chest as he sat down in the grass, his blood-stained hands raking through his hair. Tears stood in his eyes, and he hung his head in defeat.

Momentarily numb, Adelaide stared from her brother to her father, feeling her body begin to shake when two warm, familiar hands descended upon her shoulders. "Are you all right?" came her husband's gentle voice from somewhere behind her before he urged her up onto her feet and turned her around, so he could look at her face.

His eyes were soft, and yet, she saw anguish and deep concern darkening the startling green she had come to love. Gentle hands brushed over her face, down her neck and over her shoulders. "Adelaide," he whispered, lifting her chin so she would meet his eyes. "Talk to me."

"He's dead," Adelaide whispered, feeling tears stream down her face. "He's dead because of me." Then her knees buckled, and she sank into his arms, sobs tearing from her throat.

Holding her tightly, her husband whispered words of comfort in her ear while his hands brushed over her back and down her arms, reminding her that he was there, that she was not alone. A small eternity passed before her sobs grew lighter; she felt herself return from the dark place her father's death had plunged her into.

"Listen to me," her husband urged, his green eyes holding hers. "This is not your fault. It may not have been the wisest decision, but your father died because for once he wasn't thinking of himself, because for once he was looking out for someone he cared about." A gentle smile came to his lips as he held her. "What he did, he did because he loved you. For him, it was the only way to prove himself to you and to regain some sense of self-respect. He could not have lived with himself otherwise."

Hearing her husband's words, Adelaide felt drawn to the deep emotions she saw on his face. He, too, had grown up with a father who had been a cold and selfish man. A man who had died without even attempting to redeem himself. He had died without a last message to his son. There had been no regret, no apology, no declaration of love.

Nothing.

"He loved you," her husband whispered as the pad of his thumb gently brushed a tear from her cheek. "Hold on to that. Forget the rest."

Adelaide nodded, feeling fresh tears sting her eyes. For herself. For her father. But also, for her husband.

"After everything he's done wrong in his life," Matthew whispered as though they were the only two people in the world, "the loss of his life does not measure up to the loss of his family. His death is a small price to pay for him, and while it is sad for you and your brother, it might be what's best for him." He sighed. "I've often wondered what would have been if my father had lived. But now I know that after a certain point, it is impossible to forgive oneself, to start over. Even if others, if you and your brother, had been willing to give him another chance, now that he had come to realise the wrong of his ways, he might have been past the point when he could still have forgiven himself." Inhaling a slow breath, he shrugged. "How do you go on when the person who cannot forgive you is yourself? Your father did what he could to prove that despite everything he'd done, a part of him still loved you more than he loved himself. It is more than my father ever did." His arms tightened on her as he looked down into her eyes. "Let go of the past, and only remember that he did love you after all. Nothing else matters."

The sadness that clung to her husband's eyes told Adelaide how deeply his own father had wounded him and how much he would have wished for a small sign of affection. Yet, there had been none, and Adelaide knew that when Matthew had spoken of the burden of being unable to forgive oneself, he had spoken of himself. For too long, he had held himself accountable for his father's deeds, for not seeing the truth sooner. It had taken great courage to fight his way out of the darkness, a darkness made of disregard and betrayal, and not succumb to it. He had reclaimed the man he should have been, not losing himself in the aftermath of his father's death.

Today, Matthew stood tall, and although she could still see the occasional doubt in his eyes, he once again knew who he was. A kind and gentle man, who never failed to offer his help, who protected those who needed him, and who loved with all his heart and soul.

Smiling, Adelaide snuggled closer into his arms. "Take me home," she whispered, feeling her eyelids grow heavy. "I want to go home."

Then her knees gave out, and blackness claimed her.

38

A MOMENT OF CLARITY

Pacing up and down the length of his wife's bedchamber, Matthew kept glancing at the bed where Adelaide lay sleeping. Her breathing was even, her chest rising and falling, and she looked almost peaceful as she slept. And yet, Matthew could not stop worrying.

The way she had sagged into his arms at the clearing had scared him nearly witless. For a short, heart-stopping moment, he had thought her lost to him.

It had been in that moment that he had realised that no matter what had happened, he could not live without her. He did not care that she had been with Bartholomew. He didn't care that she had born that man's child. He did not care that she had kept her secret for so long.

All he cared about was her.

She and their family, and he would not make the same mistakes as their fathers. He would not give up what he had out of pride or arrogance or anger. He would not lose his family.

A soft sigh from the bed stopped his feet. His head snapped around, his eyes finding the still figure on the bed, before he crossed the distance between them in large strides, sinking onto the mattress beside her. Gently, he drew her hand in his, feeling the soft warmth of her skin.

She was alive, his mind whispered reminding him of how fortunate he was.

Her eyelids began to flutter and then slowly opened. At first, her gaze was unfocused, but when her eyes came to rest on his face, a gentle smile claimed her face. "Matthew."

Hearing his name on her lips, the way she breathed it almost lovingly, made Matthew's heart flutter with excitement. "You scared me," he told her, wanting her to know how much his heart had come to depend on her for his happiness. "You scared me when you fainted." He swallowed. "For a moment, I thought…" His throat closed up, and all he could do was look at her, his eyes drilling into hers, revealing the utter fear and pain he had felt in that moment.

Another soft sigh left her lips, and she lifted her hand to place it gently on his cheek. "I'm sorry," she whispered. "I did not mean to frighten you. I…" For a moment, her eyes closed, and he could see her features tense with relived pain as her memories returned, reminding her of what had happened, of what she had lost.

"My father," she whispered, her blue gaze seeking his, "is dead." Her voice did not rise. It was not a question. She was not asking him to confirm or deny her words. And yet, it needed to be said.

And acknowledged. "He is." Gently, he squeezed her hands. "I'm sorry."

Tears came to her eyes.

"Are you all right?" Matthew asked, wishing he could take the pain upon himself.

Drawing in a long, deep breath, Adelaide wiped the wetness from her face, her lips pressing together in determination. "I'm fine," she said, her voice a bit tense, but still strong. Then she sighed, regret coming to her eyes. "If only he had seen the wrong of his ways before now. If only he had…" She shook her head. "There is no use in thinking thus. Nothing can change the past. It is what it is, and yet, I feel as though he missed his chance. I keep wondering who we could have been, him and me. What kind of father and daughter could we have been in another life?"

Matthew nodded. "Regrets are a part of life. They speak of longing and hope. They help us see what we truly want and who we truly love." He sighed, "Only sometimes they find us too late."

Blinking back tears, Adelaide nodded. "Too late for him." She inhaled a deep breath, her blue eyes holding his, a hint of apprehension in them. "What about us?"

Matthew frowned. "What do you mean?"

"You've barely had time to think about what I…told you," she whispered, her hand resting in his tensing as she spoke, "about me, about Tillie. I will not hold it against you if you wished to…" Despite her brave face, her voice broke off, and the way she looked at him with such open longing gripped his heart.

Smiling, Matthew brushed a curl from her forehead, the tips of his fingers tracing along her temple and down the line of her jaw. "I meant what I said," he whispered, noting the tentative hope he saw in the way her lips twitched into a semblance of a smile. "You're my world, my life, my heart, and I'd be a fool to ever give you up. We are a family, and we always will be. You have my word."

Joy shone in her eyes as she blinked back fresh tears. "And Tillie? She—"

"In our hearts, she is ours," Matthew replied with conviction. "We may never be able to claim her publicly, but that does not change who we are as a family. We will find a way. If not in England, then somewhere else."

A gentle frown came to her face. "Are you certain? I would never ask you to—"

"You didn't ask," Matthew clarified. "I offered. I would never allow Tillie to take the fall for her father's wrongdoings." The thought of Bartholomew still turned his stomach.

At the mention of Tillie's father, Adelaide's eyes widened. "Bart! He—" Her voice broke off, and she stared at him, a question in her eyes which she did not dare ask.

"He lives," Matthew said, unable to ignore the part of him that felt a hint of regret over that fact. "The bullet hit him in the arm. He should be fine." He inhaled a deep breath. "Your brother spoke to him and told him to stay away."

A slight frown drew down her brows. "Do you think he will?" she asked carefully. "I still don't understand why he sought me out in the first place. I mean he never even knew about Tillie." Her eyes suddenly widened. "Or did he?"

Swallowing, Matthew shook his head, knowing she had a right to know the truth. "He does not." He sighed, trying to find the right words.

"What?" Pushing herself up into a sitting position, Adelaide looked at him, her eyes roaming his face. "What is it?"

Reaching out for her hands once more, Matthew met her eyes. "It was nothing but a game to Bartholomew," he all but growled at the memory of what John had finally confessed to him. "Apparently, earlier that same year, he fell for a young girl. He spoke to your brother about her, and then after a fight, John went out of his way to win her over." Matthew inhaled a slow breath, seeing her eyes widen with pained disappointment. "He succeeded, and she turned Bartholomew down, calling him a second son. He was furious, but eventually he forgave your brother…or so it seemed."

Her hands tensed on his as she stared at him. "It was revenge," she gasped. "He seduced me in order to get back at my brother."

Matthew nodded, hoping the knowledge that Bartholomew had never truly cared for her would not shatter her fragile sense of self-worth. "It was a despicable thing to do," he snapped, his voice sharper than he had intended. "His quarrel was with your brother. You were innocent in all of this. A gentleman would not have acted thus."

Sighing, Adelaide nodded. "As far as I can remember, he has always been a kind man." Her gaze focused on his. "He had to have been heart-broken to act as he did. I cannot believe he would have done this to me otherwise." For a moment, she closed her eyes…before to Matthew's utter surprise a relieved smile came to her lips. "I'm so incredibly glad I did not marry him."

Matthew frowned. "Did he offer for you?" The mere thought sent panic up and down his spine.

"No, he did not." Adelaide's smile grew wider as her hands gripped his with determination. "But if he had, I would have accepted him. Then. And I would have regretted it for the rest of my life. He is not the kind of man I could have loved."

Her words warmed Matthew's heart, and he pulled her closer into his arms. "He is not? Who then?" he teased, noting the sparkle that had come to her eyes.

A slight blush rose in her cheeks, and yet, she did not avert her eyes. "You," she whispered, and before he knew what was happening, her hands grabbed his face and pulled him down into a kiss. Then she smiled at him, a bit of a sheepish grin on her face. "Do you have any objections?"

"None at all," Matthew replied, his lips still tingling from their quick kiss. What would it feel like to hold her in his arms all night? "All I care about is your happiness," he whispered, brushing his knuckles over her cheek. "This is a new beginning for all of us, and we will not allow it to slip through our fingers."

Smiling, she shook her head before a hint of tension returned to her eyes. "I only hope that my brother will see it the same way," she whispered, her voice apologetic as though she feared by mentioning her brother she would break the spell that had fallen over them. "I worry about him. Too early did his life take a wrong turn, and there was no one there to guide his steps back."

"We are here now," Matthew said, reminding himself that despite numerous mistakes, John, too, had grown up with a father who had been an awful example, tempting his son to abandon all thoughts of decency and simply seek out his own desires…no matter the cost.

"He is not alone, and we will make sure he knows that…even if we have to hit him over the head with it."

Adelaide laughed, the sound contagious as she threw herself into his arms. "Thank you," she whispered, hugging him tightly. "For everything."

When she pulled back, Matthew once more brushed the tips of his fingers over her cheek, unable not to touch her. "Even though you grew apart, John loves you," he reminded her, knowing she would never find peace without resolving the issues with her brother. "I suppose everyone lost sight of that, but I have a feeling that John will be overthinking things as well."

Adelaide sighed as she leaned into Matthew's caress. "I can only hope so, for despite his mistakes, he deserves to be happy."

"So, do you."

Her eyes sought his. "What will become of us now?"

"Whatever we want." Cupping his hand to her cheek, Matthew glanced down at her lips. "Whatever we want."

A shiver ran over her as she became aware of the direction of his thoughts. "Can you forgive me? Truly?"

"There is nothing to forgive," Matthew said with vehemence, pulling her closer. "I have no regrets. I have you and Tillie, and I can't imagine my life without either one of you." Meeting her gaze, he inhaled a deep breath. "Do you want me? Here? Now? As your husband? Forever?"

Holding his gaze, Adelaide exhaled a shuddering breath. "I do," she whispered, her lips quivering as they drew up into a smile. "I've wanted you for a long time now, and I was so afraid to lose you. I'm sorry I kept this from you for so long. I should have told you, but I never thought I'd ever lose my heart the way I lost it to you. It scared me like nothing before. I couldn't bear the thought of losing you, not when I never thought I'd even find you."

Never in his life had Matthew felt such utter joy than in this very moment. Everything was perfect, frighteningly perfect. And all he had to do was pull her into his arms and never let her go again.

Gently, he placed a kiss onto her lips, feeling her arms come around him. Her hands brushed down his neck as her fingers twirled in his hair. His own traced the lines of her face, over her brows and cheekbones down to her jawline. All the while, he kept kissing her, feeling her respond first tentatively and then with more vehemence.

"Stay with me," she whispered before her lips reclaimed his and they sank back into the pillows.

Matthew could not think of a place he'd rather be.

He belonged with her.

Here and now.

Forever.

EPILOGUE

Three months later

Matthew sighed as he stepped to the edge of the terrace, Tristan right beside him.

"It is a beautiful day, is it not?" his cousin remarked as they allowed their gazes to sweep over the gardens of Hampton Hall, Tristan's rightful estate.

Matthew nodded, enjoying the peaceful scene of the falling leaves all around them. Brown, red, orange and golden, they fell to the ground into a rustling sea, blown about by a gentle breeze. Here and there, Matthew could still see the small tracks Tillie had left behind as she had chased through them earlier, her new puppy Oscar on her heels.

"Uncle Matthew, do you want some tea?" the little girl called from behind him, cheerily setting up her tea set and arranging her dolls while Oscar slept at her feet.

Matthew smiled. "I'll be there in a moment," he promised, watching as she turned back to the task at hand, her little face slightly scrunched up in concentration.

"She's a sweet one," Tristan observed before his eyes slid from Tillie to Beth, seated comfortably on a chaise right beside the little girl, their newborn daughter Ellen snug in her arms. Hovering around the new mother were not only Adelaide and Matthew's mother, but also his wife's mother and grandmother, their faces shining as they looked down upon the new life.

The death of two tyrants had freed them all and given them back the life they deserved.

"You look happy," Matthew observed, smiling at his cousin. "Being a father obviously agrees with you."

Laughing, Tristan nodded. "It certainly does," he said, his eyes glowing as he spoke of his little family. "She's been here a few days, and yet, I cannot imagine ever spending another day without her." Smiling, he shook his head in disbelief. "Not since I met Beth, have I felt anything so powerful."

"That's how it ought to be," Matthew remarked, relieved that Tristan would not be a father like his own, but loving and devoted instead, seeing his child as a blessing, one to cherish each and every day.

For a moment, Tristan's eyes became thoughtful before he spoke. "You, too, look happy, my friend. I've never seen you so much at ease."

Sighing, Matthew nodded. "Is it that obvious?"

"Happiness is impossible to hide," Tristan laughed. "You look like a man very much in love with his wife, and I should know as I'm speaking from personal experience." He clasped Matthew's shoulder. "When I first saw my sister again after she got married, I could see it at one glance as well."

"How is Henrietta?" Matthew asked, remembering the angry young woman he had always known. Perhaps he ought to write to her. Perhaps they could begin again.

"She's well," Tristan replied. "She's recovering well after giving birth to her little one."

"What's her name?"

"Bridget," Tristan laughed, "and from what Connor writes, she's as fierce as her mother."

Inhaling a slow breath, Matthew glanced over at his wife. Standing next to Beth, she held little Ellen in her arms, cooing softly to the infant, a deep smile on her face. Then she lifted her gaze and looked over at Tillie, and her eyes shown with the same deep joy that clung to Beth's features as well.

A mother's happiness.

"And you?" Tristan asked, a teasing chuckle rumbling in his throat. "When will you join the ranks? When is she due?"

Blinking, Matthew turned to look at his cousin, a frown on his face. "How do you know?"

Again, Tristan laughed, "As I said, my friend, happiness is impossible to hide."

"So, it would seem." Smiling, Matthew relented. "In the summer," he whispered, hoping Adelaide would not be upset with him for spilling their secret. "We found out a few days ago."

"Congratulations!" Tristan said quietly, understanding Matthew's cautious look as only another man deeply in love with his wife could. "I cannot say how happy I am to see our family reunited, to see us all filled with joy again. It's been too long."

Matthew nodded. "Too long indeed."

"Never again," Tristan prompted, his blue eyes finding Matthew's, a silent vow in them that touched Matthew deeply.

"Never again," he promised in return before his gaze travelled to his wife and daughter.

He knew exactly how fortunate he was.

And he would never take that for granted.

Never.

THE END

In the next instalment of this series, *Tamed & Unleashed – The Highlander's Vivacious Wife*, we will once more meet Miss Davenport as she sets out to find her child, only to receive unexpected aid in her quest from a handsome stranger. A man who seems more familiar than he ought to be. A man she has met before. If only she could remember him!

ABOUT BREE

USA Today bestselling author, Bree Wolf has always been a language enthusiast (though not a grammarian!) and is rarely found without a book in her hand or her fingers glued to a keyboard. Trying to find her way, she has taught English as a second language, traveled abroad and worked at a translation agency as well as a law firm in Ireland. She also spent loooong years obtaining a BA in English and Education and an MA in Specialized Translation while wishing she could simply be a writer. Although there is nothing simple about being a writer, her dreams have finally come true.

"A big thanks to my fairy godmother!"

Currently, Bree has found her new home in the historical romance genre, writing Regency novels and novellas. Enjoying the mix of fact and fiction, she occasionally feels like a puppet master (or mistress? Although that sounds weird!), forcing her characters into ever-new situations that will put their strength, their beliefs, their love to the test, hoping that in the end they will triumph and get the happily-ever-after we are all looking for.

If you're an avid reader, sign up for Bree's newsletter at www.breewolf.com as she has the tendency to simply give books away. Find out about freebies, giveaways as well as occasional advance reader copies and read before the book is even on the shelves!

Thanks you very much for reading!

Bree

LOVE'S SECOND CHANCE SERIES

For more information, visit

www.breewolf.com

A FORBIDDEN LOVE NOVELLA SERIES

For more information, visit

www.breewolf.com

Printed in Great Britain
by Amazon